Praise For

Barbara

Explicitly sexual, thougl   el,
Barbara, is both heart   g.
Through page after pag   y
mind was, "real." These p   grew up in
the 1960's in Florida, I ofte   een one of these people
out there on the beach discussing God, the world and everything. As I remember, we were quite certain we had the answers—if not all, at least a good many more than the "clueless"
generation that preceded us. This novel is a triumphant por-
trayal of all that is beautiful about sexual intimacy, love and
respect, even when—perhaps especially when—experienced
for the first time by unspoiled innocents. I couldn't put it down
until the last page. I envy all who still have the reading of *Barbara* ahead of them... Enjoy.
- *The Reverend Dr. Angeline Theisen*

What a rumbustious, rollicking, sweet holy monster of a book! I
admit that what I thought I was getting when I first started
reading was "Orgasms I Have Known," but what I encountered
instead – and what held me spellbound – was the story of a
man's search for self-knowledge through intimacy. This is
some of the most compulsive reading I've had in quite a few
years. I literally couldn't wait to see what would befall Tom
next, thanks to the book's cast of endearing and lovingly-
rendered female characters. And while our hero does indeed
grow sadder as he becomes wiser, there is an underlying cele-
bration of life in all its untidy, awful and exuberantly glorious
aspects that keeps the proceedings from becoming maudlin.
This is an uncommonly rich reading experience.
- *Burt Kempner—Wordtender, writer for Screen, Stage & Page*

Barbara is an erotically provocative novel that wrings emotion
from every pore. Tom, the protagonist, has decades to come to
terms with his conflicts and confusions, but the reader gets it all
in one mighty wallop. A must read!!
- *Elaine Campbell Smith, novelist/short story writer and former Senior Editor of Snap Magazine.*

Barbara

Barbara

by
R. LeBeaux

BARBARA

First WordMerchant edition published 2008.

WordMerchant Publishing
Post Office Box 1764
New Port Richey, FL 34656
www.wmpublishing.com

ISBN 1-4196-9379-4

Cover and interior design by Rick Boling

Acknowledgments

The author would like to thank the following readers and editors for their invaluable help, editing and frank critiques of this work – all good friends and honest compatriots, without whose assistance I could not possibly have completed the book:

Elaine Campbell Smith (Ecs): novelist, editor, brutally honest critic, and former member of the best writers' group ever.

The Reverend Dr. Angeline Theisen: writer, editor, minister, and essayist.

Pauline Masterton: poet, novelist, spiritual advisor, and Chakra adjuster.

Burt Kempner—Wordtender: writer for screen, stage and the page; producer of films, television and video, and a very *punny* guy.

For Barbara
- with apologies -
wherever she may be

Author's Forward

This book is a bit of penance for me, penance for the transgressions of youth, for the inexcusable insensitivity and selfishness that comes with adolescence. Since I am not a Catholic, I can't do the three million or so Hail Mary's it would take to achieve absolution for my early sins, so the words that follow will have to suffice.

I feel I must warn the reader that what you are about to read contains sexually graphic scenes, and that I hold little or nothing back in descriptions. My intent, however, was not to write a sex novel, but to create in the reader an understanding of the need for honesty and caring and empathy in any intimate encounter, especially those that might be a first experience for one or the other partner.

Finally, though the disclaimer appears earlier, I should reiterate that this is a work of fiction and that none of the characters are real. It is informed, of course, by real experiences. If you recognize yourself or someone you know, it is only because at least some of these experiences may be universal and you or your acquaintance may at some time in your lives have experienced similar things.

R. LeBeaux

"Sex holds first place in the thought of God. Its glory pervades and suffuses all Nature. It is sex that gives the bird its song, the peacock its gorgeous plumage, the lion its mane, the buffalo its strength and the horse its tail. Aye, it is sex that causes the flowers to draw from the dull earth those delicate perfumes which delight the sense of smell. It is sex and sex alone that secures to them the dazzling galaxy of shapes and colors that reflect the Infinite."

Elbert Hubbard (Founder of The Roycrofters Arts & Crafts Community)

From *The Note Book of Elbert Hubbard.* Originally "Done into a Book" by The Roycrofters: www.roycrofter.com/

PROLOGUE

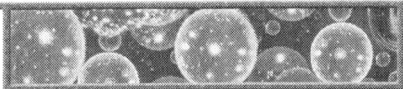

There was a time when I found a small measure of comfort in the theory that says there are an infinite number of parallel universes, each one based on the consequences of our actions or inactions at any given moment in time. If the theory is true, then somewhere out there is a universe in which I didn't make the biggest mistake of my life.

I will always wonder what that universe would be like, but wondering is all I can do because I live in this universe, and in this universe I did make the mistake. It was a mistake that could perhaps be more generously described as a small error of omission, and to be sure, I had excuses: the heat of the moment, youthful ignorance, powerful emotions that clouded my thinking. Still, absolving myself for these reasons is difficult, just as ignorance of the law is no excuse. Worse is the fact that I had opportunities to correct the error, or at least to make the attempt. But always there seemed to be some moral barrier I could not, or would not allow myself to challenge.

Whatever the cause or lack of reparation, that error spun my personal universe in a new direction and left in its wake a huge echoing cavern filled with regret so intense it can still overwhelm me with memories and speculation on how different things might have turned out had that void been filled by the most loving, honest and beautiful human being I have ever known.

If it is true that a life without regrets is a life not lived, then I started living early, because that single error— the defining regret of my life—took place when I was a mere sixteen years old. For compensation I have only one day, one incredible day of love, learning, excitement and passion that will remain crystallized in my memory forever.

My life is nearly over now, with all except one of its paint-by-number segments colored in by friends, family, and another incredible creature, so unique and nearly perfect I am often baffled by the fact that, in spite of having lived a life of, at best, dubious value, I was privileged to find her. Unfortunately, however, that one unpainted segment will forever remain blank, just as that one alternate universe will forever remain beyond my reach.

As I stare across the waters of The Bay, waters that have returned to glass after being briefly disturbed by the scattering of all—save memories—that remained of the first and forever love of my life, I resolve to record those memories, to commit them to the invisible dance of electrons that will hopefully preserve them for all time. To tell the story of that one glorious day when time stood still and the laws of this particular universe bowed to the superior power of human emotion; when two people, despite their youth and naiveté, found in each other something few couples are ever privileged to find; to tell of their lives, lived apart though not distant, lived together though not nearly as close as both had once hoped.

Here follows that story.

It is dedicated to Barbara.

Barbara's dead!"

The voice on the phone reverberated in my psyche like a cannonball shot into a room with rubber walls.

"Tom? Did you hear me? Barbara was killed in a car accident this afternoon, somewhere out by Tyrone Mall."

The air rushed from my lungs. My body began to shudder. The voice urgently continued to emanate from the cell phone as I moved it farther and farther from my ear, eventually clicking it off and placing it on the nightstand. I stared into the darkened room, oblivious to my wife, who had stirred with the ringing of the phone.

"What is it, Honey?" Rosie asked. I did not respond.

The voice on the phone didn't mention a last name, but that didn't matter. George knew it would not be necessary. Though there had been two women in my life by that name, there was only one my best friend and singing partner would call about.

I swung my legs over the side of the bed, rose painfully, went to the dresser where my shorts hung clasped in the top drawer, put them on, added my shirt from the clotheshorse by the dresser, and walked out the door.

"Tom?" Rosie yelled after me. "What's wrong? Who was that on the phone?"

By then I was at the door to the garage, which I swung open with no regard for the fact that it slammed into the wall. I stood for a moment looking into the dimmed cavern, then stepped toward my Taurus, opened the driver's side door, climbed inside, and put the key in the ignition. Then I stopped.

Rosie's voice echoed through the house behind me, as I turned the key and listened to the engine come to life. The radio came rudely alive, and I slammed my fist against it as if trying to kill an insect that had invaded my personal space. When that didn't stop the unholy sounds of Mick Jagger, I turned down the volume until his ranting about sexual satisfaction faded and finally disappeared.

Sex and satisfaction! What an appropriately gross bit of serendipity. Of all the songs in the history of Rock 'n' Roll, this was among those I hated most. In fact, I hated the Stones in general, but that didn't negate the fact that Lips Larue had found the most appropriate moment, the most appropriate few words, the most incredibly appropriate concept to lay on me at that particular split second of my existence.

Satisfaction.

Barbara.

Dead.

Sweet Jesus!

2
BARBARA   1960

I think I'm ready," Barbara said, with a demure glance at the floor of my brother's upstairs bedroom.

Less than half an hour earlier, Barbara and I had been caught making out in the master bedroom of a friend's home. The friend, Todd, and his family, like many other snowbirds, owned homes both in Florida and up north, and they lived in the southern house only during winter months. It was late August, warm, moist and uncomfortable—normal for St. Petersburg at that time of the year. Another "friend," Harry Stimson, had surprised us in the bed, Barbara with her shorts around her knees and me with my hand between her legs.

Barbara Baker and I were both sixteen and Harry, who was considered the supreme asshole of the neighborhood, was a couple of years older. He claimed to have been ordered by Todd to keep an eye on the house (crap, I later learned), and when he saw us sneaking in the back door, he decided to investigate. Being an amateur magician and escape artist, I had used my professional lock-picking kit to get in and, finally, we thought we had found a haven where we could continue our sexual explorations.

Barbara and I had only recently become intimate, though we'd been friends for some time. She had dated another friend of mine for a year or so. Brad was three years older than Barbara, and her parents had no idea they were seeing each other. They would meet at my house (next door to Todd's) whenever we had swim parties and other get-togethers for the kids in the neighborhood or from school. Brad eventually found an older girl to date, and Barbara and I hooked up on the rebound, as I also had recently broken up with Alicia.

Tentative at first, we soon found ourselves making out whenever we could be alone (which wasn't often), and both of us were anxious to further explore our changing bodies and feelings. The problem was we never seemed to get the opportunity to be out of sight of parents and other grown-ups. The last time we had gotten that chance was one evening two weeks earlier after everyone else had gone home from my sister's birthday party. The adults were socializing in the living room, while Barbara and I continued to soak in the warm waters of our pool, with only the underwater light for illumination. Eventually, the bubble blowing from underneath her legs and the silly splashing and tag playing, brought us together in an awkward embrace, and we had one of those "movie moments" where our eyes met and we kissed. It was a soft, chaste kiss, more romantic than sexual, but soon, in an imitation of what I had seen in a few movies,

I started kissing her neck and holding her tighter, to which she responded with approving little moans and movements.

Of course, it wasn't long before I became aroused, and we were so tightly entangled there was no way I could keep her from feeling my growing erection, even though I tried to pull my lower body back a little. Barbara showed no signs of outrage or embarrassment. In fact, she held my face in her hands, pushed me away and smiled, while wrapping her legs around mine and pulling my body into her even harder.

Up until then, I had only had sex with one girl, sort of the school "slut," though she really was a nice person, intelligent and thoughtful. We were both thirteen at the time, and, oddly, her name was Barbara, too, Barbara Wilson. The sex had first happened at her house while her mother was out. We were on her bed staring at the ceiling, while she told me the story of how her first boyfriend, a seventeen-year-old juvenile delinquent named Carl, had forced her to have intercourse in the back seat of a car while another friend held her down. She explained how painful it had been, particularly because Carl had a huge penis (reputed to be some nine inches long). Barbara was a tiny girl, all of five feet tall and weighing maybe 90 pounds. She had an incredible thirteen-inch waist and perfectly formed breasts. With the exception of a rather rounded nose, she was pretty. She was also poor, and her mother, known as a "loose" woman, often left her alone at night in the small duplex they rented.

That evening, I found myself sympathizing with Barbara over her first traumatic sexual experience, and I also found myself growing hard. I knew I couldn't compete with her first boyfriend's size, however I was so horny by the time she finished her story that I couldn't keep myself from asking if she might be willing to have sex with me.

The year was 1958, decades before condoms lost their illicit luster and became generally available. Besides which (unbeknownst to me due to my immaturity) I would probably have slid right out of one. Barbara, however, after careful deliberation, began to explain to me the fine art of pre-ejaculation withdrawal, and once assured that I understood the process and its absolute necessity, she agreed to an instructional session in fumbling adolescent intercourse.

I have always recalled in detail that time, which was at once thrilling and disturbing. The thrill began as she allowed me to remove her shorts and then her panties to reveal the first vagina I had ever seen. Barbara's hair was jet black, and she had a large swatch of thick black pubic hair hovering over a slitted opening surrounded by a great deal of brown, wrinkled skin. In my youthful naiveté, I speculated that the overused look of her vagina had been caused by that first, painful rape experience, and then was made even worse by a year or more of repeated intercourse. At the time, I wasn't aware of the fact that the appearance of a vagina could be influenced by many things, such as ethnicity or heredity, and I more or less took for granted this was how all vaginas would eventually look—basically nasty, though that didn't seem to have any effect on my desire to get into hers.

Barbara laid a folded towel on the bed, then lay down, careful to place her hips in the center of the towel. The towel, she explained, was to catch my ejaculation so it didn't leave a telltale stain on her bedspread. After everything was in place, I was allowed to first touch the opening of her vagina with my fingers and then to insert one, two, then three of them. I was surprised by the amount of warm fluid that gushed out, and she explained that this was to help facilitate the ease of entering her and minimize whatever pain there might be. Of course, being as small as I was at the time, pain wasn't something she had to worry about, and as I slid into her, I felt no resistance whatsoever. In fact, it felt like entering a huge, moist cavern, in which my penis swam like an eel wriggling in a large tube filled with warm Cream of Wheat.

I began to move in and out, and within what seemed like a matter of seconds my orgasm started. Feeling the contractions, Barbara told me to withdraw, which, though I found difficult, I managed to do before much if any semen escaped.

Thinking back on that night, I would often marvel at what little emotion Barbara showed during the experience, and how her lack of emotion, excitement or even response continued through the following year, during which we had intercourse whenever her mother was out and I could get away long enough to pedal my bike the eight miles or so to her house. I speculated that this emotionless sex had something to do with her rape. But I was inexperienced; maybe all girls acted that way during sex.

I would later realize that, regardless of my encounters with the first Barbara, I didn't learn much about sex. Sure, I was the first among my friends to have "gotten laid," and that brought with it a kind of celebrity and a reputation for being "experienced." But the nature of our encounters was so mechanical, so emotionless and non-verbal, they became more like masturbation for me. As for Barbara, I would never know what it did for her, since she displayed no signs of pleasure or excitement, not even the slightest bit of heavy breathing. There was almost no foreplay after the first time, so I learned nothing about how to arouse a girl. Eventually, we even stopped kissing, except when we said goodnight. Our encounters became a matter of undressing, lying down, fucking, cleaning up, and then, if there was time, doing something else like playing her piano or listening to records. In fact, about the only thing Barbara ever taught me, besides withdrawal for birth control, was how to play *Für Elise* on the piano.

Our affair ended when Carl, the rapist, was released from reform school, and Barbara once again took up with him. By then my penis had grown a good bit, however, I was still no match for Carl, and I figured Barbara would rather be more adequately satisfied than barely filled.

Next came Alicia, whom I had known since Kindergarten and who lived two blocks away. A thin attractive girl, with a playful spirit and a cute upturned nose, Alicia had been my first "love" during our preadolescent days. Together we had gone through the, "I'll show you mine if you show me yours" stage many years earlier. This was only to satisfy childhood curiosities, since neither of us was in any way sexually capable. By the time we got together as adolescents, all that had been forgotten, and Alicia was adamant about not allowing any sexual contact between us. We did a lot of making out, but try as I might I could never get my hand within two inches of her almost non-existent breasts, let alone between her legs. I have speculated that, since her breasts hadn't yet matured, she might have been embarrassed, but I couldn't reassure her because, at our age and in that time, these were not subjects opposite-sex adolescents discussed with each other.

Alicia and I broke up because she demanded I quit smoking, something all "cool" boys did in secret at the time, and something I was not about to give up. Nor was I in any way predisposed to allow a "girl" to order me around. In later high school days we would have called such a capitulation being "pussy whipped." Then, however, taking orders from a girl was basically non-macho. Besides which, Brad had just walked out on Barbara Baker, leaving her available and hurt and presenting me with an opportunity I had dreamed about for over a year.

There was something special about Barbara Baker, a radiance of soul that shone through her eyes and her actions and her obvious empathy with others. Though I could tell she was upset over losing Brad, it was she who went out of her way to comfort me over my split with Alicia. I remember with incredible clarity one night at the local YMCA dance, standing against a wall and talking to her about our mutual heartbreaks. I must have seemed emotionally in need, because when I leaned over, Barbara gently laid a hand on my back. It was a sincere effort to comfort me, that laying on of a hand, but it had an unusually sensual effect. A chill started at the top of my scalp, rippling down my body until it reached my toes, and I almost immediately had an erection, which I tried my best to hide by remaining in that bent over position while she massaged my back, making things worse.

It was her touch, but more so the emotion and caring radiating through it that clinched the deal for me at that moment, a moment I have never been able to erase from my memory and one that fills my more sensual dreams to this day. I was, however, almost positive that, for Barbara, this was a sincere effort to comfort me in my grief over losing Alicia, and had nothing whatsoever to do with any suggestion or invitation. Barbara was a good person, with an enormous capacity for feeling and sympathizing with the troubles of others.

Later that same evening, before our parents were due to pick us up from the weekly dance, we crossed paths again outside in the enclosed courtyard where kids could sneak a cigarette or find a dark nook to make out in. I had lit a

Lucky Strike and was leaning against one of the several stone pillars, assuming (I thought) the demeanor of James Dean, when Barbara came up and kissed me on the cheek.

"Are you okay," she whispered. I noticed she was a little misty eyed, and I thought my heart was about to explode, so I broke eye contact and looked at the ground. She placed a finger under my chin and lifted my head so we could lock gazes, and the expression of concern on her face brought a huge lump to my throat. I know we adults are supposed to understand these adolescent emotional volcanoes as raging hormones, infatuations, childhood crushes and the like, but at that moment I felt such an overwhelming explosion of love that it has, like her earlier touch, remained imprinted on my memory for all time. Just as my knees were about to buckle under the weight of all that emotion, she leaned over and kissed me on the mouth. Her lips, trembling and softened by tears, said all there was to say, but I was so shocked and disoriented all I could do was stand there like an idiot.

"I gotta go," she said. Then, with a smile tugging at one corner of her mouth, added, "We should talk. Call me sometime okay? Let's get together somewhere more private than this."

Again, I was sure all she wanted was to comfort me, and maybe commiserate with a friend over mutual losses, but for me that sealed it; I was a dead duck, hopelessly and irretrievably in love. I carried that feeling in my heart and in the huge cavern that had opened in my chest, all the way home that night and into my restless bed. There, I found a measure of release from the painful Hot Rocks I had developed as I masturbated—five times, if I remember correctly. And although my hormones had taken over, as they almost always did when I encountered a pretty girl those days, I knew there was a lot more going on than wanting to have another notch on my belt. This was love, Goddamnit, and it was far more important than finding a way to get into Barbara's pants.

The next few weeks proved to be happy ones for us. Barbara began coming over to swim on a regular basis, and we talked and talked about our feelings for our departed lovers, and how they had begun to fade in the wake of our new relationship. We didn't kiss again for some time, but were happy to let our friendship mature and become stronger through honest interaction the likes of which I had never known before with any friend, male or female.

During this time we made several pacts, the first and foremost of which was that, no matter how embarrassing it might be, we would always be completely honest with each other and would answer each other's questions without holding anything back. Thus it was that Barbara, with her head turned away, and in a voice so soft I sometimes had to strain to hear, told me about her relationship with Brad. It was late one Saturday evening when I finally got up the nerve to ask her the Big Question.

"How far did you go?" I asked in a guarded whisper as we sat hip-to-hip in a wicker lounge chair beside the pool. Her grip on my arm tightened in response to the question, and I started to backtrack. "Hey, listen, you don't have to tell. Really. I'm just curious, that's all."

"No," she said. "We have a deal, don't we?" And, after a long period of nervous silence, she began.

"We met over here," she said. "You remember. It was that party at the end of the school year. He was so cool, you know, older and all and good looking. I sort of got swept away and before I knew it we were kissing and making out every chance we got. At first I tried to stop him going too far, but he was so strong and insistent, and he finally tried to touch me. You know, up here." She brushed her bathing suit top with her fingers. "It seemed kind of silly to me at the time, because I didn't have much there, but apparently he wanted to anyway."

"Did you let him?"

"Well, yeah. A little. But I was so scared I couldn't concentrate on it very well. And I don't think I was quite ready, if you know what I mean."

Thinking of my first encounter with Barbara Wilson's huge hairy wrinkled canyon, I nodded my understanding of not being quite ready.

"The problem was, he didn't want to stop there." Barbara paused and looked at me. "You're going to hate me if I tell, I know it. You'll think I'm a slut and never speak to me again."

I was hurt that she would say such a thing, but I understood. In our cruel world back then, a teenage girl could become a "slut" simply through unsubstantiated, often false rumors, spread by a spurned boy. This was long before losing one's virginity became a badge of honor for some girls, or at least a respected passage into some form of adulthood.

"Listen," I said. "I won't. I mean I could never feel that way about you. What we have is so special, I don't think it could ever be destroyed, least of all by being honest with each other. If you don't want to tell me, please don't, but I really do want you to. Not so I can see or think of you in any different way, but so we can have some kind of spiritual bond or something, which I think we already do. And I would die before I would ever tell another soul anything you say to me in confidence. I mean it!"

She twisted around until our faces were close, then kissed me on the nose. It seemed like a thank-you kiss.

"Okay," she said. "I believe you. Just give me a sec to work up my nerve."

I put my arm around her shoulder and she laid her head on my bare chest. We stayed like that for a long time, until finally she began to speak again.

"It was the next time I saw him. We were at the Y and he had his car. He talked me into sneaking away with him and we ended up in the back seat, parked on one of those dark side streets a couple of blocks from The Bay. It all started the same. Making out, him touching my chest. And then things started getting a little hot and heavy. He reached down and pushed his hand inside the front of my shorts. I tried to stop him, but he was on top of me and there wasn't much I could do. Anyway, by then I was curious to see what it was going to feel like."

She looked up at me as if expecting recrimination, but I hugged her tighter and said, "It's okay, you can stop if you want to." We were quiet for a while, as she snuggled up under my neck and fiddled with what little hair had sprouted on my 15-year-old chest. Finally, I said, "So, what did it feel like?"

After a short hesitation, she answered. "Good, I think. I mean I was excited and nervous, but it wasn't bad. When he undid the back of my shorts, I started getting scared, but he kept saying everything would be all right, to relax and trust him, that he would never hurt me. And then, before I knew what was happening, I felt his finger inside me, and whoa."

I felt her shudder as if chilled, but since it was eighty-five degrees and humid, I knew she couldn't be cold. "What do you mean, 'whoa?'" I asked.

"Well, it was a whole bunch of feelings all wrapped up in one big ball. First, I was scared to death, but then at the same time it was like when the Wild Mouse hits the top of that first incline and starts going down like a rocket ship.

You know, you're scared as heck, but you're also excited and it's exhilarating.

"Anyway, he kept whispering in my ear all kinds of reassuring things while he started to move his finger in and out of me, and then I think he put in another finger in too, because it started to hurt and I got to thinking how much more it would hurt if we went, you know, all the way. So I asked him to stop. I was scared he would think I was too young for him, that I wasn't mature enough to do what he wanted, or was chicken. Most of all, at that moment, I was worried I would lose him if I didn't let him do what he wanted."

I shuddered at this, thinking back to Barbara Wilson's story about her rape, and how it seemed to have messed up her head so badly she couldn't seem to feel anything anymore. And when I thought of that happening to this Barbara, to *my* Barbara, I started to get angry. Cautiously, almost not wanting to know the answer, I said, "So what happened?"

Looking a little sheepish, she lifted her head from my chest, looked me in the eyes and said, "Not much more. He didn't stop right away, but after he saw that I was crying, he pulled his fingers out and started massaging me down there. Funny thing is, that felt better than the other, but then he stopped and took his hand away. I asked him if he was mad, but he said no, that he was just frustrated. Then he went behind the car for a few minutes. I straightened my clothes, and when he came back he drove me to the Y and let me out. And that was it."

"Why do you think you stopped him?" I asked.

She smiled at me and said, "You know, I think it was for two reasons. One was that I wasn't quite ready yet, and the other was that I realized when I did finally feel ready, I wouldn't want my first time to be with him. I know it's going to happen someday, and it scares and excites me, not to mention worrying about what the church and my mom might think, and who it should be and how they would treat me afterward. It's pretty complicated, you know, for a girl, I mean."

"Well, to be honest, I never thought about it like that," I said. "I mean from a girl's point of view." And I hadn't. Up until then, I'd never even considered what it might be like for a girl. In fact, since my first experience was with someone who seemed to have no feelings about it at all, I had come to believe girls were only there to satisfy guys. If they got something out of it too, that was fine with me, but it wasn't important as long as I got off.

"You know," I said, "we need to talk some more about this, and maybe see if we can find some information or something to explain what goes on when people, uh, do it." She didn't answer, so I worked up a little more nerve and asked, "Do you know what a climax is? Sometimes they call it an orgasm. At least I've heard it called that. But, really, do you know what it is, or if girls can have one?"

"No," she said. "I've never heard either of those words before. What is it?"

"Wow!" I said, wondering what I had gotten myself into. My dad was a doctor who kept an office full of medical books at home, so I had been privy to lots of technical information about anatomy and the clinical aspects of reproduction, but none of the books ever included feelings or emotions when they talked about intercourse. This was years before the so-called sexual revolution, so my chances of finding anything written on the subject were slim, especially in the dry, technical medical journals my dad kept in his home library.

Finally, I said, "I could try to explain, I guess, but it's going to be pretty embarrassing."

"Oh, like what I told you wasn't?"

"Right," I murmured, wondering how a boy who doesn't know shit could explain an orgasm to a girl who might not even be able to have one. In fact, when I thought about it, there weren't a lot of words to describe what an orgasm felt like. It didn't feel like anything else I knew, so it would be almost impossible to describe. "It's going to be tough," I said. "And I don't mean just the embarrassment. The feeling is so different from anything else I've felt that there's nothing to use for comparison."

"Well," she said, "I may not have had one, but I did find something to compare what I was feeling with. Remember the roller coaster?"

"Yeah, right," I said, working things around in my mind to find some way to at least get started.

"Okay, here's an idea: try to think of the best feeling you've ever had in your life. What would that be?"

She was quiet for a few moments, then her eyes lit up. "How about when I won the figure skating title in the regionals last year? That was probably the happiest I've ever been."

"Okay, good. Now let's try to put that into a more … intimate context. Tell you what, go back to the night with Brad and the excitement you felt, along with the part where what he was doing started to feel good. I guess when he took his fingers out and was massaging you. Remember?"

"Yeah, what about it?"

"Well, try to blend the two experiences. You remember the build up to the finals, how each time you won a program you went a little bit higher and it got a little bit scarier because you might not win the next one?"

"Uh-huh," she said, looking skeptical.

"Okay, that worry about the next program, compare it to the way you felt about going each step further with Brad; the fear that was really the cause of your excitement, like the

Wild Mouse when it was about to start down. Then imagine Brad never hurt you, but that each step was like the massaging, only it got better and better and better, and at the same time a little scarier, but not so much that the fear would make you want him to stop. Can you imagine that, like in a dream? Close your eyes. Try."

She closed her eyes and I could tell she was trying. Then I noticed her legs start to rub together in a slow rhythmic way. "I think I can imagine it," she said. "The feeling, I mean."

I fished around for words or ideas to get to the next level, and finally I hit on something. "Okay, now imagine all those higher levels, those more exciting programs, being spread out on the side of a mountain, and what you're trying to do by reaching each new level of happiness and pleasure is get to the top of the mountain, because that's where all the good feelings are going to come together into one huge wonderful sensation, something like you've never ever experienced before. Like an explosion, a volcano of happiness, the greatest, most fantastic feeling in the world."

Suddenly, she opened her eyes and stared at me. Her legs had stopped moving, and she looked curious. "I think I get it," she said. "Or at least I can imagine what it might be like. The big question is, how do I get to the top of the mountain?"

"That's what I don't know," I said. "Like I said, I don't even know if girls can do it."

"Well, you can, can't you?"

"Sure."

"Okay, how do you do it?"

"Ohmigod, now we're really getting into it." My throat started to close and a huge flock of butterflies began dancing in my chest. How could I explain it without showing her?

And that thought turned the butterflies into thousands of tiny military combat helicopters.

"Come on, Tommy, you started this, and you can't leave me hanging now. Listen, if nature wants us to have kids, she wouldn't make the process pleasurable only for the man. Frankly, if there weren't something in it for the woman, and if what I hear about having babies is true, women wouldn't even consider it unless there was some powerful urge. From what you describe, I'll bet it's this climax thing. If I'm right, that means girls can have them too. All we need to do is find out how. And what better way would there be than to learn from someone who already knows?"

"Wow! That's a hell of an argument. Did you come up with it or did you read it somewhere?" I was stalling and she knew it.

"It makes sense, if you think about it."

"Okay, okay, give me some time to figure out how to say this." And right then I was saved by the bell.

"Tommy, Barbara," came the sweet sound of Mom's voice from inside the house. "Time to call it a night."

In trying to jump up from our somewhat compromising position in the wicker lounge, we got tangled in each others legs and arms, spilling out onto the rough surface of the patio and laughing until we couldn't breathe.

"Okay, kiddo," Barbara gasped between heaves of laughter, "you lucked out, but this isn't over. Promise me you'll think about it and the next time we can get away, you'll try to explain."

Head hung low in an over-dramatic imitation of chagrin, I nodded. And then, she made another one of those rip-my-heart-out moves. Glancing back toward the glass doors to make sure no one was watching, she pulled on my chin until we were eye to eye and kissed me. Not so soft this time, and definitely not one of those sympathy kisses. This one was the real thing, the kind with electricity and an afterbuzz. When we parted, our eyes seemed unable to come unlocked for the longest time. Finally, Barbara whispered, "My God, Tommy. What was that?"

3

THE FUNERAL

I wanted to say a few words here today," I stammered at the crowd of mourners. "I know a lot of you don't know me, but I knew Barbara." I hesitated for a moment, trying to keep from blubbering like an child.

"Barbara and I were, well, friends. Good friends, I'd like to think." I looked up at the four-dozen or so staring faces, and decided to amend my last statement. "Forget that," I said with finality. "We *were* good friends. In fact, we were best friends."

The weather was kind that afternoon, not that it wasn't often kind here in the western reaches of the Sunshine State. Above the group of mourners, a wispy gaggle of ice-cream white clouds gathered and stretched like ephemeral gowns blown on the winds of a Disney fantasy.

As I looked back down from the sky, I saw some of the guests whispering to each other, no doubt wondering who this brash intruder might be. I knew only a few of these people, but the rest must have known Barbara, and I tried to take comfort in the fact that we were all here because we loved her.

Barbara's dad, Phillip, was in the front row. And even though he was basically an asshole, I had to assume his grief was real. Though he was stoic and stern, as always, I could discern a measure of sorrow in his eyes, even from a distance. Her mom had died of breast cancer years earlier, and even though Phillip was a general stick-in-the-mud, it seemed Barbara's death had dealt a second blow to the old man's already damaged heart.

Charles, Barbara's second husband, was there as well. Her first was killed in Vietnam, and Charles had been a rebound, never quite able to live up to the image of his predecessor. The two split after four tumultuous years. Charles was a nice fellow. I was sure he was one of the few who had caught a glimpse of Barbara's soul. Why else would he never marry again? Why else would he succumb to alcoholism and isolation and a constant vigil to see that Barbara never wanted for anything? Charles was one of the good guys, as pathetic as he might seem to those who never knew Barbara the way he and I did.

Unfortunately, Barbara's daughter, BB, was somewhere in Darfur, doing what she could to stop the genocide going on in that God-forsaken country. I sent her a telegram, but it didn't reach her in time for her to make it back for the funeral. Even if it had, she probably would have stayed where she was. BB had inherited Barbara's heart and empathy, and had spent her entire adult life trying to right the wrongs in the world.

The rest of the attendees, with the exception of George and a few others I knew casually, were strangers to me, and it made me happy that so many of her friends had shown up.

I hate funerals. To me they are basically a way for funeral providers to make a bunch of money off the grief of others at the most vulnerable times in their lives. Money grubbing pricks with no real concern for anything but their own bottom lines, pretending to be chock full of concern for those they are ripping off. It was often said jokingly, though it may have been true, that there were more funeral homes in St. Pete than there were bars. The land of the newlywed and nearly dead, we used to call it, because as soon as the kids grew up and got married, they tended to leave rather than raise their kids in the waiting room of a mausoleum that catered mainly to conservative retirees.

Among my musician friends, we never had funerals; we had what we called "musicians wakes." These were not somber affairs, they were joyful celebrations of a person's life, with music and speeches and humor and drinking and jam sessions. No burial site or coffins or any of that crap. We let the square community take care of those things and most of us ignored them while we planned for a Wake. If the deceased was someone with a young family, we would tape the whole thing so their kids would have something to play for years to come and know how much their dad or mom had meant to all of us.

But this one, this particular funeral, was going to be all there was for Barbara. It was my only chance to let at least a few people know how much she meant to me, how important she had been in my life. So there I was, talking to a bunch of strangers. That was something Barbara and I prided ourselves in, our ability to just talk. But now it was something I had a lot of trouble doing.

4
PAULA ~~~~~~~~~~~~~~~~~~~~~ 1968

H_{ey}, Tommy!" I heard the voice waft across the sultry breeze as I made my way back from the snack bar to the blanket where Paula and the kids anxiously awaited their hot dogs and Cokes. My family had grown to four with the birth of my son two years earlier. Paula, Donna and Tom, Jr. had emerged from the salty waters of the Gulf of Mexico to take a break and dry off while I scrambled over blistering sand, dodging hundreds of sunbathers on a trek to the snack bar and back with the food.

I was almost within sight of them when that voice stopped me in my tracks. No one had called me "Tommy" in years, but it wasn't the name that sparked my memory, it was the voice. There was only one voice in the world like that: high pitched, but not shrill; insistent without being demanding; warm but not the least bit syrupy. It was a voice for the ages. A voice that at once demanded attention, while at the same time conveying patience and an understanding that if you didn't respond, that would be okay, too.

I glanced at the steaming bodies and spread umbrellas, trying to figure out exactly where Barbara's voice had come from, when suddenly I felt a cool hand on my ankle. I looked down to see a vision I could only have hoped to see again. There, right at my stinging hot feet, she reclined under a small umbrella, her soft brown hair glowing in the filtered sunlight, her slender body clad in a skimpy two-piece bathing suit. Another girl shared the blanket, but I could not tear my eyes away from Barbara long enough to even sneak a glance at her.

Barbara smiled up at me and I nearly dropped the two cardboard trays I had balanced in the crooks of my arms. The first thing I noticed, besides her near nakedness, was that she still had freckles. Her smooth complexion, growing pink from the sun, was dappled with a plethora of tiny specks that gave her the adolescent look of innocence I remembered so well. Before long, however, my eyes could not help but stray from her face to the rest of her, which had changed little over the eight or so years since I'd last seen her.

Her breasts were still small, but they had filled out somewhat, and showed the effects of having been suckled. Her legs, slender and firm, stretched out in an elongated V, while she leaned back on one arm and gazed at me with a smile that nearly tore my heart from my chest.

"Well," she said, when I didn't seem able to speak. "You always did like to look. So, what do you think? Have I changed for the worse?"

"Good God, woman," I finally managed. "Have you no shame? You can't just do this to a guy like it's the most normal thing in the world."

"Shame? Hell, Tommy, you know me better than that. Besides, all I did was call your name."

"I know. I mean, sure, that's all you did, but you have absolutely no right to show up out of the blue looking as good as you do while I'm rushing on hot sand with an armful of food for my family."

My eyes, with a seemingly uncontrollable mind of their own, found their way to the lower half of her bathing suit, where a slight wisp of light brown curls had escaped. They lured me like a finger beckoning in subtle invitation. There was a faint hint of a stretch mark or two on her stomach, confirming the fact of childbirth. I suddenly realized I had an erection that must have grown to the point of obviousness under my bathing suit. Unable to do anything about it because my arms were immobilized by the food trays, I tried to scrunch sideways, while Barbara and her friend stared in silent scrutiny.

"Hey," I said finally. "I've got to get this stuff back to the kids. Are you going to be around a while? I'd really like to talk to you, if that's okay."

She looked at her friend and they both chuckled, but when she looked back at me, the humor seemed to disappear. "Sure, Tommy, I'd like that," she said. "I'll be here for at least another hour, so if you can get back without, you know, making any trouble ...." This was not said with sarcasm, but with the sincerity I had come to love many years before.

"You got it," I said. "I'll be back. Please don't go anywhere." One of my trays slipped sideways, and I did a silly dance and gyration to regain balance and keep them both from falling to the sand. Barbara and her companion got a kick out of that, but their laughter was cut short when Barbara jumped up to help me regain control. As her arm brushed mine in an attempt to move the trays to a good position, I felt an electric shock go through my body. At that moment she looked me square in the eyes.

"I see you're still a little clumsy," she said in a near whisper. "It's a good thing I'm around to help out." Then, with her body turned away from her friend, she quickly brushed my cheek with her lips. "If I'm not here when you get loose, I'm in the phone book under Robert Gallagher. This is not an invitation to anything underhanded. Rob's in Vietnam and I would never two-time him. But it would be nice to get together and talk, since I know how much you like to sit and talk." With that, she sank back down on the blanket, smiled over at her friend and waved goodbye to me, as I stumbled like a crippled clown toward my family.

That 1968 meeting at the beach was a Godsend of sorts, with the promise of a cathartic encounter, or maybe even a bit of extramarital sex, something I was damned good and ready for. Paula and I had been married for about four years by then, and it wasn't working.

When my mom and I moved to Clearwater, a few years after she and Dad divorced, we settled into a house down the street from Paula and her family. Paula was a strikingly attractive girl with a face and lisp reminiscent of Hayley Mills and an athletic body punctuated by the most incredible pair of legs I have ever seen. She had been a cheerleader at Clearwater High, where some of my friends went to school.

We knew each other vaguely, but we never formally met until a few weeks after I moved in. I was walking down the street one day when I saw her rubbing at something on her front steps. Curious, I strolled over and watched, trying to figure out what she was doing. Finally, I asked the obvious question. "What are you doing?" I said, stretching out the "are." At the time, she was bent over facing away from me, with her nicely rounded butt sticking up above those lovely legs.

"What does it look like?" she said without turning around. "I'm waxing the front steps."

I noticed a can of paste wax on the steps beside her, and was flabbergasted at the idea that anyone would paste wax a set of brick and cement steps. "Right," I said. "And why would anyone do that?"

She hesitated a moment, then looked over her shoulder at me. "Obviously, you don't know my mother," she said with an exaggerated groan.

The conversation that followed kicked off a friendship that grew for something like six months. Paula became good friends with my mom and our housemate, Angie. Over the months, the four of us spent a lot of time together, playing board games and watching TV and cooking and such.

At Clearwater High, Paula was known as an ice cube, due to the fact that no one, not even the semi-famous quarterback of the football team, could get into her pants—or her blouse for that matter. Rumor had it that many a young buck had tried his best to breach her formidable defenses, but none had ever even made it to first base. She had managed, it was said, to have graduated the previous year with her hymen and everything else intact, though the hymen part wasn't exactly true. It seems all those cheerleading splits and stretches had taken care of that long before.

At the time, and throughout my abbreviated high-school years, I was sort of a rock star around town, having recently come off a tour of the Southeast opening a chain of Peppermint Lounges. Because of this, I had a somewhat legitimate reputation for sexual conquests. I say, "somewhat," because, as with many reputations, mine was based mostly on rumor, and the fact that I was often on stage enhanced the legend.

For several months after our first meeting, Paula and I were only friends, and our friendship grew to the point of talking about a lot of things, even sex and her still unblemished reputation. Paula was the ultimate tomboy, athletic and strong and adept at many sports, especially the one the boys often wanted to play in the backseats of cars at the drive-in movies or on darkened dead-end roads in the moonlight. She usually wore shorts, with halter-tops, to guard her nearly non-existent breasts, and she almost never used makeup. She always seemed to have a few abrasions or scabs on her legs and arms, which were most often soiled from one physical activity or another. In fact, until one night about six months after we met, I had never seen her looking much like a female at all.

Had I met Paula for the first time twenty years or so later, my first thought might have been that she was a lesbian, but in those days, I didn't even know there was such a thing. Besides, I would have been wrong. Though, as I would later discover, she wasn't terribly sexual in any sense of the word. She was, however, curious, and I eventually worked that curiosity around to make what came to be known as the greatest conquest in the history of our group of friends.

It all started one afternoon, while Mom and Angie and Paula and I were working on a prolonged game of Scrabble. I had acquired tickets for the new blockbuster movie, *West Side Story*, which was premiering that night and, being in between girlfriends at the time, I was trying to decide who to invite to the movie. Paula made some suggestions, and between turns, I called a few, but all were either tied up or didn't want to go out with me, a fact I was careful to cover up on my side of the conversations, which the ladies present could hear.

Finally, with nearly all possibilities exhausted, Angie turned to me and said, "Heck, Tommy, why don't you take Paula?" I looked at Paula and we both shrugged. "It'd be a shame to let those tickets go to waste," Angie concluded, slapping down a huge point-packed word I didn't recognize.

"You wanna go?" I asked matter-of-factly. Paula shrugged again, looked down at her Scrabble tiles, and said, "Sure, I guess."

That evening, I had the shock of my life as I skipped up the once-again freshly waxed steps to her door and knocked. When the door opened, there was a stunningly beautiful young woman standing there to greet me. I knew Paula had an older sister, reputed to be a Playboy quality beauty, but she was supposed to be attending the University of Florida at the time, and I had never actually seen her. Stretching my neck a bit to peer over this lovely lady's shoulder, I asked in a sheepish little voice, "Uh, is Paula ready?"

"Don't I look ready to you?" the vision in the doorway asked. All of a sudden it dawned on me: I was actually looking at my tomboy buddy. One of the problems with recognizing her, besides the makeup and slinky black dress and coifed hair, was the fact that she wore high heels, which made her a little taller than I was.

"Oh my God," I whispered, at which she laughed out loud. After the proper greetings with her parents, a couple of transplanted country folks from Louisiana, one of which was certifiably weird and the other of which I would come to love like a surrogate father, we were off to the movies. From then on, nothing would ever be quite the same between us.

Awkward would be an understatement to describe that evening. As attractive as Paula turned out to be, I was flummoxed when it came to knowing what to do about it. I could not deny my sexual attraction, but our relationship had been so different until then, our conversations so frank and un-emotional, I found myself nearly unable to speak the entire night. The same inhibitions seemed to have afflicted her as well, and we spent most of the next few hours in almost stunned silence, watching the movie, stopping for burgers at Triplets, then, gratefully finding some refuge at home, where we ended the evening playing a game of Monopoly with Mom and Angie.

I walked her down the street to her door around 11:00, and we did the normal stop-on-the-porch bit that usually led at least to a goodnight kiss. We shuffled around a bit, both trying to think of something to say or do that would alleviate the need to perform that teenage ritual.

"So," she said, finally breaking the roaring silence be-tween us. "What did you think?"

"I, uh, gee, Paula, I don't know what to say," I said, look-ing down at my shoes. "I mean, you're really beautiful to-night, and I, well, I'm not sure how to react to all that, you know?" I had actually worn a suit that evening, something I seldom did, but Angie had warned that the premier of *West Side Story* was pretty important, and that I should not go looking like some scruffy musician, lest I find myself embar-rassed to be the only male in attendance without at least a tie.

"Well," Paula said with a short burst of laughter, "you're not so bad looking yourself, but that's not what I was ask-ing. I meant, what did you think of the movie, idiot?" That broke the nervousness, her laughing and calling me an idiot and all. Suddenly the old comfortable friendship returned, and I joined in her laughter, reaching out a hand to touch her on the shoulder, which, I realized immediately was not the best thing to do if I wanted to keep things on the level of friendly banter. That touch led to a slight grasp, which led to a movement toward each other, and we ended up kissing after all.

Looking back on things today, I should have known right then we were not exactly made for each other in the way couples are meant to be. Like her reputation, her kiss was rather perfunctory and cool, but it still stirred up my libido a good bit. And, as I would later find out, it also had stirred her budding sexual awareness. Still, her chilly countenance might have warned me that our love life, if there was to be one, would probably not be great in the long run.

Over the next few weeks our closeness waned, at least in the sense of being buddies. Our conversations tended to be a bit more stilted, and we started doing things together we had not done before, like going to beach parties as a couple and her accompanying me to gigs with the rock band I had assembled from my more musically talented high-school friends. In those days, there were no drugs to speak of in the white-bread society of middle and upper class teenagers we hung around with. The "drug" of choice at that time was beer, and our little group was renowned for its incredible capacity to put away gallons of the stuff. And, like the tomboy she was, Paula could drink most of us under the table if she took a notion to.

To make more palatable our move to Clearwater, which was predicated on my parents' divorce and Mom's subsequent inability to financially maintain the big house with the swimming pool where I grew up, I was allowed to close in the one-car garage and make a private music room out of it. Within a couple of months after the move, my friends and I had completed the room, which was lined on the walls and ceiling with acoustical tiles to capture the sound before it could reach the neighbors' ears. We added a musically themed façade on the front, and installed a sliding door that one electronically talented friend had rigged to slide open and shut at the touch of a button on the inside and the turn of a key out front.

The room, which we named "Club NAMA," was furnished with a stage, upon which sat the drum set and organ and amplifiers our band used, plus a scattering of chairs and tables and a rollaway bed/couch, where I could sleep if I wanted to. I used this couch mostly as a sanctuary from the attention of my mother on those nights when I'd had a bit too much to drink and needed a place to crash and then nurse a morning hangover. But it also served me at times when a few ladies found themselves alone with me in the privacy of the music room.

Though I always claimed, at least to teachers and other adults who might cause trouble, that NAMA stood for Nelson's Academy of Musical Achievement, a lot of the younger folks and some savvy adults knew the letters actually stood for the rather irreverent No Anal Motherfuckers Allowed.

On one of those nights when the band had practiced, entertaining a small group of friends and drinking a good bit of beer, Paula and I, both quite high, got into one of our long conversations and ended up broaching the subject of sex once again. Like many before it, this conversation was punctuated by frankness and Paula's growing curiosity to understand what "all the fuss was about." It wasn't long before the group dispersed and we were the only two left in the room. I found myself trying my best to explain the unexplainable, when she stopped me mid-sentence.

"Okay," she said with a determined resignation in her voice. "I believe you when you say it can't be described, so I guess you're going to have to show me."

Even though this was what I had been working toward for the past several weeks, her abrupt suggestion took me by surprise. "You mean, right now?" I stammered. "Tonight? Here? Do you really think we should?"

"Come on, you dummy," she answered almost angrily. "You've been working on me for weeks now, as if I didn't know what was going on. I said okay, didn't I? I gave in. So let's get on with it. Or are you saying that after all that effort you don't want to?"

Again, this was one of those signals that, had I been older, I might have recognized as averse to long-term romance. But, of course, nothing could have been further from my mind at the time. Paula's somewhat cold and matter-of-fact attitude about losing her virginity should have set off some alarms, however, at that moment, the only thing I could think about was the four-alarm fire burning in my groin.

The scene that followed was almost antiseptically unemotional. I turned off the overhead light, leaving only a small lamp with a 40-watt bulb burning several feet from the couch, while Paula stepped out of her shorts and panties, leaving them in a wrinkled heap on the floor. She did not, however, remove her halter-top, which seemed to signal her intention was not to waste time on foreplay. She wanted to get laid, and that was all there was to it.

When I hesitated to remove my own clothes, she stared me down until I finally managed to slip out of my jeans and Jockey shorts. Then she leaned over and started grabbing the pillows on the couch, tossing them to the floor one by one. As she began to tug at the strap that released the bed from the couch, I joined her, and we soon had the rather uncomfortable rollaway flattened out. I always left the sheets on the bed when I closed it up, so there was little left to do but lie down, which she did with a little flouncy jump, more like an athletic move than a prelude to sex.

"You know," I said as I lay down beside her, "this isn't going to work very well for you if we just, well, do it."

She turned to look at me then, and asked in a perfunctory tone, "Why not?"

I hemmed and hawed a bit, and then, like a teacher, began to explain what might make things more comfortable for her.

She thought for a moment, then said, "Okay." And for the first time since we started our discussion, she began to show a hint of fear.

We had done a good bit of making out over the previous few weeks, mostly in the presence of other couples at the beach or on double dates in a car, so that was nothing new for us. What was new was that this time the making out was actually going to lead somewhere. I still had never touched her sexually, which meant all of this was going to be new territory for both of us. When I didn't move for a few moments, she sighed and turned toward me. We kissed, but her nervousness and lack of warmth rendered the kiss somewhat less than sexual. Still, we went on, with me kissing her ears and neck and eventually straying toward the top of her halter.

I later learned it was her undeveloped breasts that caused Paula to be reluctant for me to touch them during sex. And that night, as I started to move down toward her still covered chest, she began to stroke my hair in a way that signaled me to stop. Then, as if becoming exasperated with the wait, she grabbed one of my hands and placed it firmly between her legs, lifting them up and spreading them in a clear indication that she wanted to move on.

I began to massage her, and eventually the stimulation started her juices flowing. When I finally entered her with a finger, I was shocked to find she was quite large, not at all like the few virgins I had known, but nearly as large as my first sexual partner, in whose cavernous vagina I had often felt lost.

As I proceeded and she became wetter and wetter, she turned to me and asked, "Is it going to hurt?" I thought for a moment, not wanting to be insulting or to say something that might hinder things. Then I hit on how to answer her without spoiling the moment.

"Well," I said, "if you were younger and not so athletic, it probably would. But since you're nearly an adult and spent most of your life doing all those acrobatics and stuff, you've gotten pretty … mature down there. I mean, from what I can tell, you probably won't experience much if any pain."

"That's nice," she said, as if I had told her she didn't have to pay me back for a loan or something. We went on like that for a while, with me massaging and fingering, waiting for some overt reaction, but for a long time she hardly moved and made no sounds at all. When her hips finally did begin to move a little, I decided to climb on top, never taking my hand away from its rhythmic work. I had earlier retrieved and unwrapped one of the rubbers I kept squirreled away under the couch, which I now began to put on, again continuing to attend to her with my other hand.

When I figured I had done about all I could do to get her aroused, I spread her legs a bit farther, pushed them up to gain better access, and abruptly entered her.

"Oh," she said, as I pushed in farther and she grabbed me in a hard hug. "Are you okay?" I asked. "Uh-huh," she murmured, with a hint of sadness and apprehension that stood in sharp contrast to her earlier self-assured cockiness. "But it does hurt a little"

"Do you want me to stop?" I asked. I had penetrated her about halfway, but stopped when she said it hurt. After a few moments of stillness and no movement, she said, "No. I want you to go on," adding, "Please, Tom, I'll be all right."

Again, I took hold of her legs and she helped while I pushed them even further apart and began to raise them up. Then, with one final thrust, I buried myself to the hilt. This time, she let out a little shriek, but I was no longer able to stop. Soon, we got into a serious slapping rhythm, each thrust being harder and harder and each result eliciting a guarded exhalation of breath from her.

Between my own gasps, I managed to ask, "Do you think you can come now? Because I'm about to."

She seemed not to hear me at first, but after a few seconds, she responded. "I think so," she said in a gruff whisper. "But please do it harder and faster. As fast as you can, okay?"

"Okay." I began to increase the speed and power behind my thrusts until the sounds of our bodies slamming together seemed to grow loud enough for the neighbors to hear. It didn't take long for me to come, and I thought she had as well, because I could feel her breath in my ear as it grew shorter and shorter in little quiet gasps. When I felt myself begin to shrink, I tried to use the last few moments of my erection in a rhythmic effort to match her waning contractions. And, when I could no longer continue, she whispered, "That was good, Tom. Really good."

That first time, as I have alluded to before, was a preview of things to come. Our sexual encounters became fairly regular, but Paula was never shy about saying she didn't feel like it on any particular occasion. It wasn't long before we ran into one of those situations where I was sans rubbers and we decided not to worry about it. Unfortunately, all it took was that one time, and within a few weeks we had resigned ourselves to the fact that she was pregnant.

Though we both seemed to sense it wasn't quite right, in that day and age there was little choice but to "do the right thing." So we hastily planned a wedding, with all our friends and parents no doubt aware of what was going on, but no one willing to say it out loud. It was a pretty big wedding, stressful for both of us, after which we settled into a somewhat chilly married relationship, with little real love or affection. After our daughter was born, sex became even less desirable for her. Intercourse was relegated to about once every two weeks or so, with her always on top so the penetration would be as deep as possible and she could regulate her own stimulation using her considerable athletic skills to rub her clitoris against my pubic bone.

This was tough for me, as my sexual appetite, even under those mechanical and repetitive circumstances, was greater than hers. I soon found out, however, that her apparent lack of interest in sex applied only to me, because it wasn't long before I caught her having an affair with one of my best friends—something I thought might have had to do with his reputedly large dick. Though we got through that little episode okay and stayed together "for the kids," I eventually became aware that her straying hadn't ended, and finally understood it probably never would.

We divorced after some seven years, but it wasn't the old male seven-year itch that did it. I never stepped out on Paula. Having lived through the trauma my dad caused my mom when he left to marry the nurse with whom he had been two-timing her for years, I resolved always to be a faithful partner. And I never broke that vow, even when Paula's extramarital activities became general knowledge among our friends.

I did come close once, but only because I happened to run into the real love of my life on the beach that fateful Saturday afternoon. Not even my solemn vow would have stopped me from committing adultery with her. No, it wasn't my unassailable will power that kept it from happening; it was Barbara who handled that bit of trauma for both of us, though even for this strong-willed and practical woman, doing so was no piece of cake.

5

BARBARA 1960

I finally found what I wanted a few days after our conversation about sex by the pool. Mom had gone out to the grocery and our maid had already left, giving me a few minutes alone in the afternoon to root around in Dad's home office looking for something, anything that could lend a clue to whether or not a girl could have a climax, and if so, how. It was in a section on sexual anatomy. A diagram showed something called a clitoris, which, according to the picture, was right above a girl's vagina. The book didn't say too much about it, other than calling it the "main organ of female sexual stimulation." The rest was complicated medical stuff, but that one phrase sounded to me like this clitoris thing might be important.

With new information in hand, I resolved to tell Barbara about it and maybe ask if she would like me to see if what the book said was true. Of course, this would involve touching it, which would be something new for both of us, and she likely wouldn't want to let me do that. Still, she was the one who was curious about climaxes, and I felt like it was my duty to at least mention the discovery.

The big problem for all us horny adolescents in those days, besides finding a girl who would let us do "it," was finding places safely out of eye and ear shot of our parents. It wasn't like you could simply take a girl up to your room and lock the door. At that age, at least one parent or adult was always around to keep a close eye out for anything that might look suspiciously like sexual activity.

In my case, with our large house and grounds in the old northeast section of St. Pete, there were probably more hiding places than most of my friends could find at their homes, but that didn't negate the fact that adults never let us out of their sight for long, particularly if there was a girl around.

That odd thing called adolescence was a strange transition. Before we turned 13 or so, we had a good bit more unsupervised freedom of movement. But once girls started to change from icky little irritants to objects of curiosity and desire, parents seemed to sense it, and all of a sudden our whereabouts and activities were subject to a new and more intense scrutiny. But there was one place I thought might be perfect.

In our side yard was a huge Laurel Leaf Rubber tree. Everybody thought it was a Banyan tree because it was so big, but it lacked the hanging vines of a Banyan and I learned early on that it wasn't. The tree had a base trunk diameter of nearly 15 feet, from which grew several huge secondary trunks, each about 3 feet in diameter at their origin. These spread up and out as they rose to support the canopy, a mass of smaller limbs and leaves that shaded some two thirds of our triple lot. Of course, this configuration invited serious climbing, and also provided a near perfect framework for a tree house, which my friends and I had started to build when I was about seven years old.

By the time I was 15, the tree house had grown to three stories, with trap doors in each floor and ladders nailed to the larger limbs so we could climb from floor to floor. We had furnished the floors with old blankets and discarded pillows, plus a chair or two and some makeshift tables and a few shelves tacked to the limbs. For the most part, the three stories were open on the sides, but we had installed two walls and had even run a long extension cord up to provide power for a radio and portable record player. In the early days of ambiguous sexual identity, boys and girls alike would climb up into the tree house to play, but once puberty began to set in, the girls seemed to be less and less inclined to join us. Still, the tree house did provide a measure of privacy and for some odd reason, this fact did not raise alarm bells with parents in the same way a locked bedroom door might. In addition to the privacy factor, parents, for the most part, weren't into climbing trees, so surprise parental intrusion was almost non-existent.

About three weeks after I found the medical book, Barbara once again visited for an afternoon of swimming and I suggested she might like to see the tree house. She agreed with an enthusiastic laugh. We changed out of our bathing suits into shorts and sneakers, and I began to demonstrate the somewhat difficult procedure for climbing up to the first level. Early on, we built a ladder to make the first climb easy, but that also made it more accessible to adults and smaller kids, so we eventually removed it in favor of the tougher first climb.

Barbara was a bit of a tomboy and she caught on quickly to the handholds and foot supports we had installed. As we climbed higher, I explained some of the history, pointing out the older supports on the lower levels and various improvements and upgrades we had made throughout the years. Once at the top level, we were essentially out of sight from the ground, and one of the walls blocked off direct viewing from the windows in the second story of the main house. It was a soft and fragrant day in late summer, with a warm breeze and brilliant white clouds that occasionally appeared through the few gaps in the leaf canopy.

At first, we stood there nervously facing each other and catching our breath, but soon our eyes locked as they had many times before and we reached out for each other. The embrace was tentative, much like our first connection in the courtyard at the Y. Then, slowly we drew each other closer and hugged. I found my mouth resting near her ear and began to kiss her neck; soft kisses, not urgent or demanding, but the kind meant to convey real affection, which is exactly what I felt. It wasn't long, however, before these nibbles became more serious and she began to respond with encouraging little sounds and body movements. This had an immediate effect on me, which I knew she could feel through our light clothes.

Embarrassed, I took her by the shoulders and pushed her far enough away to look in her eyes without breaking our embrace. Clouds suddenly obscured the afternoon sun, darkening the atmosphere around us, but the radiance of her smile seemed to light up the scene, creating a bubble of suffused illumination that seemed to surround only the two of us. It was another of those times I never forgot. I was so filled with love at that moment my body began to shudder, and that seemed to worry her.

"Are you okay?" she whispered, cocking her head in curiosity. It was all I could do to nod and squeeze my stinging eyes shut to nip a couple of tears in the bud. She pulled me back against her, and we stayed in that semi-chaste embrace for a long time, until I remembered the reason I had brought her up there in the first place.

"Hey," I said in her ear. "I've got something I want to show you." She jerked back with a look of mock alarm on her face. "No, no, not that," I said laughing. "It's a book." We untangled and I swept the back of my hand above a large floor pillow. She plopped down, crossed her legs and peered up at me with a curious expression.

From a shelf above her head, I retrieved the book I had pilfered from my dad's study earlier. "I think I might have found some answers," I said flipping through the pages to find the section I wanted. But when I turned the page to uncover the diagram, I realized how embarrassing this whole thing was going to be. My reflex reaction slammed the book on my finger and I stammered to find the right words to explain why I had done so.

"I don't know if you … if I … uh, maybe we shouldn't look at this right now." I could feel my face turning red as blood rushed to my head.

Barbara looked perplexed and tilted her head to peer into my eyes. "Why did you bring it up here then?" she asked.

"Well, I found something in there, and I thought you might like to know about it."

"Okay," she said. "But we won't know until you let me see it, right? So, what do you say we take a look?"

I clamped the book to my chest. "It's just that it's kind of embarrassing. It's a diagram of your … you know, down there." I let my head drop a little, careful not to look all the way down between her legs.

"Oh," she drew the word out until it trailed off into silence. Then, perking up, she smiled. "Well, you've already seen it, so it won't be anything new for you. Maybe if you let me look by myself first?"

"Sure, no problem," I said, giving in. I held out the book with my finger still stuck in at the page in question.

With a nervous glance up at me, hooded by her eyebrows but sparkling with curiosity, she reached out and pulled the book from my grasp, careful to slip a finger in as I withdrew mine. Then she swiveled around on the pillow and, with her back to me, began to examine the page. After a minute or two, she said, "Oh, I see now. It's a cutaway view. Like an X -ray picture."

"Yeah, on that page. On the next one there's more of a front view. But the most important thing is the parts. They're labeled with little arrows pointing at them."

Slowly, she turned the page. "Oh, gross!" she said, but her head never turned away. In fact, she seemed to be bending closer to get a better look. After a few moments of examination, she started scraping her heels against the blanket in an attempt to spin back around on the pillow. Then, with a twinkle in her eye, she said, "Okay, you've seen me, now where are the diagrams of you?"

"Wait, don't you want to hear what I found out about you?" I said in a momentary panic. "I mean, we know—or at least I do—what happens with me. What we're trying to figure out is if you can, well, you know."

"Fair's fair," she said with a pout, and started flipping backward in the book until she found what she was looking for. "Oh," she said. "This must be it. Looks about as gross as mine." Then, after a minute or two of serious scrutiny, she said, "Okay, that's out of the way. Now, what was it you wanted to show me?"

With the heat in my face growing to the point that I thought I might blister, I lowered myself onto the pillow beside her. She turned the book so we both could see, and I flipped the pages back to the female diagram, then pointed at the arrow indicating the clitoris. "Uh-huh?" she said, looking from the diagram to my face and back again.

"See the reference number? That corresponds to the text on the other page. This is number six, so look over here and read what it says next to number six."

After a moment, a small whistle escaped from her lips. "Wow," she said. She seemed to be reading it over and over, following the words with a finger, then moving to the other page to point at the diagram. Suddenly, she stopped. "That confirms it, don't you think? I mean they wouldn't use that description if women were just hunks of dead meat meant for men to enjoy." She seemed quite pleased at this discovery and her interpretation. Then, closing the book and laying it aside, she smiled at the air in front of her and in a voice slightly above a whisper, said, "I wonder what it feels like."

After a few moments of nervous silence, I said in the same half whisper, "You could try it and see."

"Me?" She said, incredulous. "What do you mean? Touch myself there? I don't think so!"

"Well," I said, "remember when you made me promise to explain how I do it?" She nodded with a sly little smile. "Okay, how do you think I could do it without touching myself?"

She pondered that for a moment. "I guess I never thought about it. But doesn't it seem weird to be doing something like that to yourself? I mean, I can't even imagine doing such a thing. Isn't it supposed to be a sin or something?"

"I don't know about the sinning part, and, yeah, it did seem weird to me at first, but the result, the feeling, is so incredible I gave up thinking it was strange a long time ago."

"Oh," she said, again letting the word trail off. She turned to look at me and reached out a hand. I took it in mine and rubbed the back of her fingers. She squeezed ever so slightly, smiled and said, "Thanks, Tommy. For telling me about this, I mean. I know it wasn't easy for you and I really appreciate it. But I still don't think I could do that to myself." Then she started to pull me toward her until our faces were inches apart, and this time the kiss was different. Her lips seemed softer, warmer, wetter than before, and she pressed them into mine with an urgency I had never felt before. Soon we began to lean backward until we were both reclining on the huge pillow and the blanket beneath it. I kissed her cheek, then her eyes, which closed when my lips neared them. And when I began to nibble on an earlobe, I could feel her shiver. From there I continued down her neck and around to the front, nipping and licking along the way as I slid ever closer toward the top button of her blouse, all the while awaiting the abrupt "Stop!" I knew was sure to come at any moment.

But she made no attempt to stop me, and the only sounds she uttered were soft, urging murmurs. When I reached the button, I felt her fingers creep up from below to unfasten it. Then the next and the next. Kissing a bra is not the most pleasant or romantic thing I have ever done, but I damn well was going to put up with it. And I did, until I felt it begin to loosen and realized she had reached around to unfasten it herself.

I stopped for a moment and looked into her eyes, where a hint of moisture had begun to appear. "Is this okay?" I asked in what turned out to be a rough whisper. My voice seemed to be deserting me. She smiled and reached out to ruffle my hair.

"It's better than okay, Tommy. So long as you like it and won't think I'm some kind of slut for letting you. It feels nice and I don't want to stop, at least not now." She ran her hand through my hair once again and turned my head back down toward her small, perfectly formed, breasts. Not having any idea what to do, I kissed, then licked and eventually began to suck on a nipple. "Oh," she moaned. "Oh, God that feels good. Oh, Tommy."

I began to wonder if she might be having an orgasm right then, though I didn't think so because, unlike the clitoris, the breasts were not labeled in the book as being an "organ of female sexual stimulation."

I soon realized I was moving up and down against her, and since she wasn't protesting, I began to insert one leg between hers. Again, no protest. In fact, as the movement intensified, she seemed to be lifting her hips to press harder against my leg. This encouraged me to take the next step, and I reached down with my hand and began to rub between her legs. Her response wasn't immediate, but she didn't try to stop me. As I rubbed with more and more pressure, her hips began to rise and fall and her moaning, though quiet, became more intense. I could feel the warmth of fluid begin to grow under her shorts, as if her body was getting ready for something. And then I noticed her lifting and turning a bit. I thought at first this was more of her reaction to my movements, but I soon realized she was trying to undo the button and zipper at the back of her shorts. It wasn't long before I felt the shorts slacken and she reached down to remove my hand and insert it under the waistline.

The angle was awkward and our scrunched position didn't help, but I soon made it all the way down to where the warm moisture had soaked through her underwear. I resumed my rubbing, and before long I managed to slip one of my fingers around the elastic and inside her.

"Oh," she whispered when I pushed my finger farther in, then she gave out a long, strained sound as I started moving it in and out. I wanted to ask again if what I was doing was okay, but her reactions seemed to answer that, so I kept it up, moving faster and faster, reveling in the little sounds she made in response.

It was then that a kind of delirium overtook me, matching her own, and suddenly I came all over the inside of my pants. She seemed to sense something at that moment—probably my rhythmic jerking against her leg, or maybe even some dampness seeping through. In any case, I was suddenly spent, exhausted, and all sexual desire began to vanish, as it always did after a climax.

As I slowly removed my hand from her pants and stretched my neck to kiss her on the lips, she tightened her arms around me, patting me on the back as if she were comforting me after some major ordeal. I immediately flashed back to that time at the dance when she had nearly brought me to tears with the same gentle touch, and I felt a huge shiver run up and down my body. Moving my lips around to her ear, I whispered, "I'm sorry."

"There's nothing to be sorry about, Tommy," she said, holding me tighter and stroking my back like a mother comforting a child. "That was wonderful." And then, after a few minutes of sweet silence, she said, "Was that it? Did you have a climax?"

Still nestled in her neck with her damp, chlorine-scented hair around my face, I nodded. "I wish you could have, too," I said after a while, and next to my ear I felt her lips curl into a smile.

"There's time," she said. "There's time."

And then, as if destined to be—and only because that moment was one of the most incredible of my life, one I wished could last forever—the shrewish voice of our maid Thelma rang out over the side yard. "Where you two at?" she yelled. "What're you up to? You up in that tree? You better get down out of there before your momma comes home and finds you're not swimmin'"

6

BARBARA

When I arrived back at our beach blanket, it took me a few moments to hand out the hot dogs and Cokes and make sure the kids were settled, all the while trying to think of some excuse to get back to Barbara. The breeze picked up and a few dark clouds began rolling across the horizon as our typical afternoon invasion of thunderstorms began its slow trek in from the western Gulf.

Paula was reading a book and the kids were in the beginnings of a food fight, when George appeared at the edge of our blanket. "Hey, gang." he said. "Anybody seen Allie?" George was my oldest and closest friend, and he had recently hooked up with Alicia, one of my off-and-on steadies since grade school. A big, bronzed, strapping fellow, George was a guitarist of the first degree, with a sweet, melodic voice reminiscent of Art Garfunkle that blended almost perfectly with my bluesy baritone. After I married Paula and we had our first child, I went "legit." I'd given up on Rock 'n' Roll and abandoned the road to take a "real" job. And, to make sure we didn't lose complete touch with the music scene, George and I started working together writing music and performing at small local venues.

Paula perked up and did a once-over of George's chiseled body. Of all my wife's extramarital efforts, George was probably her most frustrating. Paula's infidelity was well known in our little group, but George and I were much too close for him to consider her less-than-subtle flirting.

"I thought I saw her a little earlier playing volleyball, George." Paula nodded toward a gaggle of legs and arms and flying sand about fifty yards away.

"Thanks, Paula. I'll check it out. Hey, Nelson, wanna grab a beer?" George said to me, jerking his head back toward the snack bar. I looked at Paula, and she shrugged. Fact was, she probably felt more comfortable here on the beach without me to inhibit her habitual flirting. This bit of serendipity was perfectly timed, as I now had an excuse to get away and meet up with Barbara. George wouldn't mind a bit playing the shill for me once he found out who it was I wanted to see.

It was funny how I felt I had to hide this from Paula. In spite of all her extramarital activities, or maybe because of them, she was extremely suspicious and jealous of me with other women. I learned this a few years earlier when I happened to see Alicia at a prom party where George and I were performing. She was there with her first husband, and we managed to step away for a few minutes to catch up. All we did was talk, though she did give me a light peck on the cheek as we parted. And somehow that innocent rendezvous got reported to Paula by one of her girlfriends, and she lit into me as if I had committed murder.

As George and I slogged off through the sugary sand, I started to explain what I needed to do. "You'll never guess who I just saw," I said after we were out of earshot of my family.

"Barbara," he said, as if answering a question on a verbal test.

I looked at him, but he kept on trudging through the sand, toward where I had seen Barbara and her friend on the blanket. "How the hell did you know?" I asked.

"Why do you think I showed up to drag you away from your old lady's prying eyes?"

It turned out that George had seen Barbara earlier and had told her he thought I might be at the beach. He saw me staggering across the sand with an armful of food, so he faded into the crowd while we had our surprise meeting. Figuring I was going to need some cover, he made up the bit about missing Alicia, who he had actually been with all day, and came by our blanket to extricate me from the family so I could have a little uncontested time with Barbara.

"Man, you are something else," I said, as we approached her blanket and he began to peel off toward the volleyball crowd. "You owe me a beer, buddy," he said over his shoulder with a quick wave to signal "no problem."

Hi," I said, as I flopped down on the blanket next to Barbara. Her friend had disappeared, leaving us with a semi-private situation.

"Hi, yourself," she said. "How've you been?"

"Okay, I guess. And you?"

"Ditto. Not great, not even really good. Just okay."

We sat for a few moments in nervous silence, as old lovers who meet later often do, but then I began to realize how silly the nervousness was. Though our relationship had lasted only about a year, I had never known anyone as well or as intimately as I had known Barbara, and of all the people in the world, this was one I should not be nervous around. Still, the setting wasn't the best for a quiet conversation, and there were some private things I wanted to talk about.

"Listen," I said, venturing to place a hand over one of hers. She didn't withdraw. Instead she looked down at our hands, then up at me with one of her heart-wilting smiles. "Listen," I started again, "I don't have a lot of time right now, and there's so much I'd like to talk about. Can we meet somewhere more, well, private sometime?"

She did one of those little head tilts then, and her expression changed from a smile to a look of admonishment, as if she were preparing to berate one of her kids for suggesting something bad. But before she could speak, I went on. "Look, I heard what you said before, and I respect that, I do. Maybe I should mention that I have never committed adultery, and I have no intention of ever doing so. But Barb, I need to know some things, like why you disappeared, how you're really doing, what your life's been like since—"

"Tommy, Tommy, Tommy, don't get so worked up. I'm only teasing you a little. I know you've never two-timed Paula. And I know she hasn't returned the favor, and that your life together hasn't been the greatest."

"How the hell could you know all that?"

"I have my sources," she said with a sly smile. "Actually, I guess I know more about you than you do about me, judging from your questions, at least."

"Hey!" I said. "Don't think I haven't tried. You probably also know, considering your 'sources,' that I tried for nearly a year to contact you. I even hung around your school sometimes, hoping to catch a glimpse of you, and I used to cruise your neighborhood like a stalker. Even after Alicia and I got back together—I assume you know who Alicia is—I could-n't let go. But, God woman, you disappeared into thin air."

"Well, you've got that about right," she said looking down at our hands, which were now intertwined and carry-ing on their own tactile conversation. "And you're also right that this is not the time or place to be discussing all that. Do you think you can get away sometime for a couple of hours at least?"

"Hell yes I can. There's not a power on the face of this earth that could keep me from it. Not even the formidable Mrs. Nelson and her cadre of spies." As an afterthought, I added, "She's not the most trusting type, but you probably know that, too."

"I do," she said. "Though I don't understand it, what with all her, well, you know, activities." She withdrew her hand and inserted a finger in one of the leg openings of her bathing suit, stretching it downward. "I hate this thing," she said to the blanket. "It's so damn small, and it doesn't cover my—" She stopped in mid sentence and looked up at me with a shocked expression. "Holy crap, Tommy. I'm sorry about that. I don't know what got into me."

"Well, I do," I said with what I hoped was a reassuring smile. "You had a little flashback, that's all. We never could keep from saying what we felt at any given moment, now could we? It was our most important pact, remember? And I'm thrilled to death that it still seems to be alive for you." And I was, though I have to admit I was also disappointed to see that wisp of hair disappear.

Over Barbara's shoulder, I saw her girlfriend approach-ing, and Barbara followed my eyes to glance backward. "Give us a few more minutes, will you June?" she said be-fore the stunning blond reached the blanket. June nodded and, without losing stride, spun on her heel and disap-peared into the crowd.

"So, what do you think? Day or night? My place or yours?" Barbara said this with a provocative little grin, as if she were being picked up in a bar or something.

I thought about it, then said, "I think neutral territory might be best, don't you? And daytime is definitely better for me."

At the time, I was working as a manufacturer's rep for a greeting card company, and my days were mostly spent traveling around my territory, which stretched from Gainesville to Lakeland, all the way down to Ft, Meyers and back up the coast to the St. Pete-Tampa area. I was often gone by eight in the morning, and sometimes didn't get home till after seven in the evening. But the best part about the job was that I was essentially my own boss. My nearest superior was in Atlanta, and all he ever worried about was the bottom line. He could care less if I worked six days a week or three, as long as the numbers were there. This meant I could, if I chose, work my brains out for three days, then take a couple off. I normally did this only when there was some family activity planned, but I could do it anytime and Paula would never be the wiser.

"Here's an idea," I said. "How about we meet some day down at The Bay?" 'The Bay' referred to a stretch of waterfront on Tampa Bay, about two blocks from the house I used to live in down in the northeast section of St. Pete; the house where Barbara and I had first met and where we had gone on to have many memorable encounters. We'd spent lots of time at The Bay, climbing over the seawall and finding hiding places among the huge sea grapes and other foliage on the narrow strip of beach below. "I could meet you there almost any weekday."

"That would be nice," Barbara said, a flit of nostalgia flashing across her upturned face. "Tell you what, I'm working with my dad now, so I'll have to come up with some excuse, but I think I can handle that. Could you maybe give me a call, say Tuesday or Wednesday? It's Baker Glass, you remember. It's in the phone book, and if I don't answer the phone, ask for me. Lots of customers ask for me." With that she scrunched her legs up and grabbed hold of them in a hug. "Oh, Tommy, I've missed you so much."

I wanted to ask why, then, she had walked out on me. Why she had worked so hard to stay lost. How, after all we'd been through and all we'd meant to each other, she could leave me hanging like she did. But I didn't. Instead, I grabbed her hand again and looked her in the eyes. "You have no idea, Barbara. You have no goddamned idea."

I crossed the wide expanse of grass between Beach Drive and the waterfront, and it wasn't long before I caught a glimpse of Barbara's back as she sat on the seawall throwing food to a swarm of seagulls circling overhead. She had let her hair grow some, and it brushed her shoulders as the warm breeze caught and ruffled it. She wore a simple flow-ered peasant blouse and, when I came alongside, I saw she had on sky-blue shorts. Not short-shorts, but of a length al-most identical to those she used to wear back when we were younger: chaste and proper, suggesting only comfort.

"Hey," I said, squinting out over the water that shim-mered and gleamed in the late-morning sunlight. "Hey yourself," she answered, tossing the rest of a handful of bread high in the air and watching the gulls scramble and dive for it. "Wanna go for a walk?"

"Sure," I said. I reached down to take her hand and pull her up to stand on the seawall. We looked at each other long and hard then, and she seemed to be searching my eyes for something. Then she hopped off the wall, trailing my hand behind her, and started down the long sidewalk.

After we'd walked for a while, reveling in the breeze and sunshine, I ventured, "Are you really just okay, like you said? I mean, what keeps you from using words like great or fine or something more positive?"

"Oh, lots of things, I guess," she said. "To be completely honest, I think I got spoiled by us."

"Spoiled?" I said. "You mean what I did, what we did, ruined your life?"

She stopped and pulled me back to a bench we had passed. We sat and she continued. "That came out wrong, Tommy. I didn't mean that at all. I meant spoiled like some rich kids get spoiled when they're given everything they could possibly want. It makes it hard for them to appreciate anything ordinary. And that's how my life has been since we last saw each other, just ordinary."

"So, if it was that great, why did you leave?" I hadn't wanted to broach the subject so soon, but her lead-in was too opportune and my curiosity too strong to wait. "I've wracked my brain trying to think of something I did to turn you against me, and the only thing I've ever been able to come up with was the fact that I stole your virginity, maybe at the wrong time for you—too soon or something."

"Come on you nitwit. You know better than that," she said. "You were there, too, weren't you? And I was the one who almost begged you to deflower me. Besides, at the time there was never a problem with that for either of us. Well, there were a *few* problems." She looked at me and we both laughed. Then she continued. "But they weren't the kind that could have made the experience bad. In fact, in case you don't remember my saying so at the time, those were some of the most beautiful and spiritual and loving hours I ever experienced. I told you that several times back then, I think, and nothing has changed since, at least not for me."

"I remember all right. I remember." I let my voice trail off into the soft breezes like the fade-out of a love song. Then I turned and took both her hands in mine. "But listen, Barb, that makes what you did afterward all the harder to understand. Nothing but that one note—which I still have, by the way—and all that did was tear my heart out and leave me with a ton of questions you weren't around to answer. At least, if you *were* around, you did a hell of a job of hiding."

"I know, Tommy, and I'm sorry. I sometimes sit up nights and cry thinking about it. It was horrible for me, too, you know. But I had no choice." She looked up at me, and as I was about to respond, She placed a finger across my mouth. "No, wait," she said, her voice beginning to choke a little. She swallowed hard and continued. "I'm going to explain, I promise. But it's hard for me. It's something I swore I would never tell you as long as I lived. But I've done a lot of growing up over the past eight years, and I realize now that it's not fair. To you I mean. I've found through lots of bad experiences that keeping secrets can be one of the most damaging things human beings do. And to make it worse, we never had secrets, you and me. We promised not to and I broke that promise. That's why, or at least partly why, I couldn't face you again. I would have been so conflicted it would have killed me. Actually, it almost did."

With that, Barbara raised her left arm and turned it over to reveal her wrist. She nodded toward it, and I looked down. I didn't see anything at first, but then, as my eyes refocused, I began to make out some vague, almost invisible white lines, like the lace on a fine handkerchief. It didn't click right away what those lines were, what they meant, and when it did my heart nearly exploded and I burst out crying like a baby. She quickly drew her hand back, then grabbed me and pulled me toward her until we were wrapped in a hug so powerful I could hardly breathe.

"It's okay, Tommy. It's okay. I'm here, aren't I. I'm still here." I nodded against her shoulder and she started rubbing my back to comfort me.

"Thank God," I whispered. "Thank dear God!"

7

BARBARA 1960

I look back on that time when Barbara and I were in the tree house and Thelma interrupted us, and I wonder why some memories remain vivid, while others seem to waver and flicker in the shifting and ever-thickening mists of time. I cannot, for example, remember my first successful attempt at masturbation, though it must have been a powerful experience. Nor can I remember other important firsts, such as my first solo bicycle ride or my first solo singing performance, both of which, like sexual encounters, must have been preceded by great anxiety and followed by intense euphoria. Still, it seems that only the sexual encounters themselves are indelibly imprinted in the synaptic network of my brain. And of all these, the strongest has always been the afternoon with Barbara Baker a few weeks later, when we were first caught almost in the act, then were miraculously presented with a second opportunity.

As we walked back toward my side yard after being humiliated by Harry Stimson, who had caught us making out in the master bedroom of my neighbor Todd's house, neither of us spoke. I took Barbara's hand and led her through a narrow gap in the Ligustrum hedge at the edge of our property, and her gentle squeeze of my fingers reassured me we were still in this weird and scary thing together. We passed under the big tree with its looming canopy and plywood façade dripping memories of the day we were interrupted by Thelma. Our steps slowed a bit then, and we glanced at each other, silently agreeing that tree climbing was no longer a great idea. That glance told me we were definitely not done, even though shaken and more wary than usual because of being caught. And right then Thelma's frantic voice rang out once again.

"Tommy! Tommy, where are you?" she screamed, as if I might have fallen down a well somewhere and was in the process of dying. But this time it wasn't me causing the shrill terror in her voice, nor was it an assumption that Barbara and I were again doing something clandestine. As Thelma emerged from the side door, I could see she was crying and clutching her purse and coat in a mad dash toward her old '49 Ford in the driveway.

"Oh, thank God, there you are," she said as she jerked at the driver's side door.

"What's wrong?" I asked when we came alongside the car.

"It's my boy," Thelma said. She cranked the engine and it moaned until it finally caught and started up. "He's been in an accident and I have to go. You two stay inside and don't do anything you'll be ashamed of later." She shifted the car into reverse, then looked out the window at both of us. "Your mom won't be home till after five, and I got no choice but to leave you here alone. So please, please stay out of trouble." The wheels spun on the cement driveway as the car swayed sideways, then found traction and flew backward out into the street. With one last glance out the window, she yelled, "You hear me?" We both nodded our heads in unison, as she slammed the transmission into first gear and flashed out of sight.

Barbara and I stood there with the smoke from Thelma's exhaust wafting over us in the warm breeze, afraid to look at each other as the reality of the situation settled in.

Despite my irritation at Thelma's constant scrutiny of my activities and her repeated admonishments and interruptions, she was a nice person, and I loved her the way kids come to love a family friend. I knew her boy, Gerald, too, and I was worried about what had happened to him.

Inside the house we found a note she had scribbled and taped to the fridge, where she knew I would find it because the fridge was always the first place I went upon entering the house. It said Gerald had fallen at the playground and broken his arm, and she had to leave for the hospital. This was a relief to me, erasing my initial thoughts of his bloody body smeared all over some street along with the remains of a mangled bicycle or car or something. Broken bones were tough, but fairly common among kids, and I knew he would be okay.

I could feel the relief settle around us as we read the note together. And with that relief came a gradual opening of space in our minds for other thoughts. In particular, the fact that it was only 1:30, and Mom wouldn't be home until after five. Our hands, which had come apart when I opened the kitchen door on the way in, began a tentative, nervous groping, until they connected again and mingled chilly coatings of perspiration. Still, we didn't seem able to look at each other yet. Then, without speaking, Barbara pulled me toward the stairwell next to the fridge—three stairs that led to a landing, from which we could either step down into the living room, or go left and climb the long dark stairway to the upstairs bedrooms.

As I think back on that moment in the stairwell, where we waited for one of us to make the first move, I'm often amazed that I felt so scared when Barbara paused on the landing. It had been only a few minutes earlier, in Todd's house, that we seemed primed and ready to carry things to their inevitable conclusion, though there was no real way to know if we would have gone "all the way," as the saying went back then. Now, however, there was no obstacle, at least in the sense of having to hide out in someone else's house or worry about being discovered by adults in my own. That sudden freedom, which should have caused only relief and eagerness, seemed to raise a new kind of fear -- a fear of being unimpeded on our way to whatever it was we intended to do. It was clear to both of us that by climbing those first three steps we were *not* on our way to the living room.

The long narrow stairway could not comfortably accommodate us side-by-side, and our hesitation grew as we waited to see who would lead. Finally, after what seemed like an eon, but could only have been a few seconds, Barbara took the first step, holding my hand behind her and pulling me along. As we reached the hallway at the top, we stopped and turned to face each other. With the bedroom and bathroom doors closed, even at midday there was little light to see by, and the atmosphere was more like a romantic night-time movie scene than a secret afternoon encounter between two scared adolescents.

We kissed then, a trembling kiss colored by fear and anxiety and desire that soon gave way to an intensity that found us opening our mouths and exploring with our tongues, while our bodies pressed together with clear indications that kissing would be only the beginning. When we parted and our vision had adapted to the dim light seeping from doorjambs and the stairwell, I could make out Barbara's reassuring smile.

Next came another thing I have never quite been able to understand. Instead of heading for the doorway of my own room, I began to lead Barbara toward the room that had once been my older brother's. Neal had recently married and he and his wife, Lucy, had moved to Gainesville to attend the University of Florida. Perhaps it was because I knew that, of all the four rooms on the second floor, only Neal's had its own bathroom. Or maybe it was some latent fear that, should Mom get home earlier than expected, she would look first in my room to find us. It might even have been because I knew Neal's room had a big double bed, while mine had only a narrow single. Whatever it was, we soon found ourselves in the much brighter atmosphere of Neal's room where, after locking the door behind me, I turned to look at her.

With the romantic dark of the hallway left behind, the stark brightness of the room might have killed the mood, but as the long white curtains swirled behind her in the breeze from the open windows, Barbara looked to me like the most beautiful thing I had ever seen. Her fluffy white blouse, ruffled by the wind, became a silken gown in my anxious imagination, and her smile reassured me I had not assumed too much by ushering her into this sanctuary and locking out the rest of the world. I went to her then, reached out my arms to hold her by the shoulders, and tried to find some appropriate words to say. But when I opened my mouth to speak, she stopped me with a quick shake of her head.

"I think I'm ready," she said, glancing down at the floor, a gesture that spoke of embarrassment and innocence so pronounced I felt a rush of emotion akin to that moment when she touched my back at the Y.

Without asking the question to make sure I knew what she meant by her declaration, I said, "Do you want me to close the blinds?"

She looked up at me then, her smile beginning to fade a bit and her shoulders shaking almost imperceptibly. She glanced around at the bank of windows behind her as if taking stock of the situation, and when she turned back her face had grown more serious. "No," she said, shaking her head. "If we're going to do this, I think I want to see you and I want you to see me."

I had never been terribly modest in the past. In fact, Barbara Wilson and I had often taken off our clothes in front of each other in well-lit circumstances without giving it a second thought. But here, with this Barbara standing demurely before me, fear began to rise in my chest at the thought of disrobing in plain view like some exhibitionist. There was also the fact that I had never seen her naked either, with the exception of a few stolen glances at a breast while we made out. But my fears were of no consequence as, again, it was she who made the first move.

Without taking her eyes off my face, she reached around and began to undo the button at the top of her shorts. I heard the whisper of her zipper and after a moment she let the shorts glide to the floor.

I saw all this in my peripheral vision, as I could not seem to bring myself to move my eyes downward. She then began undoing the buttons on her blouse until it hung open. She hesitated a second before shrugging it off, and at the same time she stepped out of her rumpled shorts.

My heart felt like a cannon ball in my chest as we stared into each other's eyes. Though it might have seemed a bit mechanical in the midst of such a nervous and significant moment, Barbara's innate desire for proper decorum took over and she bent in a legs-together curtsey to retrieve her shorts from the floor. She carefully folded and laid them on the chair next to her, following with her blouse, which she draped over the chair back to make sure it wouldn't get wrinkled.

These simple acts, though certainly not intended to be sexual, had an incredible effect on my libido. My erection pressed painfully against my jeans, and my embarrassment grew as she turned once again to face me. Any modesty on her part seemed to fade as she spread her legs and placed her hands on her hips. Then she smiled and cocked her head to the side, as if to say, "Your turn." I looked up at the ceiling for some respite, in hopes of buying some time, but when I looked back her stance and expression had not wavered.

I started with my T-shirt, which I pulled up and over my head. In an imitation of her neatness, I draped it across the clotheshorse by the door. I realized I was not going to get away with much more hesitation, so I reached next for my belt buckle, released it, undid the button at the top of my pants, and lowered the zipper. In order to get them off, I had to remove my shoes, which I did without bending over by prying them off with my feet. I felt sweat grow under my arms as I resolved to continue without showing the shyness I was experiencing, and quickly stepped out of my jeans. I lay them across the clotheshorse, then turned to face her.

A jumble of emotion rolled around in my mind and my chest as she glanced down at my underwear, where my erection seemed about to explode and rip them open. I returned the favor and looked down at hers. They were antiseptic white, with ruffles around the leg openings, and a light-brown shadowy bulge at the front. I was so anxious and excited, I didn't know how to proceed from there, so I nodded toward the bed and said, "Do you want to get under the covers?"

She looked over at the bed, then back at me. "No. I don't think that would be right. I think we need to look at each other before we do anything. I mean, we've never seen each other, and I think that should be part of this, don't you?"

At first I didn't understand what was so important about seeing each other, but then it dawned on me: she wanted to see what she was in for before we went any further. And for the first time in my brief sexual life, I began to wish I were smaller, rather than larger as I had always wanted to be with Barbara Wilson. Because of the intensity of the situation, I imagined I was larger at that moment than I had ever been in my life, and my thoughts began to switch from my own modesty to a fear of how painful this might be for her. If there was anything I did not want, it was to hurt her—emotionally for sure, but now it was the physical part that worried me most.

As if she had grown tired of waiting for me, she reached around and unclasped her bra, pulling it off and turning to lay it on top of her shorts. When she turned back, her arms were covering her small breasts, but with a sigh of resignation, she dropped them to her waist and stretched the waistband of her panties, pulling them over her hips and down to the floor. After she had placed them atop her bra, she hesitated before turning around, and when she did, she seemed to have gained a measure of confidence. She spread her legs a little and stood with her hands at her sides, staring into my eyes as if daring me to look down.

Rather than give my eyes a chance to react, I responded by pulling my underwear down, releasing my erection into open view. I laid them on top of my jeans, and when I turned back to face her, I found it hard to meet her eyes. When I finally did, they were no longer staring at mine. For a long time she seemed to be scrutinizing my erection, tilting her head to the side as if to view it from different angles. Since she wasn't looking at my eyes, I decided to examine her as well.

Her smallish breasts were round and firm, not jutting or anything lewd like that. The light brown nipples were small as well and appeared almost like what I thought a much younger girl's might. As I allowed my gaze to wander down below her waist, she raised her eyes to follow mine. An almost imperceptible flinch rippled through her body, but she made no attempt to cover herself.

With the exception of once when I was about seven, playing pre-adolescent games with Alicia, this was only the second time I had seen a girl's pubic area. Unlike Barbara Wilson's, which was covered with a thick black rectangle of wiry curls, Barbara's was adorned with a small wispy mound of soft, light-brown hair that seemed as innocent as the locks on the head of a newborn baby. I was fascinated by this, and was contemplating the fact that not all vaginas were alike, when Barbara spoke up.

"Tommy," She said in an almost reluctant half-whisper. I looked at her face and caught the fear that had crept into her eyes. "I'm scared."

Immediately, my heart tried to jump out of my mouth, and I felt a tear attempt to squeeze its way out of the corner of my eye. I took a deep breath, choked back the growing lump in my throat and managed to say, "Look, we don't have to do this, you know. We can wait. We can wait years if you want. I mean, I'm okay with that. All I want is for you to—"

But she didn't let me finish. "That's not what I meant, Tommy. I said I was ready and I am. I don't *want* to wait any longer, especially for years. It's just that, well, it looks so big." She glanced down and back up again. "I mean, it hurt me even when Brad only used his fingers, you know?"

I knew, and I began to feel my erection subsiding. "I don't know what to say, Barbara. I really don't. I mean I don't want to hurt you. I can't even imagine hurting you, not for any reason, not even as much as I want to do this right now. And believe me, I want to do it." She smiled at me and cocked her head again in that cute little gesture I was coming to love.

It was then that the word "love" began to creep to the front of my thoughts and emotions. I had used the word before, with Alicia and with Barbara Wilson, but that was more a manifestation of what we expected grownups to say to each other, an imitation of the movie stars we had seen professing their undying love for one another. It was never said with any understanding of what love might actually be, and because we didn't know anything about it, there was no depth or sincerity to it. Here, though, the thought came into my head in a direct stream of emotions from my heart.

"I know what you mean," I said finally, "and I only want you to be happy. I swear it, Barbara. I swear that's the God's honest truth. I want to do what you want to do, not what my feelings are telling me to do right now." I waited a moment to let this sink in, then cleared my throat of the enormous ball of phlegm collected there and said, "I think I love you, Barbara. I mean, I'm not exactly sure, but if this isn't it, then I can't help but wonder what else is out there that could be any stronger than the feelings I have for you right now."

She smiled then, a big one. "Can we—?"

"Wait!" I said. "I'm not finished." I looked down at the floor as my thoughts rumbled around inside my head. "There's one more thing I want you to know and know for sure. I want you to know I'm not saying any of this in order to get you to do anything or to make you feel better about doing whatever we're going to do. I meant it when I said I'm willing to wait. Even if it means we might never get together. What I want is for you to be happy, and I want that more than anything in the world. This thing we have, our friendship, the honesty, the caring—it's more important to me than any sex thing, even though I want to have sex with you so bad it hurts. I also want to admit that I've told other girls I loved them, but I don't think it was the least bit real. But now, I'm pretty sure I know what it means, and it means a hell of a lot more than sex. Whatever happens here, now, today, or whatever doesn't happen, I want us to keep that thing, and if having sex is going to interfere with it, I *don't* want to have sex." I was crying now, embarrassed by my unmanliness, but not about to try to hide my feelings.

Through the blur of my tears, I saw her lift her arms and reach out to me, and I started toward her. When we embraced this time it was different. There was no urgency, no arousing movement, only a gentle intertwining of arms and bodies and emotions that nearly ripped my heart out. Even our naked bodies against each other did nothing to change the moment. By then I had no erection at all, and feeling her skin against mine was wonderful.

"I believe you, Tommy," she whispered in my ear. "I think I love you, too." She broke our embrace then, and pushed me away, holding onto my arms and looking so deep into my eyes I felt she was examining my soul. "And you know what?" she said. "I don't think you could hurt me even if you tried. I mean, it will probably hurt if we, you know, but I guess it does the first time for any girl. And if girls never got past the hurt, there wouldn't be any babies or families or anything, and the world would come to an end one day."

I stared at her with my heart in my throat and my body shaking so bad I knew she could feel it. "Tell you what," I said, "let's sit down for a while and talk about this. I don't know what to say exactly, but let's talk a little first, okay?"

"Okay," she said, and let me lead her to the side of the bed, where we sat side-by-side, without hugging or kissing or anything for a while. Finally, she turned to me and said with a little smile tugging at her lips, "Well, you wanted to talk, so say something."

"I said I want to talk, Barbara, but what I really want is for you to talk to me."

8

THE FUNERAL

*T*alk, I thought as I continued to stare out at the funeral crowd. It's something a lot of people don't know how to do well, especially in situations like this when what needs to be said is particularly important. Barbara and I knew how to talk, at least to each other, but she wasn't here to help me, and I was nervous as hell trying to figure out what to say. Then it came to me: I had to pretend I was talking to her. Not having a conversation, but talk as if she were listening. So I cleared my throat, jerked my tie to loosen it a little, and dove back in.

"Barbara and I were best friends." I said in a quavering voice. "And I loved her with all my heart." I let that sink in for a moment while I tried to gain control.

"We were young, fifteen I think, when we first met. We lost touch for a few years, but we met again later in life, and our friendship grew stronger with each year that passed. Of course, as with most teenage couples, it was our adolescent emotions that first brought us together, but as time went by we got past all that and became close friends. I have to admit the transition was a tricky one, especially for me. But Barbara? She knew the trick.

"Barbara, you see, was a good person. There are few persons on this earth about whom I can say that with absolute certainty. But Barbara, folks, was one of them."

I took a deep breath of the fragrant spring air, complicated by the dozens of baskets and vases of flowers that surrounded me on the church lawn. The smell reminded me of those summer days when the magnolias and hibiscus were blooming and their scent mingled with the chlorophyll smell of laurel leaves and Ligustrum as Barbara and I swung on the tire hanging from my huge tree, or sat among the leaves on the ground and contemplated life. I shook the memories from my mind.

"Barbara was not, however, a saint," I continued. "She had her moments when she might have said or done the wrong thing. But she always managed to see those things and do whatever she could to fix them.

"Another thing I want to say is that Barbara, though she was a devout Christian in her early years, came to doubt some of her beliefs later on in life." This caused an immediate low grumble among the crowd, and I looked over at Phillip to see angry consternation growing on his aged face. Barbara's family had always been devout, as had mine, and any suggestion that his daughter might have been drifting toward disbelief was tantamount to blasphemy.

"Now, wait a minute," I said, raising my hands like an evangelist. "Don't jump to any conclusions. What I mean is she had questions, questions I think she carried until her dying day."

That seemed to calm things down a bit, so I forged ahead.

"Regardless of that, Barbara was one of the most Christ-*like* individuals I ever met. And to me, at least, that's the essence of Christianity: to *live* as Jesus lived, to *act* as Jesus acted."

A rumble of thunder in the distance drew my eyes heavenward. It seemed God might be sending a signal of approval; at least that's the way I chose to interpret it. And with that in my mind for support, I looked back at the upturned faces with a new confidence.

"Barbara lived her life that way, not because she wanted others to *think* she was good, but because she simply *was* good at heart. As I said, she had questions she probably never found any satisfying answers to, but that didn't deter her from trying her best to live up to the Christian ideals she had set for herself. You see, finding the answers wasn't Barbara's ultimate goal. In fact, there wasn't any ultimate goal for Barbara. To her, the journey was the thing, the living of one's life. She felt she should do her best to be good, to be kind, and not only apologize for her mistakes, but do something to remedy them."

The first few huge drops of rain began to fall then, slapping the podium and lawn with powerful little explosions, and we knew we were in for one of those typical afternoon thunderstorms that would soon turn into a deluge. In response, the minister stood and walked to the podium beside me. "Folks," he said. "I think we'd better retire inside, for a while at least." And with that the ushers began leading the crowd toward the large wooden doors.

Right at that moment, as the storm went into second gear and began driving the rain sideways, I caught a glimpse of Alicia. I had seen George, and I knew he wouldn't have missed this for the world, but I was surprised to see Allie. They had married some thirty years before, and, thankfully for both of them, the marriage seemed to have worked. But seeing her here, among a bunch of strangers, in a religious setting where I knew she had to be uncomfortable, was a revelation for me. In fact, it brought tears to my eyes thinking she would make such a personal sacrifice.

It's funny how seeing someone at a funeral can often be more emotional than the funeral itself. I remembered seeing George and Phil—another good friend, and the drummer in our high-school rock group—at my dad's funeral way back in 1964, and what a powerful impact that had on me.

My dad and I had never gotten along. Unfortunately for us, he was an athlete and I was an artist and musician, for whom athletic coordination was something I might achieve every week or two for about 30 seconds. When I was born, what my dad had hoped for was a clone of my older brother, a six-foot-two athletic powerhouse, who starred in high school basketball, baseball and football, then went on to play for the University of Florida Gators as an All-American tight end. To make matters worse, Dad was tone deaf and color blind, which left us with almost nothing in common.

After he divorced Mom and married his nurse, I more or less wrote him off as a human being. We still saw each other once in a while, usually at the hospital, where we would meet for coffee before his morning rounds. But, except for those few strained meetings, I had pretty much lost all contact with him during the few remaining years before he died of a stroke at age 53.

I did not shed a tear until that day at the funeral when George and Phil unexpectedly showed up. Their appearance finally released what I assumed at the time was a lot of pent-up emotion. I later realized my tears were not for my dad, but because I was so overwhelmed at the thought that these two friends, who had never known him, came to the funeral to show their support for me. It was that emotion that hit me again when I saw Allie at Barbara's funeral

As I joined the minister to bring up the rear of the crowd shuffling toward the sanctuary, he said, lowering his voice so no one might overhear, "You were on a roll there, you know?"

I was so lost in thought about Alicia and the memories her presence invoked, I wasn't paying much attention. But then, as the present came back into focus, I managed to answer. "You think so?" I asked. "I thought I was getting lost there for a while."

"We're all lost, son," he said as we approached the doors and the storm raged behind us. "We're all lost."

9

ALICIA   1952

The sun speckled bright flashing darts through the leaves onto the Spanish-tile roof where Alicia and I lay. We had earlier climbed the tree next to her house and now lay side-by-side on the roof, talking about school and movie serials and comic books and other things kids found to talk about at age eight.

We had first met on the way to school one day, when our bicycle paths crossed. Alicia was a thin, perky kid, with a penchant for sarcasm and humor that intrigued me, though I couldn't let on at the time that I liked her. It wasn't long before I started stopping by her house as we rode home from school, and we struck up a shy, reserved friendship.

Though we were far too young to know anything about sex, we were both curious, and on that day the conversation worked its way around to a tentative challenge. It was that old one most pre-adolescent kids make at least once in their lives: "You show me yours and I'll show you mine." Days like that one left me with recollections I carried for the rest of my life. And one of the most vivid was my first glimpse of a girl's pubic area.

"That's weird," Alicia said as she gazed at my tiny penis. "Oh, yeah?" I countered, "Well, what about yours. Does yours look any better?" At that time in my life, I had no idea there was any difference, at least anatomically, between girls and boys. It had only been a few years earlier when girls had started worrying about covering up their chests—or, to be more precise, when their parents had started worrying about it. Until then, girls' chests looked the same as boys', and since we couldn't see anything else in the flesh, there was no reason to believe they looked different anywhere else.

"What do you mean, 'mine?'" Alicia asked, perplexed.

"I mean your thing."

"My thing?" she asked.

"Sure," I said. "You have one, don't you? Or is there something wrong with you?"

"Well," she said as she began lowering her shorts, "I don't think there's anything wrong with me, but I sure don't have one of those." She pointed at my naked crotch. When she finally got up the nerve to take down her panties, I let out an involuntary gasp.

"Gosh, Allie," I said in startled disbelief. "There's nothing there."

"Yeah," she answered, "that's what I told ya."

We stood there for a while, staring in awe at each other's bare crotches, before we both shrugged in unison and began to put our clothes back on.

Later, sitting next to each other on the roof, we attempted in our juvenile way to figure out what might be wrong with our bodies. They were different, for sure, but why? Then, after a while, the portable radio we had brought with us began to play a new song we had never heard before, and we forgot all about our innocent sexual explorations and laid back against the tiles to listen to "Mr. Sandman."

1954

What's that on your wrist?" said my friend, Neal.

"Oh, nothing," I answered, turning my hand around so he couldn't see. We were on the playground at school. It was lunch recess and the bell was about to ring; something we could all sense even without watches.

Neal was asking about a bright smear of lipstick on the inside of my wrist. It had become a ritual for some of us boys to steal lipstick from a girl's purse and draw a line on our wrists to indicate we had been successful in doing so. I would later realize this ritual was a prelude to what would become known as "going steady," a pre-adolescent promise of fidelity to one person. The fact that we only stole lipstick from girls we liked never dawned on us at the time. All of us, boys and girls alike, were still in the stage of thinking the opposite sex was "icky."

Still, the lipstick that now adorned my wrist was that of my soon-to-be "girlfriend," Alicia Woods.

1956

Rain had begun to fall as Alicia and I stood in front of the Florida Theatre. The movie had let out earlier than we expected, and my mom wasn't due to pick us up for another 45 minutes, so we decided to explore the darkened storefronts along Central Avenue.

The movie was one called "Pardners," a Dean Martin and Jerry Lewis film we would both later come to love and would see several times before it left town. But on that particular night, we had managed to sneak way up into the far reaches of the balcony (where kids our age were not supposed to go) and spent the evening making out, in an imitation of what we thought grownups might do.

There was lots of kissing and hugging and me nibbling at her neck, while professing my undying love for her in as dramatic a fashion as I could manage. This, on my part, was a vain attempt to move my hand into a position where I could touch her breasts. Alicia's arm, however, acted like a vise during all this, capturing my hand in a grip so strong and defiant I often had to give up for fear my circulation would be cut off and I would have to have my arm amputated.

It's funny how we never talked about any of that back then, and why it never seemed to cause any real trouble or argument. It was part of the ritual for us, I guess: making out, speaking words of love, and me working my butt off to try and get my hand on her training-bra-protected breasts.

As we spun in the sparse rain and danced into one of the long glass-lined entrances to a closed store, we ended up in a movie-like embrace and kissed, as if we were stars in a Broadway musical who had only then realized they were meant for each other.

That scene remains in my memory as the single most romantic of my near-teen years. Even then I was a performer, both on and off the stage. Having begun my career at age five doing solo work for the church choir as a boy soprano, I had eventually graduated to magician and escape artist, after seeing the movie "Houdini," which featured two of my favorite movie stars, Tony Curtis and Janet Leigh. I had fallen deeply in love with Janet Leigh, and I thought Tony Curtis was about the coolest thing since chocolate Coke.

That night I was using all my skills as a dramatist in an attempt to woo Alicia into some kind of sexual contact, and having no success whatsoever. Still, our embrace—in the semi-dark, lit only by a dim streetlight, with rain falling and wind blowing as if we were on a movie set—was thrilling for me, even though I still could not manage to scrunch my hand past Alicia's iron grip.

"Hey, you kids," said a gruff voice from the outer reaches of the glass hallway. "You come out of there now. Your folks are going to be looking for you." The voice was that of Charlie, the off-duty cop hired by the Florida Theatre to keep order and see to it kids like us didn't get lost or into trouble before and after movie showings. Charlie was a nice guy, and as we walked toward the entrance, he grabbed me by the back of the head and ruffled my hair. "Come on, now," he said, "get yourselves under this umbrella and let's head back to the theatre before your folks get there and have a conniption fit."

1961

Hey, Tommy," said the voice in my ear.

I was over at Billy Anderson's house and he had been talking to some girl on the phone for several minutes, when he held out the receiver to me. "Here," he said. "There's someone who wants to talk to you."

Billy's father was one of dozens of funeral home owners in St. Pete, a town where obituaries outnumbered birth announcements by about four to one. They lived at the funeral home, and there was a huge playroom above the quarters where numerous funeral directors competed for each incoming call. The room was furnished with so many toys and games that Billy and his friends could indulge in almost any childhood activity, including ping-pong, pool, wrestling, boxing, and, for me at least, listening to and playing music.

I had been concentrating that afternoon on the 45 of Chuck Berry's *Johnny B. Goode,* playing it at 33-1/3 speed to slow it down, hoping to figure out how he got that dual and triple string sound into his leads. I leaned my Fender Stratocaster against the amp and strolled over to where Billy sat next to the phone table. I took the heavy Bakelite hand-piece from him and stared at it. "Who is it?" I asked.

"Go on." he answered. "You'll figure it out in a minute." I tentatively raised the receiver and pressed it to my ear.

The voice seemed familiar, but I couldn't quite place it at first. Then it dawned on me. It was a little deeper and more mature than I remembered, but this was definitely the voice of my old steady, Alicia Woods. "Hey, Allie," I said. "What's up?"

Alicia and I had enjoyed several years of off-and-on relationships, starting way back in grade school. The last one had broken off about three years earlier over a spat about my smoking. Since then, with the exception of a few minor dates that never seemed to work out, I had been involved with only two other girls, both named Barbara. At age thirteen, Barbara Wilson had provided me with my first opportunity for sexual intercourse. A few years later there was Barbara Baker, the love of my life, with whom I learned what real love was all about before she disappeared shortly after our last, incredible afternoon together. It had been about a year since then, and I spent most of that year trying everything I could to find Barbara to no avail. Still hanging loosely onto a broken heart, I hadn't dated anyone since, and I had no desire to do so.

"What's up with you?" she answered. "I hear you're going on the road with some band or something."

"Yeah," I answered, "maybe. But first I've somehow got to manage to be eighteen so I can get a police identification card and play in nightclubs." I had turned seventeen the month before and some promoter fellow had heard me at one of our gigs. He liked my voice and the fact that I could play organ (which I hated, but was something that filled out background music better than my guitar, so I had taken it up in order to give our four-piece group a bigger sound). At the time, this promoter guy was looking for musicians to put together a group that would travel around the south opening up Peppermint Lounge franchises.

"How're you gonna manage that?" Alicia asked.

"I'm not sure yet. Mal offered to loan me his driver's license and Social Security card, and we're about the same size and all, but I'm kinda scared about walking into a police station with someone else's ID and trying to pass myself off as him."

"No kidding," said Alicia. "You could get in a lot of trouble if you get caught. Are you gonna do it?"

"Probably. I don't know. I'm trying to work up my nerve right now. I mean it's a hell of an opportunity, you know, getting to go on the road and play in a professional band for a change. How about you? What've you been up to?"

She hemmed and hawed a little, then said, "Not a lot. You know I broke up with Devin don't you?"

I'd heard some rumors about Alicia and Devin dating, but I didn't pay too much attention to all the gossip kids at our age seemed to revel in. Devin was one of the most handsome boys at St. Pete High, a baseball star with a strong physique and, according to the girls, "dreamy eyes." His only drawback as far as I could discern, was that he was dumb as a stump and failing most of his classes.

"No," I answered. "I hadn't heard. What, did you order him to quit smoking, too?" I said this with a little sarcasm, a tiny jab I felt she deserved for her stop-smoking demand three years earlier. Fact was, I knew Alicia had later taken up the habit herself, so she had no room to criticize now.

"Okay, Tommy, you got me there. I'm sorry about all that, but at the time I, well, I thought it was the right thing, you know?"

"That's okay, Allie. I've gotten over it. By the way, I've dropped the 'Tommy' now and I'm asking people to call me 'Tom.' Sounds a little more like an adult, you know, and if I'm going to be able to work out this road thing, I don't want to be called 'Tommy.'"

"Okay Mr. Grownup," she chuckled. Then maybe you could stop calling me 'Allie,' since it sounds like I'm a place where people keep their garbage cans."

"You got it, Alicia," I said, putting strong emphasis on her full name.

We bantered on for a while and somehow, by the end of the conversation, we made plans to meet at a beach party that night. As I handed the receiver back to Billy, it occurred to me he might have wanted to date Alicia himself. "Hey, man, I'm sorry about that," I said. "One thing led to another, if you know what I mean?"

Billy grinned. "You still haven't figured it out, have you?"

"Figured what out?" I said

"That whole little thing was planned for you, idiot! I've been talking to Allie ever since she heard we were hangin' out. She said she wanted to get back together with you, so I set this phone call up for her."

"Oh," I said, surprised. "Why?"

"It's general knowledge about you and Barbara Wilson, plus you're this big rock star around town with girls falling at your feet, right?"

"I haven't noticed any falling," I said, though I knew what he meant. Being on stage had its benefits, even for a skinny five-foot-nine shrimp like me. Rock musicians of the day all enjoyed a little Elvis rub-off; even the ugly ones didn't have any problem getting girls. I was probably known on the underground female grapevine as some kind of sexual stud, even though I hadn't done anything in that department since I lost Barbara Baker. Then it dawned on me what he was talking about.

"You mean Alicia wants to get together with me because of my supposed experience or something?"

"Well," he said, "I can't be absolutely sure, but I wouldn't bet against it. I mean, she's not exactly what you would call a loose woman or anything, but I'll bet that handsome stud she just broke up with at least got a finger or two in her. Wouldn't you think?"

I suddenly felt something stirring in my jeans. Ever since Barbara had disappeared, I had thought of no one but her, and all my sexual fantasies had been centered on the last day we'd spent together. I was surprised to have another girl intrude into that sacred realm, mainly because I was not nearly over Barbara. It felt like a betrayal of sorts, getting a hard on over Alicia, but I soon realized that wasn't going to stop me, and by the time I left Billy's I was determined to finally get into Alicia's pants.

10

THE PEPPERMINT LOUNGE 1961

I was scared shitless as I entered the tiny Madera Beach police station on that bright afternoon in October, hoping my experience on stage would serve me well as I acted the part of Mal Jenkins. One thing I had going for me that I wouldn't have a few years later was the fact that driver's licenses at the time didn't have photos on them. Mal was five-eleven and I was five-nine, so I had stuffed some napkins in the heels of my zipper boots, which had about 1-1/2-inch heels of their own. Other than that, we both had brown hair and brown eyes, so the written description on the license was almost perfect, except for the fake height. I was worried they might make me remove my boots, which would be a dead giveaway, but to my great relief, the clerk who accepted my application never even looked up at me while she filled out forms and shuffled papers. Apparently such a brash and bold violation of the law was never considered, probably because they thought the possible consequences would deter any idiot foolish enough to pull something like that while standing in an actual police station.

With my newly minted ID in hand, stating I was now eighteen years old, I skipped along the street in front of the station like a grade-school kid, until I realized some of the cops might be watching and slowed to a casual stroll. I hopped over the door of my 1955 Thunderbird convertible and plopped into the driver's seat. The police station was only about five blocks from the nightclub, which was being redecorated for its grand reopening as the first Peppermint Lounge in the Southeast. The Twist was all the rage at the time, and the thematic atmosphere they planned was one that would be the predecessor to what would later be called disco: lots of twirling lights and mirrored balls and a stage with two circular pedestals on either side where the dancing girls would demonstrate how to do The Twist.

As I strolled in the front door, the promoter, Terry Lanning, caught site of me. "Hey, man," he said over the hubbub of carpenters and training wait staff. "You eighteen yet?"

"Just turned," I said, holding up my new ID.

"Good, then let's get that organ of yours out here. Rehearsals start day after tomorrow."

I glanced around to see a couple of guys up on the stage setting up amps and microphones and drums. "Come on over here a minute, I want you to meet some of your band mates," Terry said. I followed him to the stage and he made the introductions. Both musicians were older than me, probably in their early twenties, but they greeted me warmly, as if our age difference didn't matter.

"So," said Jimmy, a tall, lanky blond fellow I assumed was the drummer because he was expertly twirling a pair of drumsticks in his long fingers. "You play organ, huh?"

"Well," I said, "I play *at* it. I mean I've played piano since I was six, so keyboards are not a problem. I've been fiddling around with the bass pedals now for a while and I've worked out a few runs, but I wouldn't expect any kind of virtuoso if I were you, at least not until I get a little more practice under my belt."

"Oh, hell, man," said the other fellow, Paul. "This baby-shit Twist crap only requires knowing three and four-chord progressions. Plus, we've got a bass player, so you don't have to worry about the pedals for now." With that he hit a riff on his Fender Jazzmaster that left me staring with my mouth open. "I hear you play guitar too," he said as the screeching sound faded.

"Well, yeah. I mean I've been playing now for about five years. But I'm sure not in your league."

The two musicians looked at each other and laughed, then Paul looked back at me. "Tell you what, if we get some time, I show you a few riffs. How 'bout that?"

"That would be great," I said. Then I turned to Terry. "Do you think I might get some help lugging my organ out here? It's a Hammond B3, you know. A real monster. And I've also got a Leslie speaker, which is no small item itself."

"No problem, man," said Terry. "We've got a crew and a truck right outside and that's what there here for."

"A B3?" said Paul and he glanced over at Jimmy. "Far out!"

I would later learn the Hammond B3 was considered to be the king of rock and blues organs. We acquired ours from the church when they installed a huge pipe organ in the sanctuary and had no more use for it. Dad bought it and put it in our music room off the pool patio. That room also contained the Baldwin upright I had spent several years practicing on while I took mandatory lessons from an old fart of a teacher I came to hate with a passion. My big problem with piano lessons was that I had a good ear for music, and could memorize almost any tune after playing it or hearing it once. Consequently, by the second time I played a piece, my eyes would wander, and my teacher had a habit of smacking me with a ruler on the knuckles whenever she caught me not looking at the music.

I liked to say I came away from three years of piano lessons having learned only how to find Middle C, but that was a bit of an exaggeration. It was true, however, that within about six months of picking up my first guitar, I taught myself about ten times as much music as I ever learned from those piano lessons.

Opening night at the Peppermint Lounge was an incredible scene, with huge floodlights sweeping the night sky out front and a crowd that stood in line for blocks waiting to be let in. We practiced daily for about two weeks leading up to that night, and the group was pretty tight, at least on the two dozen or so songs that were to be the mainstay of our repertoire. There was lots of Chubby Checker and Chuck Berry and Hank Ballard and the Midnighters stuff (unbeknownst to most, The Twist was written and first recorded by Hank Ballard, and the Chubby Checker version was only a cover). We also had a few slow tunes in the bag, like "Oh Donna" and "In the Still of the Night," which I sang to give the exhausted customers a chance to rest and get better acquainted.

Our "Dance Teachers," Annie and Ginny, were older girls I knew from high school who'd tried out (along with about a hundred others) and won the positions due to their looks and abilities to gyrate in a semi-sexy manner. For the most part, they stood on their pedestals demonstrating the twist, but when customers seemed to be having trouble catching on, they would go down into the crowd to help them out with a little one-on-one instruction. The scene was carefully planned by corporate powers who financed the whole thing, and there was a mandate that said the sex angle had to be handled with kid gloves. Nothing too overt or revealing, and never any interaction between our girls and the customers after the club closed.

All in all, it was one of the most thrilling experiences of my young career in music, and it wasn't long before I realized how sexy being a semi-famous rock musician could make a person seem. By the time our first two weeks were up, I had been propositioned no less than ten times, in some cases by ladies many years my senior. But I had always been a faithful guy, motivated by the trauma of my parents' divorce, and by then Alicia and I were once again going steady, so I managed to fend off the attention from the females, many of whom had become regulars at the club.

The first hitch came when we wrapped up after six weeks. The plan was to open a chain of Peppermint Lounges across the state and then up into Georgia and the Carolinas. Since we were the founding group, our job was to assemble and train other musicians and dancers to take over, while we repeated the process at a new location. My excitement was so great I never considered the fact that I was going to have to leave Alicia to go on the road, probably for several months without a break or a visit home.

I was pretty committed to Alicia by then, and our relationship had matured quite a bit. Unfortunately, life on the road would put a serious dent in that commitment and, in her numerous letters and phone calls over the following several months, she would often mention that the song she listened to most those days was Del Shannon's hit, "Runaway."

11

ALICIA 1961

After that first beach party, where Alicia and I spent most of the time filling each other in on our activities over the past three years, things started getting intimate between us. Having spent so much time together growing up, we had little trouble falling back into our routine of making out. The difference was that this time Alicia seemed to have lost her vice-like arm-clamp, and our make-out sessions included a considerable amount of sexual contact above the waist, and even a little below, though down there it was strictly through clothes. When it came to actual intercourse, she would balk. We had worked out many clandestine scenarios in order to be together in settings would allow us to "go all the way," but every time we got close, Alicia would stop me.

Then, one night, when we had snuck away with another couple, each girl having told her parents she was spending the night with the other, we ended up in adjoining rooms in a big hotel on Clearwater Beach. As we lay beside each other on the bed, something happened that gave me a little insight into Alicia's reluctance. After a while we got to that point where everything was leading to final consummation, and she started to pull her old routine of wrapping blankets around her legs and turning away so that it was impossible to continue. I rolled off and this time I made no effort to conceal my anger and frustration.

"You know what they call girls who do that, don't you?" I asked while she lay with her face toward the wall and her back to me.

"Yeah," she said.. "Prick teasers!"

I was surprised at her candidness, but I was determined to get answers. "Can you tell me why?" I asked, a little less anger and a bit more sympathy creeping into my voice.

"Look, Tom," she said. "Why don't you just do it? I mean, why don't you hold me down and, well, do it?"

"What? You mean rape you?" I said, lifting up on an elbow, grabbing her arm and turning her to face me. Her eyes glistened with tears as she tried to answer, but it seemed like she was having a hard time talking right then, so I went on.

"Why, in God's name, would you want me to force you? Don't you *want* to do it? I mean, are you scared or something, or worried it might hurt and can't do it unless you're forced?"

That opened the floodgates and tears began to stream down her face. She grabbed me around the neck and squeezed so hard I thought my head would pop. "Oh, Tom, I'm so sorry," she sobbed. "I don't mean to be this way. But I don't know any other way. I mean what are you going to think of me if I give in like some kind of whore or something?"

"Whoa," I said, struggling to get her to release my neck. "Whoa, let's wait a minute here and get this straightened out." I finally managed to remove her arms and held her out in front of me. Then I kissed her eyes, tasting the salty warmth of her tears. When she had calmed down a little, I said, "I'm sorry, too Alicia. But I can't do that—can't use force I mean. And I won't think you're a whore if you let me. Where did you get the idea the only way to do it is to have someone force you?"

She looked down at the covers between us and shame radiated from her body like waves of electricity. Then, in a near whisper, she said, "Because that's the only way it's ever happened before."

I reached over and lifted her chin with a finger. "Someone forced you? Is that what you're saying? Are you trying to tell me you were raped?" She kept her eyes closed as if afraid to look at me, then began to nod her head. When she started to grab me again in one of those bear hugs, I stopped her. Then in a much softer voice, I asked, "Can you talk about it? You don't have to get into the gritty details or anything, but maybe it would help if you told me what happened."

"You'll hate me if I do. I know it."

"No I won't, silly. We've been friends for, what, over ten years now? For most of our lives, in fact. What in the world would make you think I could hate you over something like that? Hell, kid, I'm no virgin either, you know, and you don't hate me because I've been with other girls, do you?"

"No," she said, drawing out the end of the word in a low growl. "But, this is different."

"Come on, what could be so different? I mean, sure you're upset about it, and you have every reason to be, but you made it through and you're here with me now, and I'm certainly not going to hold anything like that against you. You know that, don't you?"

Again she nodded, then laid her head on my shoulder and stared to pull us down against the pillows. After a few moments of silence, she whispered, "It was my brother."

Luckily, I managed to keep my surprise and revulsion under wraps. "Okay," I said after only a slight hesitation. "That's not so good. But it's not the end of the world, Allie—" I accidentally slipped back into using her old nickname "—I mean … oh, hell, I don't know what I mean. I want to help if there's any way I can. You maybe want me to kick his ass for you?"

Ass kicking wasn't my best suit. In fact, in the few fights I had not managed to talk my way out of over the years, I always ended up with the ass that got kicked. Still, I knew her brother and he was a shrimpy little asshole I had come to hate because of his snotty act of superiority. He was, I figured, about 20 by then, but he was only five-seven or so and I had maybe twenty pounds on him. Besides, I was so angry right then, I probably could have kicked George's ass—at least a little.

"No," she said. "I don't even want him to know I told anybody. It was about a year ago, and he was drunk at the time. I was trying to help him get his clothes off and into bed before Mom and Dad got home and found him like that, when he grabbed me and started tearing at my clothes. I was so scared I didn't know what to do. He kept begging me to let him touch me, and I was trying to talk him out of it, but then he slapped me, and something seemed to snap in my mind. After that I closed my eyes and tried to shut everything out, and when I came back to my senses he was passed out on top of me. It wasn't until I got back to my room and saw the blood that I realized what had happened."

"Goddamnit!" I shouted, slamming my fist down on the bed. "That little scumbag! That little egotistical buttwipe."

"Calm down, Tommy—" she too seemed to have reverted to our old familiar names "—It's, well, it's over now, and nothing can change it, not ever."

For the second time in my life, I was hearing a story of adolescent rape. I started to wonder how much of that kind of thing actually went on in the world. Back then, we never heard the term "juvenile sex offender," mainly, as I would later come to understand, because such acts were swept under the rug and never reported to authorities. It wasn't until late in the 20th century that people became aware of how common inter-family rapes of adolescents were, and that the trauma could mess up a woman's future sex life.

When Barbara Wilson had told me about hers, it was in a matter-of-fact way, with no tears or regrets I could discern. Of course, her rapist wasn't a family member, and she went on to have a fairly long-term relationship with him. Still, it came back to me then how unemotional sex with her had been, and how she never derived any pleasure from it, at least in ways I could recognize. Over the years, I came to think it must have been her rape, or at least the way it happened, that subsequently robbed her of her ability to feel much of anything, emotionally or physically.

And here I was again, this time with more knowledge and experience, but still wondering what was the right thing to do. It felt like a heavy burden had been dropped on me that I had no idea how to carry. I sure didn't want to make things any worse for Alicia, but I had no idea what might cause her distress or what might help.

"Okay," I said finally. "We should probably stop now and, I don't know, maybe not do anything else, at least for a while." When I looked down at her, the tears had started to flow again.

"But I want to, Tommy. I do." She blubbered this out between swollen lips drenched with tears and moisture dripping from her nose. I reached over to the nightstand, pulled some tissues from the box, and started to dry her face. She let me do this without protest, and when I finished, I said, "There now. Better?"

She nodded and the hint of a smile began to crack the corner of her mouth. She reached up and put her hand behind my head, pulling me down until we kissed. Her lips were soft from all the crying, and it was a long gentle kiss, more like affection than foreplay. When she drew back she said, "I want you, Tommy. I want you really bad. And I promise I won't try to stop you this time. I promise."

"I want you, too, honey," I said, a bit of fatherly sound creeping into my voice. "But I'm not sure this is the best thing to do right now. I mean, I can't even imagine how horrible it must have been for you, and I'm sure it left scars—I don't mean physical scars, I mean emotional ones—and I don't know how to make things better and not worse."

"Do you love me?" she asked.

"Sure" I said, and I did in a way, like an old friend, but at least I could say it without feeling like I was lying. "You know I do. We've loved each other for a long time. Even when we split up and all, I think we both knew there would always be something special between us."

"Well, then, that should make everything okay. I mean if you love me and I love you what could be wrong with our having sex?" And then, as if she had grown exasperated with my hesitation, she grabbed me and pulled me down on top of her. "Just fuck me, will you? Please?"

Odd how the word "fuck" had an immediate effect on a young man's libido. It's only a word, after all, a word we never said around girls and that girls never uttered at all, at least to my knowledge. There was something carnal about it, especially coming from Alicia's lips, and I almost immediately gained a tremendous erection. Unfortunately, both of us still had our clothes on, so there was a lot of fumbling and unromantic repositioning before we were ready, but Alicia seemed determined to get on with it, and it wasn't long before I was between her legs, working my way up by scrunching my knees against the sheets. This was one of those situations I had learned before was not the best configuration for adequate penetration, but things were moving so fast, I didn't feel I should stop and get all technical about it.

When I finally reached her vagina she let out a little gasp before I had even begun to enter her. I raised up then and looked her in the eyes. She smiled a little, and I said, "Do you think you might be able to spread your legs a little?" Without speaking, she slowly began to open herself up to me, then surprised me by reaching down to help guide it in.

I had thought, with the rape and all, she would probably be stretched or maybe even damaged down there, but as the tip began to enter her, I realized she was tight. *That little prick*, I thought, *he must have a dick about the size of his brain*. I pushed a little harder until the head popped past the outer folds and slipped inside. She let out a little cry when this happened, and I looked down at her closed eyes to see a few tears squeeze from the edges. I kissed her eyes again, and before I could ask, she said, "It's okay, Tommy. It hurts a little, but only when you move."

"Well, Kiddo, I'm kinda gonna have to move, you know." I said this in a jocular voice, attempting to bring a little levity to the situation.

"I know that, silly. But try to go slow, okay?" Going slow was one of those things I guessed girls took for granted a boy could do, but I didn't want to explain the nuances of male sexual arousal at the time, so I resolved to do my best. As I pushed deeper, her little cries became less pronounced and I could feel her juices, which had begun to flow before we began, start to increase. Encouraged by the fact that I now felt she was more lubricated, I lifted up and spread her legs even farther, then began to push them forward into a more upright position.

I hesitated for a moment, then looked down at her and asked, "Are you ready." She gritted her teeth and nodded, so I took one last deep breath, leaned over to peck her on the mouth, and made the first deep thrust.

"Aaahhh," she sighed in obvious pain. "Oh, oh my God, Tommy, It hurts, it really hurts now."

"It's going to be okay, though," I answered in a rough whisper. "Hold on for a little while and it's going to get better." With that I pulled back and thrust again, this time slower and with more deliberation. When I neared bottom, her sigh was less guttural and more like a pant. Again I rose up and pushed, and this time she brought her hips up to meet me. "Is it getting better," I whispered.

"Uh-huh," she said, and when I went even deeper she added, "Oh, yes." I increased the speed and depth of each thrust until she was gasping for air like a sprinter after a run.

"Oh, God," she said in a loud whisper. "Oh dear God." And she wrapped her arms around me, pulling me against her even harder with each penetration.

"Are you okay?" I asked through heavy gasps of my own.

"Yes. Oh, Jesus. Yes," she shrieked.

"Okay, then, here we go." I said, and we sped up into a frenzy that ended with an explosive orgasm I knew had happened for both of us at the exact same moment.

"Oh. Oh. Holy shit," she whispered as I began to slow down. "Jesus, Tommy, don't stop now. I mean if you can help it. It feels soooo good. Soooo good." Her voice trailed off into a delirium of mumbles, while she hugged me and scratched at my back and kissed me and snuggled against my neck. Things finally began to wind down, but I made no effort to rise, though I knew my erection was almost gone and I was about to slip out. When I looked down one last time at her face, I saw she was asleep, still mumbling in intelligible little murmurs, but definitely out of it. Careful not to disturb her, I rolled off, keeping my arms around her as she drifted into a deeper and deeper sleep.

12

ANNIE

1962

"Hey, man, Gimme a hand here." Jimmy was lugging his trap case toward the stage, with his high hat slung over his shoulder while trying to carry a tom-tom in the other hand. We had arrived in Cocoa Beach, at the Satellite Motel, where we were to set up the second Peppermint Lounge franchise in the motel's former piano bar. As I ran to help Jimmy, we both looked around at the tiny space, then at each other.

"Man," said Jimmy. "How're we going to do our thing in here?"

Right then Terry Lanning came through the door, talking quietly but gruffly with a short bald guy I assumed must be a bigwig at the motel. They finished their conversation, and Terry turned to us. "Okay, guys," he said, "stop right there and start packing up." The little guy looked shocked at this and started tugging at Terry's sleeve. After a few minutes more of heated conversation, the bald guy nodded several times and backed out of the room like an underling trying to demonstrate deference to a royal.

"Well, fellas," Terry said to us after the guy was out of earshot. "It looks like we're going to get to take a break." We both looked at him with curiosity and he continued. "Seems these folks misled us a little when they told us about the room. What they first described met our specifications, but it looks like they were talking about the room *after* the planned renovations. Renovations, it now appears, were scheduled to take place in another month or so, which put them in breach of contract." He swept his arm around the tiny piano bar. "What do you think? Is there a chance in hell we could make our scene work in this space?"

Jimmy and I followed his gesture, then said in almost perfect unison, "No way!"

"Right," said Terry, shaking his head in disgust.

We stood there for a minute, and finally I said, "So, what's going to happen."

"Well," said Terry, "things could have been worse. We might have been on our way back home to wait for the next franchise site, which I hear won't be ready for at least eight weeks. But I told the guy he was going to be out about ten grand, and that seems to have bumped up his renovation plans a bit. According to him, he's going to have the carpenters here tomorrow to start busting out those walls." He pointed at two interior walls that faced a strip of rooms stretched out in a cross from the lounge. "And, he says, he's going to pay double overtime to keep them working 24-hours a day until everything's finished"

"How long do you think it's going to take?" Jimmy asked, still not moving toward the stage with his trap case.

"Well, according to the little twerp, they should be far enough along for us to get started with our interior decorating in about three days, so guess what?"

We looked at each other, then back at Terry.

"You guys get to take a three-day paid vacation."

The Team," as we were now being called, was supposed to work on the road like a carney troupe. Since we'd all been in on the construction and set-up of the first franchise, everyone was asked to pitch in on the subsequent set-ups, which meant that, in addition to rehearsing and training others to take our place, the musicians and dancers were required to help with the other stuff that would transform a new venue into a Peppermint Lounge. There was some grumbling about this, and none of the entertainers were particularly enamored of the idea, but we knew which side of the bread our butter was on, so we accepted the new responsibilities with a fake cheerful resignation. The news that we would now get a break, after the grueling teardown, packing and travel, was met with universal relief.

As mandated by our contract, we had comp rooms at the motel, though we had to share. And in my case that meant I had to share a room with Annie, one of our dancers. For anyone else, this might have been a good thing, but for me it was pretty scary. I was committed to Alicia, and the temptation of rooming with Annie would hold my feet to the fire on that score.

It would have seemed logical for Ginny to share a room with Annie, but Ginny and Jimmy had become an item and he managed to get the room assignments altered to accommodate that. The other guys in the group were all married, so that left Annie and me.

Annie was a tall, thin, girl-woman, with large breasts and a cracked front tooth that, rather than detracting from her looks, gave her a cute, innocent schoolgirl attractiveness. She was also a card, with a great sense of humor and a candidness that often shocked the rest of us. In fact, she was only the second female I had ever heard use the word "fuck," the first being Alicia on our night of sex at the Clearwater Beach hotel. Annie did not use the word as a sexual suggestion, she used it as a straight-out swear word, though always with a hint of humor or sarcasm, which made it hard for anyone to protest. She was, however, a sensible girl, and never used it except among the close-knit members of The Team.

Despite my vow to never cheat on any woman, I was attracted to Annie. Not so much because of her looks, but because of her personality. She reminded me of Holly Golightly, Audrey Hepburn's character in *Breakfast at Tiffany's*, a movie Alicia and I had seen the year before, after which I decided I would be willing to walk barefoot over a mile of broken glass for the chance to meet the lovely Miss Hepburn.

That first night of freedom, we all wanted to check out the clubs along the beach, so about twenty of us set out on a walking trek to do so. Terry even tagged along, probably more to keep an eye on us than to join in the fun. With the space program on Cape Canaveral in full bloom, Cocoa Beach was like a California gold-rush boomtown. Bars and nightclubs sprouted up all over to accommodate the drinking and partying of the thousands of space workers and support personnel. At night the atmosphere was like a constant *Mardi Gras*.

We had spent an hour or so in each of three bars, with lots of curious young space workers eyeing the girls, when one of the local cowboys decided to hit on Annie. I had no business whatsoever playing her protector, but this redneck was so rude and profane in his approach, I became immediately incensed. I would later come to understand that Annie could handle herself quite well in such situations and didn't need me to be her knight in shining armor. But several beers and a few shots had rendered me unable to control my ego, and I ended up challenging this large fellow to join me outside and "settle the matter."

It was, of course, a disaster. Not only was I less than adept at fighting, but before I could even begin to try my usual negotiating, the guy took a swing at me that clipped my eye and tore open a two-inch gash, the resultant scar from which I will carry until my dying day. Blood streamed into my eye, and his next blow, which caught me above the nose, rendered me essentially blind. I staggered around, trying in vain to wipe the streaming blood from my face, while he took pot shots at my stomach and head, most of which missed because I was flailing around like a beached fish. About that time, the rest of The Team arrived on the scene and, unfortunately for my opponent, showed him no mercy whatsoever.

The redneck, I would later learn, ended up in the hospital with a couple of broken bones and a few lost teeth, while I was examined by a paramedic who stopped the bleeding with some crap that stung like hell and then applied what they call a butterfly bandage to the gash over my eye. Had I known of the permanent scar, I might have agreed to be taken to the hospital for stitches, as the kindly paramedic suggested, but at the time my pride was so incredibly damaged I insisted I would be okay, that the bandage would be fine and I didn't need to go to the hospital. Because of my refusal, I ended up in considerable pain for several days, and with a lovely battle scar that rippled across my eyelid like a shriveled worm.

That night, however, I thought I was going to die, not so much from the pain, but from embarrassment at having been nearly killed by an ignorant redneck I had stupidly challenged to a duel. All I wanted was to slink back to the motel, crash, and nurse my damaged pride. But Annie would have none of that. Assuring the rest of The Team they should continue partying, she took me by the arm, pressed an ice pack to my head, and led me back to the room we had been assigned.

"You didn't need to do that, you dumb fuck," she said as she refreshed the ice pack from the bucket in our room. "I mean, that twerp wasn't worth it: some ignorant fucking redneck with shit for brains? What the hell were you thinking anyway?"

"I wasn't—thinking, I mean. I was reacting." I said this through a moan of pain, which got worse when she not so gently applied the new ice pack.

"You know," she said, with a bit less anger this time, "I can almost understand, but it takes a little stretch of the imagination for me. You guys, you men, always seem to think we women can't take care of ourselves and that you have to come to the rescue. Well, I'm here to tell you, in case you didn't know, I have a black belt in Shotokan Karate, one of the deadliest forms of martial arts. I could have ripped that shithead's nuts off and stuffed them down his throat before he had a chance to raise a hand. But, like I said, he wasn't worth it."

That was another one of those moments I never forgot. Annie ministering to me like an exasperated parent, and me sitting there in a huddled mass of embarrassment, accepting her reprimands without protest. But it wasn't the embarrassment or the nursing that branded the night indelibly on my memory; it was what came later.

Annie eventually got me into the bathroom and ordered me to take a shower. I wondered at the time what was so urgent about my bathing under the circumstances, but I would later find it wasn't because she thought a shower might make me feel better, or that I needed to further cleanse my wound (over which she had taped some plastic).

I had no power to resist, having begun to fear her a little, so I complied with her wishes and took a long hot shower, which did make me feel a bit better—that, and the three aspirin she had made me swallow before entering the bathroom. I emerged, red as a lobster, with a towel around my waist and my embarrassment shifting from the fighting episode to my near nakedness. But Annie ignored me. She had changed into a nightgown sheer enough to perk up my sleeping libido.

"Here," she said as I turned sideways a bit to hide what I could feel beginning to grow under the white motel towel. "Drink this." She held out a plastic cup, filled to the brim with a warm, golden liquid.

"What is it?" I asked, as I accepted it and peered over the lip.

"It's whisky, dummy. What did you think it was, Kool-Aid? Hair of the dog, or so they say. I figure right about now you're coming down from all those beers and shots, and you're about to start hurting even worse." She smiled at me for the first time since we'd left the bar, and I was nearly bowled over by the fact that she seemed to want to take such good care of me; and more so because she seemed to know exactly how to do it.

I lifted the cup and took a small sip. It tasted strong, but after years of pretty heavy drinking, I handled it without grimacing.

"No, no," she said. "If it's going to work, you have to toss it off. Drink it all quickly." I looked at her, then back at the nearly full cup. Finally, I shrugged, took a deep breath, and drained it. This caused a three-alarm fire to break out in my esophagus, but again, rather than display any unmanliness, I managed to keep my cool with only a squint. In fact, the sensation wasn't all that bad, and within a few seconds I felt the warm glow of alcohol as it made its way to my still-aching brain.

"Good," she said. "You'll feel better in a minute." She waited a few seconds, then said, "What do you think of me, Tom?"

"Whu, ah, what do you mean?" I stammered.

"I mean, what do you think of me? Do you like my looks? Do you think I'm a profane bimbo? Are you sexually attracted to me?"

My head began to spin, probably because of the alcohol jolt, but also because I was shocked by her candid questions. "Give me a minute, will you?" I managed to mumble as I made my way to the chair in front of the dresser and plopped down like a wet sack of potatoes. I tried to think of an answer, but she didn't give me long.

"Okay, you're freaked, I can see that. I'm sorry for putting you on the spot. I never have been one for all the preliminary bullshit that goes into eventually having sex. Believe it or not, I haven't had many sexual partners—three, if I count correctly, but two of those were way back when we were fumbling adolescents who had no idea what we were doing. The last … well, you don't need to hear about that disaster. I probably scare guys off before they can learn to handle their own over-inflated egos, and I may be about to scare you off too. Be that as it may, what I want to know is—and I want you to be absolutely honest—do you want to have sex with me? Because I want to have sex with you, but not if you find me unattractive or repulsive or anything like that."

Jarred into stone silence, I stared at the floor and tried my best to get my mouth working. Unfortunately, it would not comply, so I glanced around the room as if there might be something on the walls that would help me think, speak, do anything other than sit there like a dumb clod. My hesitation didn't seem to bother Annie, who raised her eyebrows in anticipation of my answer.

Finally, I said, "Annie, I'm not myself here, so you probably shouldn't take anything I say seriously. But, yes, I want to have sex with you, and no, I don't find you repulsive or unattractive. The only problem, besides the fact that I've recently had the shit kicked out of me, is that I'm sort of committed to someone else at the moment, and I don't know exactly how to deal with that."

She thought for a minute, then said, "Sort of? What the hell does that mean? If you can't say anything stronger than 'sort of,' then you're really not committed at all, are you? You might be screwing someone and you might like her a lot, but you're definitely not committed unless you can tell me right now there's no way in hell you could convince yourself to fuck my brains out."

Of course, there was no way in hell I could convince myself *not* to fuck her brains out, so I gave in. I stood shakily and walked toward the bed, where Annie sat awaiting my decision. And that's when things got strange. Instead of taking complete control and directing me as I thought she would, she shook a little when I put my arm around her and seemed to be waiting for me to take the lead.

"Remember," she whispered in my ear as we fell back on the bed, "I'm not as experienced as you might think with all my tough talk. So please take it easy with me, will you?"

So, with all manner of conflicting thoughts banging around in my head, I began a slow and deliberate session of sex with one of the most intriguing and interesting human beings I had ever met. And man was it good. Annie, though she professed to be inexperienced, moved like a cat in bed, quickly learning all the little tricks that made me want to finish, but that allowed her to hold me off until she was ready. And she was ready, many, many times over the next few hours.

She talked a lot, but not in a way that interfered with the mood or intensity of the moment. Her subtle questions and suggestions always came at the right time, heightening my excitement while tempering my immediate need to forge ahead. It was as if she knew precisely those moments when I would be driven past the point of no return and, without frustrating me or making me angry, she would find a way to slow things down, using her hands, and sometimes her tongue, to keep me on the most pleasurable edge possible.

I'm not quite sure because the evening became a blur of prolonged orgasmic sensation; but I think she had about eight orgasms that night. And I know she managed to revive my libido from a near-dead state at least four or five times. There was a lot of tongue work on both our parts, but there was also quiet time, during which she patiently waited or inquired or experimented with gentle and loving touches and licks and silly little comments, aimed, it seemed, only at making things better for me. I knew the experience was one of the best she'd had, or, as it turned out, would ever have. She confirmed this decades later. But that's another story.

I've thought about Annie a lot over the years, often comparing her brash candidness with Barbara's subtle and compassionate honesty. The comparison is not fair. Barbara could never be as abrupt or rude or demanding as Annie, though she could be candid and unabashed when the circumstances called for it. In fact, at times she was equal to Annie in that regard. The difference was not in blunt talk; the difference was in the fact that Barbara *cared*. Regardless of her need to be honest, she often realized honesty could hurt. At those times her empathy took precedence over total honesty.

Annie, on the other hand, had almost no empathy, except when it came to a partner's sexual needs. She, like many intellectuals who spend minimal time delving into the humanities, the arts, or the suffering of humankind, felt that total honesty at all times under any circumstances was the only proper way to interact with others. An intriguing philosophy that sometimes works in the short run.

A few days after that amazing first night, I saw her reading a thick paperback. When I asked what it was, she turned the cover toward me, then turned it back to continue reading. It was "The Rise and Fall of the Third Reich," a tome I knew little about until many years later when I read it myself.

On our way to Daytona Beach, I noticed she was reading a different book, and I asked her what "Rise and Fall" had been about. "It was about this little twerp who thought he could take over the world," she said, as if describing a second-rate novel. "So he killed a bunch of people, lied to a bunch of world leaders, and started a world war. He had some interesting ideas, but he wasn't competent enough to pull them off."

The conversation Barbara and I had—sitting naked side-by-side in the somewhat scary atmosphere of my brother's bed-room—has stayed in my mind for decades. Not because of the emotion or the nakedness or the intensity of the moment, but because Barbara became so practical about things. She even apologized at one point for ruining the mood. She said we could always get the mood back, and we might be able to eliminate some of her fear if she knew what was going to happen and how.

"Look," she said, "I guess I know what it is, but I want to avoid nasty surprises. I need to know how it works first." Her voice and attitude had taken on a whole new tone; humorous and gentle, as if it were I who needed reassuring. "What exactly do we do? How do we start? Do we make out until I'm ready and then, I don't know, just do it? Or could we break me in slowly? What would be best, or the least painful for me?" She looked at me and smiled, then she laid her head on my shoulder, grabbed my hand, and asked, "What do you think?"

Unfortunately, I couldn't think too well at that moment. Things had gotten all jumbled in my mind: the love, the affection, the sexual desire, the fact that we were actually sitting together naked on a bed calmly talking about how we were going to have sex. Finally, I said, "You know, I have a feeling it's only going to hurt in the beginning. I mean when we first start. But I don't know if that's true. How could I?"

As part of our earlier pact to always be completely honest with each other, I had let her tease me into admitting to my previous sexual relationship with Barbara Wilson, though I had not gone into gruesome detail, and that's exactly what she wanted now—details. So, after a few false starts, I managed to explain that Barbara had not been a virgin, and I told her about the rape, about her boyfriend's huge penis, and how I thought that was why I felt lost inside her. She got a kick out of that, laughing, then apologizing, then laughing again. I went on to explain to her, however, that I was sure I was much larger now, at which time she looked down between my legs and said with a sly grin, "You don't look so big right now."

"Yes," I said. "And wouldn't it be nice if I could stay that way for our first time?" Of course, as we talked my erection started making a comeback, and she looked at me with a grimace of feigned regret. "Oh, well," she said, "I guess that option's out."

After a few moments of thought, I asked her, "What is it, do you think, that scares you the most. I mean, I know it's probably the pain and all, but maybe there's something else, something you haven't even thought of yet. Like the blood, or that I might not be able to stop if you want me to?"

"Blood?" she shrieked. "What do you mean, blood?" I realized then that she didn't know anything about this, and that not knowing what to expect might be her biggest fear.

"Okay, okay, calm down a minute and let me explain something to you." I knew from street talk and from my dad's medical books that a virgin had a thing called a hymen—which on the street was called a cherry—and that when a girl lost her virginity, this little membrane would often tear and bleed. In fact, after I thought about it, I figured most of the pain for a virgin was probably caused by that tearing. I took her hand in mine and began to massage it, trying to think of the best way to tell her.

"You see," I said finally, "there's this thing, a thin piece of skin that partly covers the, uh, opening, if you know what I mean." She nodded and I continued. "Maybe it's there for protection of some sort in younger girls, I don't know, but when a girl first does it, this thing gets torn and it sometimes bleeds a little." Actually, I didn't have any idea if it bled a little or a lot, but I thought it might be best at that moment to go with "a little." Though I didn't want to give her a false sense of security, and I was definitely not trying to talk her into anything, I added, "It's one of those things that happens and you can't get around it." She laughed at my unintended pun, but I ignored her and continued. "It's something that signals your going from being a girl to being a woman."

Barbara thought for a minute, then said, "Okay, so there's going to be some blood. I guess I can deal with that. Heck, I deal with it every month now. But you said something about maybe not being able to stop if I wanted you to, remember?"

"Yeah." I tried to think of some way to explain how hard it is for a boy to stop once he gets started. After some concentration, I thought I might have found a way.

"Remember when I described orgasms and getting to the top of a mountain?" She nodded. "Well, for a boy it's like the reverse, like going down a mountain instead of up. Once a boy gets started, it's like rolling down a steep hill in a car with no brakes. You feel like you have to get to the bottom no matter what." I then went into a detailed explanation of the withdrawal method Barbara Wilson had taught me, and how it was hard to do even though I knew I could still have an orgasm.

Ever since the other Barbara and I had split up, I'd tried to get some rubbers, so I would never have to go through that frustrating withdrawal bit again. I finally found them in the bathroom of a local gas station, where I could lock the door and buy them from the machine for a quarter. Of course, all I did was end up socking them away (literally, in a sock hidden at the back of my closet), as the opportunity for intercourse had never come around again. Until, perhaps, today. It came to me then that it might be a good idea to go get them before we got started and I forgot.

We hadn't broached the subject of a possible pregnancy, which seemed weird to me at the time, but I guess Barbara trusted me to know about these things and take whatever precautions were necessary. In fact, my discussion of pregnancy prevention using the withdrawal method didn't even seem to pique her interest, because her response had nothing whatsoever to do with that.

"That's what I was talking about, that thing about not being able to stop," she said. "I think what worries me most, beside the pain, is not being in control—having it hurt a lot and not being able to stop it myself. I mean, you're supposed to be on top right?"

"I guess," I said. "I've never done it any other way, but I suppose there are other ways. Wouldn't you think? I mean some ways that would make it possible for you to stop things if you don't want to go on? Don't get me wrong. Even though it would be hard to do, I think I could stop if you wanted me to. I mean, the way I feel about you now, I bet the love would be stronger than anything else, and I wouldn't continue to hurt you unless we both wanted to get past some point where the pain might go away."

She seemed to be thinking hard for a while, then she said, "Okay, let's do it a little and see how things go. But try not to go too far at first. We can experiment. Would that be all right?"

"Sure," I said. "Anything you want." But all the talk had killed the mood for me, and I didn't know how to begin. Again, Barbara made the first move.

"Can I touch you?" she asked, averting her eyes and letting her shyness manifest itself for a moment.

"Okay. Yes. Certainly," I said, and watched as her hand moved toward my once-again-growing erection. She touched it gently at first, then wrapped her hand around it as if to check and see how thick it was.

"It's growing bigger right now," she exclaimed as if I, too, might be surprised by this.

"Uh-huh," I said. "That's what happens when I get excited."

"Oh, sure, I guess I know that. But, well, seeing it happen is kind of strange. Boy, is it getting big now." For a moment she stared at it, fascinated, then she said," This top part, it's a lot bigger than the rest. Do you think that's what hurts?"

"Probably," I said. "But I don't know if it's only that or if going in too far hurts too. Geeze, Barbara, I don't have any idea. Maybe it's both or maybe something else altogether. Maybe it's your hymen and after we're past that everything will be okay."

She considered that for a moment, then said, "I think that's it. Think about it. If it was anything else, it would hurt for a long time, maybe forever, and girls wouldn't do it at all after the first time. But they do, or we wouldn't have any babies, right? So I'll bet it's a first-time thing when the hymen gets broken. And even if that's not all the pain there is, whatever else has to get better pretty fast, dontcha think?" Her mood had once again turned humorous and jaunty, as if she were ready to handle anything by looking it straight in the eye and staring it down.

"I guess so. That makes sense to me," I said. "But I'm not sure about any of this, and I don't want you to hate me if things don't go exactly like we hope they will."

With that, she squeezed me hard and took my chin in her other hand, turning my face towards her. "Does that hurt?" she asked.

"You bet," I answered with a grimace.

She squeezed harder. "Do you hate me?"

"No, I could never hate you," I said, my voice rising an octave.

"Do you get my point?" she said as she slowly released the pressure, to my great relief.

I nodded. "I think so," I said.

"You *think* so?" she said, reaching to grip me again.

"Okay. I get it. I get it."

And she once again grabbed my face and looked me in the eye. "Look, you numbskull, what I'm trying to say is, I love you as much as you love me, and no amount of pain or mistakes or anything else is going to change that. Got it?"

"Got it."

"Okay. Now I have an idea."

14

BARBARA

1968

Barbara held me for a long time, rubbing my back, oblivious to the curious eyes of a few elderly passersby on their daily walks at The Bay. Finally, when she felt my sobs subsiding, she ruffled my hair and whispered, "We're kinda making a spectacle of ourselves here, aren't we?" I couldn't have cared less that we were hugging in public, but after a little hesitation I managed to release her. "That's all over now," she said when she saw my eyes drift back down to her arm, which she had turned so I could no longer see the scars.

"But, but, Barb, why?" I stammered. "What could ever make you do something like that?"

"That's what I'm going to tell you, Tommy. Please be patient with me." She looked skyward, where some of the gulls still circled under the powder-like clouds. Then she cleared her throat and continued.

"You said you remember that day, and if you're like me, you remember every minute, every second, everything we did."

I looked up at her. "Of course," I said. "The whole day is indelibly seared into my memory. I could no more forget one moment than I could forget my own name."

"Well," she said, "if you remember what we did, do you remember what we didn't do?"

I began shuffling through those memories, playing them like a newsreel across the wide screen of my mind, but for the life of me, I couldn't figure out what she was talking about. "What we *didn't* do?" I asked after a few seconds. "Gosh, honey, I thought we did about everything there was *to* do."

"Yes," she said. "We just about wrote the book on, well, at least on everything we could come up with at the time. But think for a moment. Think about socks."

"Socks?" I said, trying to concentrate. "Your socks? My socks? What socks?"

"Your socks, Tommy, but not the ones you were wearing."

Then it hit me. I had mentioned to her, before we'd gone too far, about the necessity for protection, and about what I had stashed away in that sock at the back of my closet. But we were so involved in each other, so oblivious, I forgot all about that not-so-minor detail. "Oh," I said as I started to put two and two together. "Oh, my God, Barb. Oh, shit!" The tears started to come again and she touched my cheek.

"Tommy, please, please don't take this all on yourself. It wasn't only you. I forgot, too."

"But, but, did you get ...?" I grasped her arm and turned it over. "Is that what this was all about?" It was her turn for tears now and I lifted her hand to kiss that delicate spider web of ivory white scars, then pressed it against my cheek. After a moment or two, she seemed to regain her composure. She stared down at her lap and continued.

"When I got home that day, while I was cleaning up and all, taking care of the residual evidence, so to speak. That's when I remembered."

"But, why didn't you call me? Why didn't you tell me right then?" I whined like a little kid.

"Because, Tommy, I didn't want to worry you. I knew my period was due in a couple of days and that that would probably take care of it. So I decided to wait. What I thought was, why should we get all worked up over something that might not even happen?"

"But it did happen, didn't it?"

"I think you know that now, don't you?"

"Jesus," I said. "It must've been hell for you."

"It was," she said. "I did a lot of praying over the next few weeks, hoping God might see His way clear to lend a hand, to make it be a disease or something. I even asked Him to take my life at one point, so I wouldn't have to put you or my folks or your folks through all that. Unfortunately, He didn't seem to be around at the time." She smiled a little and took me by the hands. "But you have to understand, Tommy, I'm still here and I'm okay, really I am. There's nothing you did wrong. After all, what could wrong with two people who love each other making a baby?"

The breeze started to kick up, and the acrid scent of ozone in the air signaled that rain was on its way. I knew she could feel my hands shaking, and when the first crack of thunder shuddered in the distance, she said, "Listen, why don't we find someplace a little more private? That will give us some time to calm down and talk. What do you say?" It was clear she meant me when she said, "calm down," but with the first spattering of raindrops beginning to fall and my mind in a quagmire of grief and love and emotional upheaval, I decided she was right.

As the wind grew stronger, we started off hand-in-hand toward the street. When we reached my car I quickly opened the door for her. By the time I got around to the driver's side, the rain had started coming down hard, and I swung into the seat and slammed the door behind me. We sat for a few minutes, looking out the blurry windshield at nothing. Finally I said, "Where should we go?"

She thought for a minute, then said, "I've got an idea." I started the car and looked at her in curiosity. "Drive, okay? Stay on this road and drive."

With the late-morning storm swirling around us, I drove slowly, and Barbara guided us until we ended up on Fourth Street, headed north. After we had traveled a few miles, she pointed out a street on the left and told me to turn. Two blocks down, she directed us into the driveway of a small house with a For Rent sign out front.

"My dad bought this place about two years ago as an investment," she said as we sat in the car and waited for the rain to slacken. The house, from what I could see through the sheets of rain, was of gingerbread design, with curly white wooden appointments and a porch surrounded by white picket railing. "It's a neat little place. In fact, I was the one who picked it out and decorated it for him. It's furnished and the rent's fair, but it hasn't been terribly successful as a rental. You want to make a run for it?"

"Sure," I said. We counted to three, jumped from the car, and battled the rain as we made our way up the walkway. Once under the protection of the narrow porch roof, we stopped and turned to look at the rain-drenched front yard. Barbara leaned over and shook out her hair, spattering water like a dog after a bath. I stood there watching this little ritual and fell in love all over again. When she finished, she brushed her hair back with her hands, wiped them on her shorts, and reached into her purse for the key.

Inside, musty air hung like the atmosphere in an empty church sanctuary. "The electricity's off," she said, as we wiped our feet on the inside doormat, "but that won't matter." She took me by the hand and led me across the varnished wood floor, past the coat closet and into the small living room. She ducked into the adjoining kitchen and returned with two towels, tossing one to me as she rubbed her hair with the other. After we had both dried off as best we could, she sat on the overstuffed couch and patted the space next to her. I sat and took one of her hands in mine.

She stretched and sighed and leaned back against the huge fluffy couch pillows. With her damp hair splayed all around her face and her slender body stretched out below, I couldn't help myself, and I leaned over to kiss her. She didn't protest, but when our lips parted she said, "Remember what we promised, Tommy." I made an exaggerated, sad sack face, and she reached up to stroke my cheek. "Poor Tommy," she said as if comforting a kid who had been denied ice cream before dinner.

The silence, enhanced by the white noise of rain, had begun to roar around us when she finally continued with a sly smile, "Hey, kiddo, don't think I don't want to jump you right here and now, because I do. But we're both married now, and Rob is over there in that hell hole dodging bullets." Her eyes began to moisten and she turned her face away. "I couldn't betray him, Tommy. I couldn't. Not even with you."

I squeezed her hand a little. "I know you couldn't, honey. I know. I have to be honest though when I say that, even though I've never been unfaithful, I could easily justify it here with you right now. Especially since fate seems to have given us the perfect opportunity."

But there, on that rainy summer day, when everything seemed to have fallen into perfect place for a renewal of our love affair, the strongest influence fate had to offer was Barbara's unflinching loyalty and respect for her marriage vows.

15
ANNIE   1962

The hardest thing for me to handle about my affair with Annie—an affair that stretched on for nearly a year—was the fact that I was, for the first time, being unfaithful. Not only that, I lied about it. I often think back on those times and remember that rainy morning in 1968, when Barbara refused to commit adultery, and I'm ashamed I'm not as strong as she.

It isn't like we're engaged or anything, I used to tell myself in a vain attempt to justify the affair. But when Alicia's first letter arrived, filled with fear and loneliness, accompanied by a copy of Del Shannon's "Runaway," I resolved right then and there to break it off with Annie. Unfortunately, my determination could not hold a candle to Annie's persuasion. Her logic, twisted as it sometimes was, combined with her dominating countenance, made me feel helpless. That, along with her expertise in the methods and mechanics of sexual simulation, melted my resolve.

Over the next few months, we had sex almost daily. Mostly in the early afternoons when we first awoke, me groggy and hung over from the booze and cigarettes and the cacophony of the night before, and Annie seemingly unfazed by any of that. Our schedule, like that of most entertainers, was shifted around, what with not getting out of the lounge until three or so in the morning, then hitting the late night diners and breakfast joints along with the waitresses and bartenders and all the other workers whose lives revolved around the nightclub scene. Often we were too exhausted to think about sex when we finally crashed around five in the morning, so sexual activities were relegated to those hours of the afternoon before rehearsal.

We did a lot of experimenting during that time. Annie had bought a copy of the Kama Sutra, and seemed bound and determined to work her way through it until we had tried everything it had to offer. I can't say I was against this, but all those gyrations and supposed nuances of lovemaking seemed unnatural to me. For one thing, it often required nearly superhuman stamina on my part; that is, an ability to delay an orgasm for prolonged periods filled with stimulating acts, both physical and mental. This was complicated by the fact that Annie refused to let me use rubbers. Of course, the removal of that dulling barrier made sex more enjoyable for me, but it also lessened my ability to wait for her. To ward off pregnancy, Annie used a douche, usually within minutes of any ejaculation, which had another less-than erotic impact on my ability to make a comeback.

Unlike our first night, multiple erections became more difficult for me with the addition of the technical procedures dictated by the book. This was frustrating for Annie, whose stamina and needs never seemed to wane. In fact, it was my problem with what she called "getting it up" and "premature ejaculation" that started most of our arguments. More than once I faced angry tantrums, thrown shoes and other objects, and lots of silent sulking after sex.

Still, I can't say I regret those days. I learned a lot about myself and about how to please a woman (and how not to), and I did enjoy our friendship, which, despite the sexual tension, was filled with great humor and many long philosophical conversations and stimulating debates.

Politically, Annie was an unambiguous conservative, holding many views that conflicted with my own, while seeming not to care much about what went on in the world outside. She was also a passionate atheist, which greatly influenced my own views. At times her opinions and attitudes seemed almost cruel, and social empathy was a trait for which she had no use or respect. She appeared unable to sympathize with the poor and homeless, viewing them as simply too lazy to get off their asses and work their way out of their own mess. She had an incredibly high tolerance for physical pain, which she assumed others did as well, and she had no patience with "whiners" who complained of any ailments.

It seems odd to me now, how I could be attracted to such a cold and critical person, but I was, mainly because she was a blast to be around. Then, of course, there was the sex, which no doubt colored my view. In fact, Annie and I never lost touch, and often corresponded later in our lives. We also got together occasionally, whenever I found myself in Atlanta, where she eventually settled.

The tour had come to an end in Atlanta, after we had opened some six Peppermint Lounge franchises along the

East Coast, and Annie fell in love with the city. Despite her adherence to the use of her douche, that method of birth control proved to be about as effective as the withdrawal method (Barbara Wilson, who first taught me that method, later became pregnant with Carl's child, and they ended up in a disastrous marriage that lasted about a year and culminated in both violence and divorce). Annie missed her period a week or so before we arrived in Atlanta, and by the time we were wrapping things up, she'd resigned herself to the fact that she was pregnant.

Ever the pragmatist, she was not about to allow pregnancy to interfere with her life, and it wasn't long before she found a doctor willing to perform an illegal abortion. In fact, after the tour broke up, she went to work for the same doctor as a receptionist (and, I speculated, a lover). Eventually she decided to attend the University of Georgia, from which she graduated with a degree in journalism and mass communications.

About nine years later, right after my marriage to Paula had fallen apart, I got a letter from Annie. It was passed along to me by her sister, with whom I had struck up a casual friendship over the intervening years.

"Hey, kiddo," it said in the opening. "Guess what? I'm getting married. He's a budding politician, and I've been working for him as a campaign manager for about a year now. He's going places, too. I know this because he was smart enough to hire me. He's tall, handsome, and well endowed, if you get my drift. He also has a lot of staying power (jab, jab), so I know he can probably handle the rigors of a long-term political career. It's not love, exactly, at least not in the dreamy sense most women (except me) fantasize about. It's more like a business arrangement with a side order of fantastic sex, but I do like him a lot and we get along better than I do with most human beings.

"Anyway, there's an invitation on the way, so if you want to take a break and see the Big City again, I'd love it if you could come (to Atlanta, that is)."

She went on to fill me in on the previous few years and ask how my love life was and all, then closed with:

"You know, kiddo, I've never forgotten our little road trip. The sex part for sure, but more so the fun and companionship. I will always think of you as a friend, and even if you can't make it to the wedding, I hope we can stay in touch.

"Love ya,

"Annie

"PS: I'm enclosing a photo so you can see what you're missing."

The picture was of a stunningly sophisticated looking Annie, arm in arm with a tall, good-looking gentleman. Her smile revealed the fact that she'd had her cracked tooth fixed, which was a disappointment to me because it took away the last vestiges of her girlish cuteness. Still, with the formal attire and more mature facial features, she was almost movie-star beautiful, and I felt a slight tug in my pants knowing I'd once had the privilege of, as she used to put it, fucking her brains out.

I did manage to make it up for the wedding, and Annie and Bob and I struck up a friendship that would last our entire lives. With Annie's brains and enthusiasm behind him, Bob went on to become a US senator and, though we had nothing whatsoever in common politically, he seemed to enjoy bouncing ideas off me and listening to my liberal viewpoints. He didn't even seem to mind the fact that Annie and I had been lovers, something that, in her practical and honest way, she had told him about (in pretty graphic detail, she said) before they married.

About the only thing I ever did regret about my relation-ship with Annie was that with her I abandoned my cher-ished ethics and honesty. Even though Alicia never caught on (that I knew of), I carried that self-loathing with me for a long time. And, while on the tour, I spent a lot of money on phone calls to Allie and gifts for her to try and make myself feel better. What complicated matters on that score, was how I left her with a burden she didn't deserve and should-n't have had to deal with on her own.

16

ALICIA   1961

There's something we have to talk about," I said, after Alicia and I woke from our spontaneous post-coital nap.

She turned her head and kissed me on the neck. "Tommy, er, Tom," she said, ignoring me. "Is it always going to feel that good? I mean, that was incredible. I can't imagine anything ever being able to match it."

"I don't know, kitten," I answered, trying without success to think of some way to turn the subject toward what I needed to say. "Not to get your hopes up or anything, but logic would seem to say the more experience you have the better it will get."

"Wow! Wouldn't that be something?" She said with a drowsy dreamy lilt in her voice, as if she were thinking out loud. Then she reached over and laid a hand on my now flaccid penis. "Do you think we can wake him up again, he seems to have fallen asleep?"

"Yes, for a guy that's what happens afterwards. But if you keep rubbing him like that, he'll probably come to life again soon, and that's what we need to talk about."

"You mean about doing it again?" she asked.

"Not exactly," I answered. "It's about the first time. We, or maybe I should say I, forgot something."

"Don't tell me there's more stuff we can do. I mean, is there?"

"Oh, sure, there's lots more to do than we did, but there's one thing we should've done that we didn't."

She snuggled against my chest and said, "Okay, I give up. What?"

I reached my arm up and over her head, so I could pull her close to me. "Now listen, it's probably going to be okay. I mean I don't want you to get all worried or anything. But … well, I forgot to use a rubber."

Her reaction wasn't immediate. In fact, I had begun to wonder if she even knew what I was talking about, when what I said finally seemed to sink in. She jerked her hand away from my penis as if it were a snake about to bite her. Then she lifted up on an arm and looked down at me. "Oh, shit!" she said. "Shit, shit, shit! I can't get pregnant. I can't. My mom and dad would kill me. Oh, Tommy, what're we going to do? What the hell are we going to do?" And with that she burst out crying. I held her and let her go on for a while, until her great heaving sobs seemed to be getting out of control. "It's going to be all right, Allie," I said, rubbing her back and knowing what I said might not be true. "It was only once. Some married couples try for years without, you know."

"Yeah?" she said, her sobs beginning to subside a bit. "Really?"

"Really," I answered.

"But is there anything we can do now, or I can do to make sure?"

"I wish there were, kitten, but I don't think there is." I waited for the next round of tears, but she seemed to be contemplating everything. "Can you tell me when your last, I mean when you had your—"

"My period?"

"Uh-huh."

"It stopped about three days ago, why?" She hesitated for a moment, "Oh, I know. That's how we'll find out, right?" Then something seemed to dawn on her and tears began rolling down her cheeks. "Oh, Tommy, you'll be gone by the time I'm due again." She laid her head on my chest and began to sob.

When what she said sunk in, I realized I was facing a monumental choice. On one hand, I was looking at the chance of a lifetime: to go on the road with a professional Rock group. On the other, I would have to leave her to face this dilemma alone. Finally, I said with resolve, "I'll stay. I'll tell them they have to find somebody else. It'll be okay. I won't leave you. We'll deal with this together. Whatever happens, I'll be here for you."

"You'd do that for me? Oh, Tommy, I love you so much." We lay there silently for a while, then she seemed to come to some conclusion. "But I can't. I can't make you do that. I know how much this means to you, and I didn't want you to go in the first place. But I couldn't live with myself if I were the cause of your losing out on the opportunity. I can handle it, Tommy, really I can. Besides, we can talk on the phone, can't we? I mean you were going to call me, weren't you?"

"Absolutely!" I said. "But, Allie, I can't take off and leave you now."

By then she seemed to have gained a measure of determination, and I felt her shake her head against my chest. "No," she said in a quiet but final tone. "I won't let you stay. I'll be okay. I will. Besides, like you said, the chances are pretty slim. Just promise me you'll call whenever you can. I'll tell Janet and she can give me moral support, and we'll pray it doesn't happen, okay?" When I didn't answer, she said again, "Okay? Tommy?"

It was one of the toughest decisions I had ever had to make in my young life, however, I eventually let her talk me into going. I felt like a rat leaving a sinking ship, but I kept justifying my decision by telling myself she probably wasn't pregnant and that Janet would help out and if it turned out she was pregnant, I would quit the tour and drive back immediately. After we'd settled things and the anxiety had dissipated a bit, she snuggled up and stared nibbling on my ear. I was in no mood for any further sexual activity, but when she whispered, "Can we do it again?" I found I couldn't refuse for fear of making things worse for her than they already were.

"Sure," I said. "If you want to."

"I do, Tommy. I really do." She reached down and touched me with the tips of her fingers, as if she were scared she might be doing something wrong this time. I let my mind go and eventually, despite my anxiety, I started to get hard. Even though whatever damage there was going to be had probably already been done, I fumbled through my jeans until I found a rubber. She seemed fascinated by the little round tin, as I tore it open and extracted the gooey circle of latex.

"Can I touch it?" she asked in an amazed whisper. I held it out for her and she tentatively placed a finger on the protruding receptacle end. "What's that for?" she asked.

"It's there to catch the, uh, sperm, so there's less chance of it breaking," I answered.

She thought about that, then said, "You mean they break?"

"Sometimes," I said. "But not often."

"Oh," she said with fascination in her voice. "How do you put it on?"

I started to apply it, then took her hand and showed her how to roll it down. "So you know how to do it if you need to sometime in the future," I said with a smile.

"Okay," she answered and then she surprised me by swinging her leg over and climbing on top.

Seeing the somewhat shocked look on my face, she asked, "Is this okay? I mean you said there were lots of things we didn't try the first time. Is it okay if we try it this way?"

"Yeah, sure," I said, aroused by her aggressiveness. She lifted up and I positioned myself, then placed my hands on her shoulders to urge her downward. In response, she began to relax her legs, letting out a little gasp as the tip went in, but not stopping until the gap between us had closed and her hips rested on my legs.

"Now what?" she asked. I reached down and grasped her by the waist, pulling her toward me then pushing her back again. Before long she seemed to catch on and her movements, tentative at first, became more confident and rhythmic. As her body began to respond to the arousal caused by rubbing against my pubic bone, her eyes closed and her head tilted back. I joined in, pushing upward with each sliding movement to penetrate deeper, and it wasn't long before she shuddered and came, arching her back and squeezing me with each receding wave. Unlike the frenzied orgasm of our first time, her movements were slow and deliberate, as if she were trying to prolong and deepen the pleasure of every contraction. When she seemed to have exhausted all possibility of extending her orgasm, she leaned down to kiss me, then moved her mouth around to my ear.

"That was nice," she whispered. "Different, but really nice."

As it turned out, Alicia wasn't pregnant after all, though we did have a few nervous moments when her period was late, and I nearly kept my promise to leave the group and come home. We talked on the phone almost every night during the week leading up to her time and the anxiety filled five days before she finally started. All the while with me screwing Annie like a crazed sex fiend, which made those conversations (for which I used a phone booth outside the motel office) almost painful for me.

In the end, my absence proved too much for her, however, and within six months she once again hooked up with Devin. She wrote me a Dear John letter, full of apologies and concern for my broken heart (which wasn't all that broken). In the letter she said, in what she seemed to hope was a complimentary way, she had enjoyed having sex with me so much she needed to find someone to at least fill in while I was away. Besides, she said, this would release me to do whatever I wanted on the road, instead of having to refuse the hundreds of propositions she was sure I had been turning down.

"To be honest, Tom, I was incredibly horny, that's all," she wrote. "And I needed to have sex again. Devin and I were at a beach party and one thing led to another. You know how it is."

Of course I knew how it was, since I was banging Annie almost every day and loving it. I wrote her back, trying to convey sincere regret and ending the letter by saying I would recover somehow and wishing her and Devin well. Unfortunately, their relationship, which eventually led to divorce, remarriage and divorce again, was no picnic, but her story did have a happy ending when she married my best friend and they managed to make the marriage work.

When I think back on Alicia and the other partners I've had over the years, I always feel indebted to Barbara and her innocent, yet astute, attitude about sex. Regardless of my sexual exploits with Annie, which were somewhat unemotional and perfunctory, I learned more from Barbara on that single glorious afternoon in 1960 than I ever did from any other woman in my life.

17

BARBARA 1960

Barbara had an idea.

As we sat naked on Neal's bed, with her hand on my penis and my libido recovering from her less-than-gentle treatment of it, all I could think was: *God this is weird: giving up control to a **girl**, for Christ's sake, letting her dictate how we should have sex.* Of course, after several decades of life and sex and relationships, it became commonplace, desirable even, to have a partner tell me what turned her on or off and, in some cases, demand certain actions or accommodations. But back then it was considered wimpy for a boy to do anything but stick his dick in a girl and get off any way he could. Anything different could get you labeled "pussy whipped," and I tried to appear as macho and in control as possible to my peers. Of course, I reasoned, my peers were never going to know anything about this; I would die before

I ever let even a tiny bit of it become general knowledge, a fact that reinforced my thinking that I was truly in love for the first time.

Barbara had an idea, and I was damned sure going to listen to it.

"How about this?" she said, a bit of demure modesty creeping back into her voice and demeanor. "How about if you sit down on that chair and I stand over you? Then I lower myself onto you. That way, if things get too painful, I can always stand up again. I could stop whenever I wanted to."

It was such an astute and logical plan, I could do nothing but agree. In fact, Barbara had come up with something that would relieve me of almost any responsibility for hurting her. With this plan, if there was going to be pain, she would inflict it on herself, without my having much to do with it. But before I could respond, she continued.

"Now look, I know this wouldn't be so great for you, and I also know it won't be very romantic, but I only mean we should try it so that I can get past the hymen thing then think about how it might be if we make love the right way." As an afterthought, she added, "If there is one right way." And with a wistful glance at the ceiling, she speculated, "Maybe there's lots of ways and maybe some are better for the girl than the old boy-on-top way."

When I finally managed to get a word in, I said, "Yes!" To which I added, "Perfect. Incredible idea!" Unfortunately, it turned out to be none of those things.

Because of the possibility of blood, we decided a chair in the middle of the carpeted bedroom might not be the best place, so I came up with the idea of retiring to the bathroom, where I would sit on the closed lid of the toilet and any stains would end up on the tile floor. That way we could easily clean things up and she could jump right into the shower. But all this logistical stuff, when added to the unromantic setting of a bathroom toilet for our first time, led to additional problems.

First, there was the problem of my gaining an erection, something I had never in my life failed to do, but I soon found that the location, combined with the methodology, were enough to keep Pete from rising (Barbara had earlier started referring to my penis as "Pete"). In response to this unexpected turn of events, Barbara decided to stroke Pete a little, and soon he stood at attention once again. But then, as she began to lower herself onto me, with her hands on my shoulders and me holding Pete in the right position, we ran into a brick wall, so to speak.

"It won't go in," she said. She didn't appear to be in pain, but her ineffective squirming and wriggling seemed to leave her perplexed. The problem, we both realized, was that she was dry. Unlike the time we had made out and I had used my finger, there was nothing slippery there, and we finally had to admit it was not going to work. Of course, we could probably have found a lubricant, such as the bottle of Lanolin Plus that stood only a foot or so away on the bathroom counter, but in our naiveté, neither of us thought of that. Instead, we gave up and returned to the bedroom, where we again sat chastely on the bed, deep in frustrated thought.

"You know why, don't you?" I asked, after a few minutes of contemplative silence.

"I think so," Barbara said. "It's my fault, isn't it?"

"What do you mean?" I snapped. "How could it be your fault? You didn't do anything! After all, it's not something you can control, now is it?" I scratched my head trying to come up with the right words to convey what I wanted to say.

"I guess not, but—"

"There's no guessing about it, Barb. You can't make yourself feel sexy if you're not. It's that kind of feeling that causes you to, you know, get wet"

"No, Tommy, I didn't know, at least not before now. I never knew all that mess was there for a reason, and that without it we could probably never ... oh, you know what I mean."

"So?"

"So," she said as she again locked her eyes on mine. "Let's just do it! Let's do what we've done before and let things happen as they will."

This time, it was me who took her chin in my hands. "Do you mean that?" I asked. "That we should make out and then go ahead and do it?"

"Look," she said, trying in vain to turn her head away, "I'm probably as horny as you are right now, and I'm getting tired of waiting for the absolute perfect time, or situation, or whatever. I love you, Tommy, and I want badly to make love with you. If it's going to hurt, then it's going to hurt, and there isn't anything we can do about it."

I kissed her then. Hesitant at first, she soon began to return the kiss, and together we fell back on the bed. Without releasing each other, we squirmed around until our heads reached the pillows, and before long our kisses became deeper and more intense. I had begun to nibble at her neck when she put her hand behind my head and started to push it down toward her breasts. My mouth found one of her nipples and she moaned with pleasure as I licked and kissed and made love to it.

"How can I make love to you?" she whispered after a while, between quiet gasps and rhythmic leg movements.

I didn't know how to answer, since no girl had ever actually made love to me. "I don't know," I said. "I guess you could touch me, down there maybe. But don't squeeze too hard." She chuckled in my ear and reached down to take hold of my erection.

"I'm not sure what to do," she whispered again.

"Well, don't do too much or it'll all be over before we get started."

"But isn't that okay?" she asked, "Isn't it good for you to, you know, have an orgasm?"

"Sure, but, well, if I do have one, I get all satisfied, and then I don't want to do anything more. At least for a while. And I don't want that to happen before you get some pleasure out of it, too. Understand?"

She thought about that for a while, then said, "No. Not exactly. I mean if you get satisfied, it will make me happy, and if it takes a while for you to want more, then that's the way it's going to be, right?"

"I guess," I said, not knowing if what she said was logical, but not willing to contradict her either.

"Okay, so, how do I make love to you?"

Without speaking, I began to instruct her hand in the ways of male masturbation. She seemed reluctant at first to draw my circumcised skin up over the top, probably because she thought it would hurt me, but eventually she fell into a rhythm and before long I came with an incredible burst that squirted almost to my chin. As I shuddered and jerked and let out a few deep sighs, she seemed fascinated by the whole thing.

"Wow," she said, looking over my glistening chest. "No wonder you have to pull out. With all that it would probably shoot all the way up to my throat."

I was shocked at the candor with which she described my ejaculation. But when I looked at her, she chuckled and held on to me while I shrunk. "I see what you mean about things changing after you have one of those orgasms," she said, smiling at me, not with frustration or sarcasm, but with genuine interest. "Do you think that happens to a woman, too?"

As far as I knew, Barbara Wilson never had orgasms, so how was I to know if she "shrank" after one? "Maybe," I said. "I mean if it happens to men, it probably happens to women, too. Don't you think?"

"I wonder," she said as she rose from the bed and went into the bathroom. She returned a few minutes later with a warm damp washcloth, with which she cleaned up the mess I had made. Flabbergasted, I lay there and watched her do this, thinking to myself that there could not be another female on the planet as kind and loving and uninhibited as this one. She finished what she seemed almost to feel was her duty under the circumstances, and when she came back, she said, "Was that good for you? I mean, did I do good, or is there something else you could teach me that would make it better?"

My attempt to answer caught against the growing lump in my throat, so instead, I drew her against me for a long, non-sexual, kiss. We stayed like that for a while, hugging and snuggling and whispering little jokes in each other's ears. And it wasn't long, not long at all in fact, before I began to feel aroused again.

"See," she said as she felt my erection returning against her leg, "that didn't take too long, did it?"

18
BARBARA 1968

Oh, Tommy. What am I going to do with you?" Barbara said as she stared up at the ceiling of the little gingerbread house in frustrated consternation.

"You don't have to do anything, Barb," I answered. "I was only venting some frustration. I wasn't trying to talk you into anything. We know each other better than a lot of couples do after a lifetime together, and I certainly know you well enough to understand you would never cheat on your husband, whether he was in Vietnam or right next door safe and sound. What I don't understand is why, after all we went though, after all we meant to each other, you could drop me like a hot sack of shit."

I realized a little too late I had let my anger come through, and before I could do anything to remedy it, she started to cry. I reached out a hand, but she brushed it aside and turned away from me.

"Hey," I said trying to convey remorse rather than anger. "I didn't mean that like it sounded. I didn't mean to be nasty or anything. It's just that I've been so frustrated over these past eight years or so. Not knowing anything or being able to figure out what happened has been like trying to grasp that ring on the merry-go-round, which is especially frustrating for a short guy like me, if you know what I mean." I waited for my little stab at humor to elicit a response, but when she continued sniffling and sobbing I decided to go on.

"Look, Honey, what happened was my fault, not yours. I was the one who forgot, and I did realize it a little later. I tried to call, but your mom kept saying you weren't there. Then your phone number stopped working altogether. And when I called the business, your dad was never available. It was like you had shut me out of your life, and try as I might, I couldn't figure out why. Can't you understand how frustrating it was for me?"

She continued to sob, but finally turned back to face me. Her tears glistened in the dim light, and my heart melted into a small lump at the bottom of my stomach. I reached out for her then, and she let me take her into my arms. "I can explain all that," she said in my ear. "And I will, if you give me a minute."

"Sure, Barb. I didn't mean to rush you. Take all the time you need. Do you want a glass of water or something?"

She shook her head, then smiled a little. "The water isn't on either," she said with an apologetic shrug. We sat there, looking into each other's eyes, until she seemed to regain her composure and cleared her throat.

"When I got home that night and realized what might have happened, I was scared, you know?" I nodded. "But then I thought how silly that was. After all, the chances of that one time—my first time—resulting in pregnancy seemed pretty slim. So I decided to wait until I started my period and everything would be okay."

She reached up to wipe her face on her sleeve, but I caught her hand. "Don't mess up that pretty blouse," I said, grabbing one of the towels we had used and drying her tears.

"Thanks," she said before continuing. "Anyway, my period didn't come and with each day that passed I got more and more scared. At that time, I was into the whole God and Jesus thing, and all I could think to do was pray. I prayed and prayed until Mom got curious why I was spending so much time alone in my room, and about the only thing I got out of all those prayers was a reminder—I'm sure now it came from my own mind—a reminder that I'd made a promise to Mom to always be honest with her. It was a commitment, Tommy, like ours, and when she caught me one night kneeling beside my bed crying, she asked me to remember my promise.

"By then I was so desperate I didn't know what to do. I mean, there wasn't anything I could do, was there? I thought about calling you. I even picked up the phone a few times. But then I realized there wasn't anything you could do either, not at our ages at that time. All it would do was ruin both our lives and turn us into outcasts." She choked back another round of tears, then continued.

"So I decided I had to tell Mom. She was incredibly understanding, Tommy. She didn't get mad or anything. In fact, she admitted she and Dad had sex before they married, which was a real revelation for me and made me love her all the more. She said I should calm down, that there were lots of reasons a girl might miss her period, and that we would go to the doctor the next day to find out if I was pregnant, or if there might be something else going on.

"After a while, she got me into bed and I was able to sleep a little, but the next day was a real nightmare. At the doctor's office they did all kinds of embarrassing things to me, and when they were finished, they couldn't even give us any answers. They said the tests would take about a week, so we went back home knowing nothing. That week was the hardest of my life. Mom kept saying I shouldn't talk to you, at least until we knew something, and she made sure she always answered the phone before Dad could. But when the tests came back positive, she said we had to tell Dad.

"I begged her not to, but I knew there was no other choice. And when she finally did tell him, he went through the roof. He called me all kinds of names and said I was going to hell and threatened to call your parents, but Mom got him calmed down and I was banished to my room while they had a long conversation.

"That's the closest I ever came to calling you. I felt so alone and scared, and even though I knew you couldn't do anything, I needed you so badly I almost climbed out my window and ran to find you. And that's when I—" she turned her scarred wrist up again "—did this."

She tried to continue, but reliving the nightmare seemed to have exhausted her, so I said, "Hey, let's take a break for a minute, okay?" She nodded and we both fell back on the pillows, staring up at the little chandelier with its fake candle-flame light bulbs and thick coats of white paint. Eventually she sat back up and continued.

"When they'd finished their talk, Mom came upstairs and found me in the bathroom. It turns out I wasn't too good at suicide, and the little pocketknife I had didn't cause much damage. There was a lot of blood, but Mom seemed to know it wasn't serious, so she helped me clean up, bandaged my wrist, then held me close while she told me what was going to happen. She said they had decided the best thing to do was to have me go somewhere and have the baby, and that they would find a good family to adopt it and take care of it.

"You can't possibly have any idea how that made me feel. For one thing, it was *our* baby, not theirs to do with as they chose. What I wanted more than anything was to tell you all about it and maybe the two of us could run away and, oh hell, I don't know, build a life together. Of course, when I thought about it a little more, it was clear neither of us was ready to grow up and that it would probably end in disaster. So I decided to go along with their plan."

"Holy shit!" I said, more to myself than to her. "Holy fucking shit!" At that moment, I wanted to run out of that house, find her goddamned father and strangle the son of a bitch with my bare hands. I was so angry I started to shake, and Barbara, seeing this, reached out to hug me.

"I know what you're thinking, Tommy. I felt the same way for a long, long time. But you have to understand that my dad came from a conservative religious background and he also had a thriving business at the time. A scandal like that would've been devastating to their standing in the business and social community."

"Fuck him!" I said. Then, thinking better of it, I said, "I'm sorry, Barb, I didn't mean to say that. But you said it yourself: he had no right to decide what to do with our baby. *Our* baby!" And then it dawned on me: I had a child somewhere. My own flesh and blood, and I didn't even know its name or where it was or anything. For seven years there had been a human being out there that was part of me, and I had been denied the opportunity to ever even see it.

Knowing I was about to explode, I tried my best to calm down before I asked, "What happened? Where is he, or she? Hell, I don't even know the gender."

That opened the floodgates again, and we kept up our embrace, hugging and crying and letting all our pent up emotions spill out. Finally, she managed to compose herself, leaned back against the cushions, and said in a calm clear voice, "His name is David Lee Tate. He was born in Mexico Beach, Florida, and his parents are good people. I know because I lived with them for seven months before he was born."

David Lee Tate," Rosie said as she sorted and folded towels on the dining room table. "And you never found him?"

"Nope," I answered.

"Did you try?"

"Yep."

"What did you do, exactly?"

Rosie and I had been married for about three years. I had told her about my son long ago as part of our pre-marriage agreement to have no secrets. She didn't delve into it at the time; there was so much I had to relate about my past that I suggested we had the rest of our lives to fill in the details and she accepted that. Since she was seven years my junior, she'd had fewer life experiences and secrets to reveal than I did, the most difficult of which was telling me that she had undergone an abortion at age 18, something she felt sure would cause me to hate her. In fact, she was so devastated by what she had done, my casual reaction shocked her, and I began to think she might break up with me because of my unfeeling attitude.

"I did about everything I could think of," I said. "I got as much information as I could from Barbara. I looked in the Mexico Beach phone book at the library. I even drove up there and asked around. Short of hiring a private investigator, which I couldn't afford, I think I covered all the bases."

Rosie also knew about Barbara. In fact, she knew about all my former girlfriends and lovers. Not the intimate details, but I gave her the essence of each relationship, even the fact that I still carried a latent, unrealistic flame in my heart for Barbara. She was okay with this, or at least she said she was. Rosie was the closest thing to Barbara I had ever found, which is why, shortly after we met, I convinced her to marry me. I wasn't about to let another one like that slip away.

We had been talking about having kids lately, something I had promised her before we married, but that, upon later reflection, I realized I didn't want. During this particular conversation, I mentioned the fact that I already had two kids, but she interrupted me to point out that I actually had three. The subject had then turned to my mysterious third child, and she asked what I knew about him. I told her all I knew was his name, David Lee Tate, and that he had been born sometime in 1961 in a little Panhandle town by the name of Mexico Beach.

"And you never found even a trace?" she asked.

"Nope. The address Barbara gave me turned out to be a vacant lot where they were clearing land for a new supermarket. I went to the county courthouse and looked through the recorded deeds, but it seems the owners of the house were not named Tate. Their name was Jenkins, and they were apparently absentee owners who rented the property. No one I could find remembered ever even meeting the Jenkins family, or the Tates, for that matter. The Jenkins' legal address was in Fitchburg, Massachusetts. But when I called up there trying to get their phone number, there was no listing."

"Mmmm," Rosie murmured. "That's odd, wouldn't you say? Mysterious even. Are you sure Barbara gave you the right information? Maybe she lied so you wouldn't be able to find him."

"Barbara, my love, does not lie. Of course, it may be the Tates lied to her, but she spoke so highly of them I doubt it."

"Do you mind if I do some checking around myself?" she asked.

"Why?" I said. "What's got you so curious all of a sudden?"

"Well, there's a little piece of you out there somewhere, and I'd like to at least know where all your pieces are. I mean, maybe he's in need or something. Maybe he's looking for you. I don't know, Tom, but I think we should at least try to find out if he's alive and well and where he lives, even if you never get to meet him."

That was Rosie. Not since Barbara had I ever met a woman with such incredible empathy and caring. There was no way she could contemplate suffering of any kind without agonizing over it herself and trying to alleviate it. This went for animals as well as humans, and we were always taking in stray dogs and cats and spending money we couldn't afford on vet bills to get them healthy enough so she could find good homes for them. Likewise, she could never pass a bum on the street without figuring some way to help out, like making me drive straight home so she could fix sandwiches, which we would take back and deliver.

"It's okay with me if you want to," I said with visions of monstrous phone bills and other expenses flashing through my head. "But try not to spend a bunch of money, okay?"

She turned to give me an innocent smile, then, without answering, went back to folding the laundry.

I met my second wife on the rebound. Around the time Paula and I were in the throes of divorce in 1971, I realized I didn't know how to meet girls. I had romanced many in the past, but it never seemed to take any effort on my part. Early on, it was the fact that I lived in a huge house with a swimming pool that became the gang's gathering place, giving me lots of opportunity to impress the opposite sex. Then later, after I started performing, playing gigs took care of my social life, and I never had to do much of anything to attract females. By the time Paula and I split, however, I was an ordinary salesman who dabbled in folk music with George. George and I had been concentrating on writing music and trying to get it published, and we seldom if ever performed live anymore. To make matters worse, I attended no church or social club where I might meet women.

After giving the matter some thought, it dawned on me: I had never in my life walked up to a girl, introduced myself and asked her out. And I now realized I was scared to death to do it. Maybe it was because I feared rejection. In most situations, socially or in business, I made sure whatever I had to ask for was already in the bag, so to speak; I laid the groundwork so well that total rejection was nearly out of the question. Even if I miscalculated, I always planned some way to keep my foot in the door. Not that I hadn't been turned down when asking for dates in the past, but that was always with someone I knew pretty well, and the let downs were usually tempered by excuses I could buy, or that I could at least convince myself were not actual rejections of me as a person.

When I finally figured it out, the realization, prompted by a growing horniness, made me determined to somehow get back up on stage. I still had connections in the close-knit community of local musicians, so it wasn't long before I put together a tight little group we called The Blue Notes. After the early Rock days had failed to make us stars, my other musician friends knocked around the local music scene, doing studio work and playing union gigs here and there. When I announced that I wanted to get back into the business, we coalesced into what turned out to be one of the best bands I ever played with.

By that time, I had acquired a Krueger bass unit for my B3 Hammond organ, which transformed the pedals into a virtual bass guitar and eliminated the need for a bass player. Kenny, our guitarist was somewhat of a local legend, with Clapton-like rock and blues virtuosity, and Billy, our sax player, was a Julliard-trained musician and an organist of the first order. Even though I was our organ *player* (I would never call myself an organ*ist*), about half the time Billy would take the organ while I acted as front man. Our drummer, Jimmy, was an old buddy I had traveled with on the earlier tour, opening up Peppermint Lounges around the South.

Given our backgrounds and Billy's extensive training, our repertoire was huge. Even if someone requested a song we didn't know, Billy could almost always find a way to fake it, and I usually knew enough lyrics to do a fair rendition. This was aided by an assortment of what were called "fake books," loose-leaf collections of sheet music the four of us had acquired over the years that covered everything from the early Hit Parade days to the present.

We soon established ourselves as the house band at a local Tampa club called Anthony's, and before long we were packing the place almost every night. Rosie was a regular at the club, well known for her dancing ability and her sparkling personality, and it was there that we met. On our first New Years Eve at the club, she accepted a dare from a girlfriend and at 12:00 midnight, she ran up on stage and kissed me—an interesting bit of serendipity, since I'd had my eye on her for some time.

Rosie was tiny, four-feet-eleven max, and maybe 85 pounds fully dressed. She had short, dark hair, which she wore in a bob, and her face was reminiscent of "That Girl" star, Marlo Thomas. I had previously asked Jimmy, who was a major ladies man, what he knew about her, and he had answered with one word: "Aces!" This term, coming from Jimmy, meant she was wonderful, not your typical brainless barhopping groupie. After that on-stage kiss, I approached her on our next break and asked about it.

"It was a dare," she said as we stood at the end of the bar where the musicians ordered and picked up their drinks. My return to the nightclub life, coupled with the emotional trauma of my pending divorce, had increased my drinking considerably, and I was in the habit of tossing off two or three of the club's watered-down CCs on the rocks between each set, then taking another up with me to the organ to help keep my vocal chords lubricated. After I had my third drink in hand, I signaled with my head in a suggestion that she might want to join me in the band's dressing room. She shrugged, then followed.

Alone in the relative quiet of the dressing room, we sat on the ratty couch and I asked her, "So, why me in particular?" She looked down at her sequined shoes and said, "Well, you're kind of cute, you know. Plus you kill me when you do that Gary Puckett stuff: 'Young Girl' and 'Woman,' and all that."

Though I had become a die-hard rock and blues singer on stage, my early training had started with church and boy choirs and the like, and I had gone through three years of classical voice training before I was twelve. I used to say I was singing in Latin and Italian before I could sing in English, which wasn't all that far from the truth. When Rock 'n' Roll came around, I abandoned what my mom felt sure would be a successful opera career in favor of Chuck Berry, Ray Charles and the dozens of other rock and blues stars I had come to love. I still retained a good bit of my classical training, however, and when acts like Gary Puckett and B.J. Thomas and The Righteous Brothers hit the scene, my voice was particularly suited to their more operatic vocalizations, so I used to get tons of requests for their songs.

"Yeah?" I said, trying to convey a bit of modesty, "Is there anything in particular you'd like to hear?"

She thought for a minute, then said, "Well, there's one song I like a lot that I've never heard you do. You know that Neil Diamond tune, 'You'll be a Woman Soon?'"

I had never performed that particular song, but was familiar with it, and I knew Billy could handle the arrangement in a flash, so I said, "It's not on our song list, but I'll see if I can work something out."

"Would you really? For me?" She turned her head down and brushed her cheek on her shoulder, as if I had embarrassed her.

I'm not sure if I believed her, but Rosie often said my off-the-cuff rendition of that song was the catalyst that clinched our eventually getting together. Billy had no problem with the chords and it turns out, the lyrics were lodged somewhere in my memory from it having received so much airplay. So I did the stand-up bit and put on a real show, all the while staring at Rosie with a good deal of emotional long-ing.

After the next set, we met again at the back of the bar, and I asked her how she liked it. She looked up at me all dreamy eyed and said, "It was incredible, Tom, It really was. I hope you add it to your song list."

Still nervous about making the first move with a girl, I assured her we would add it, and then somehow found the nerve to ask, "You hooked up with anybody in particular right now?"

She shuffled her tiny feet and looked around as if to make sure no one was watching, then said, with a good bit of remorse in her voice, "Yeah. Sorry. I've kind of got this hang up over a guy I met a few months ago."

"Hang up?" I said. "Hey, kid, you're way too young to have any hang ups. What're you gonna do, marry this fel-low or something?"

"I, uh, well, I'm not exactly sure, but Dave—that's his name—he's a really good dancer and he's a flight controller over at the Tampa Airport, which is exciting, and I like him a lot." Then she added, "There *is* one little problem with the whole thing, but I don't want to talk about that."

What I heard in her voice was a vague echo of the hon-esty I had known in Barbara, and I was immediately in-trigued. Not that her being lovely and young weren't factors as well. Then, of course, there was the fact that I had re-cently failed at a seven-year marriage and was in need of a serious ego boost. All that, coupled with Jimmy's "Aces" comment, somehow gave me the sense that Rosie might be a real find. I didn't want to push too hard at the time, what with her having a steady boyfriend and all, so I decided to play it cool and try to take on the persona of an older friend or brother who might lend some advice to a young girl about her love life.

"Okay, you've gotten to the 'I like him a lot' stage. That's pretty serious. So, what seems to be the problem? I promise anything you say will remain sacred, between you and me."

She looked up with clear skepticism in her eyes. There was no getting around it, what we called the musicians' grapevine, which included a large network of entertainers, bartenders, waitresses, agents, groupies and other hangers-on; well, that grapevine could be brutally fast, not too accurate, and cruel at times, much like those we experienced back in high school. "You know," she said, after some thought, "I'd love to believe you, but it's hard."

"Listen," I answered, taking her arm and pulling her back into the darkened hallway that led to the dressing room. "You need to know something about me right now. For one thing, I never break confidences, no matter what." This, of course, was not precisely true, since I *had* stepped out on Alicia, but I told myself that wasn't a breaking of confidence in the purest sense. I cheated on her, true, but I never told anyone about our affair, at least not any of the intimate details. And I did have a thing about not revealing anything told to me in confidence. "I know that may be hard for you to believe," I continued, looking her straight in the eyes. "But it's the God's honest truth."

She smiled then, one of the sweetest smiles I had seen since Barbara's, though it was still tinged with disbelief. And when she looked down again and shrugged, I decided to be straight with her. "Okay, let me be completely honest and say right here that I would love to get together with you, but I am not about to mess with anything serious you have going on at the moment." When she didn't look back up, I reached out and tapped at the bottom of her chin. "Do you think you can look at me?" I said, with what I hoped was concerned curiosity. When she finally looked up, with her eyes still somewhat obscured by her lowered lashes, I said, "I get a feeling we've already connected on some less-than-superficial level, don't you?" This time she nodded. "And," I continued, "I think that connection might lead to friendship if we give it a chance." Her nod became somewhat more pronounced, though she still wouldn't meet my eyes. "Remember, now, I said friendship. I'm not propositioning you in any way. You can believe that. What I'm saying is, I think you might be able to use a little honest advice right now from someone who has a few more years of life experience. And, if that's the case, then I'll be happy to fill that role."

I let this sink in, hoping most of it was true and promising myself that, no matter what, I was not going to push things and that I did want to make friends with her, even if it meant we might never get together sexually.

Break time was about over and I needed to get back on stage, so I said as I started down the hallway, "You think about it, okay? Then, if you want to talk sometime, let me know. I'm no genius, but I might be able to give you some decent advice."

Okay, I admit it. I was playing a role at that moment, but there was still something nagging at the back of my mind that said this was the right thing to do. I had an inkling of what she was talking about when she said there was one little problem in her relationship with the flight controller, and I resolved right then and there to get it out of her.

Two weeks passed before I saw Rosie again. She and her two older sisters came to the club for a Saturday night of dancing. Her sisters both lived out of town, but had traveled to Tampa for her father's birthday and a little R&R. Sarah was a model-like blond bombshell and aspiring actress. Glenda was less attractive. She lived in The Midwest somewhere and owned, with her husband, a small chain of cloth-ing stores. Rosie's steady went home sick that afternoon, and was unable to meet her as he usually did after his shift at the airport, which left me free to talk to her with no chance of any jealous encounters.

When Rosie invited me over to their table and introduced me, Sarah was friendly, while I could tell Glenda, the oldest, was skeptical of this lowlife musician who might be bent on seducing her innocent younger sister. I couldn't blame her for being protective; after all, we musicians had pretty bad reputations when it came to getting into the pants of group-ies and other female customers. Glenda and I never did manage to get along well, even after Rosie and I had been married many decades.

As things wound down at the club and we started pack-ing up and securing our instruments, Rosie came up to the stage and asked if I wanted join them at the 24-hour pancake house nearby, where most of the late-night workers ended up after closing time. "I'd suggest that we meet somewhere more private," she whispered in my ear, "but Glenda seems to think she has to protect me from you, so it might be better if we go along with her. Besides," she added, "It will give you a chance to turn on the charm and maybe win her over."

Of course I agreed, and her suggestion that I might try to "win over" her sister, left me thinking there might be some-thing going on between us above and beyond my "friendly" offer of advice.

At the restaurant, I did my best—over the cacophony of clanging dishes and boisterous conversation that always ac-companied our after-hour breakfast get-togethers—to be clever and intelligent, but I never made much headway with Glenda. Sarah, on the other hand, seemed fascinated by my banter, and time and again complimented me on my singing.

It was at once nervy and ego inflating. My attempt to be all things to all who were there left me exhausted. When the party started to break up, I glanced at Rosie to see if I could make eye contact. She winked at me, which I took to mean I should maybe offer her a ride home, but when I finally got up the nerve, Glenda said, "She's going with us!"

"Oh," I answered. "But I thought—"

"Glenda," Sarah interrupted, drawing her name out in a long, slow reprimand that sounded like it might have been preceded earlier by a spat over this very idea.

Glenda looked over at Rosie and me standing side-by-side, not touching or even looking at each other so as to appear as innocent as possible. "Okay, I guess," she said finally, exasperation evident in her voice. "But listen, Rosie, you be careful, you hear? You know how musicians are." Then, without even a hint of remorse for having insulted me in front of her sister, she drilled me with her eyes and continued. "And you, Mr. hot shot rock star, you watch yourself, or I'll have your balls on a spit over my fathers charcoal grill before you can sing *Will You Still Love Me Tomorrow?*"

My initial instinct was to split this little bitch in two with my rapier wit and intelligence. Sensing this, Rosie reached out a hand to touch mine, and with a slight shake of her head, let me know that I should keep quiet. Feeling her nervous touch, and knowing that giving in to my impulse would only make things worse, I decided to take the high road. Or at least give it a shot.

"Yes mayam," I said, in a poor imitation of the nanny in **Gone with the Wind**. "Why, Miss Rosie here and I are only friends, and I would never dream of doing anything untoward with her." With that, Sarah and Rosie burst out laughing and Glenda was forced to grumble her way back to their car, shooting me dagger glances all the way.

What followed was an evening I will never forget, though "evening" is not quite correct, because it was four in the morning by the time we arrived at her tiny apartment. This indelible memory was not caused by the sex that would later occur (though that was pretty incredible), but because it was another one of those encounters that signaled things to come. The scene at Rosie's apartment broadcast loud and clear that we would not be June and Ward Cleaver.

Even so, I had already made up my mind that, come hell or high water or shitbag sister, I was going to make this thing with Rosie work. As I said, having lucked into finding a near clone of Barbara, I wasn't about to let her slip away.

20
BARBARA
1960

I remember looking over at the clock that afternoon, as Barbara and I lay on my brother's bed, both wondering what might come next and realizing what an incredible opportunity fate had presented us with. It felt to me like several hours had already passed, so I was relieved to see it was only 2:45, which removed the sense of urgency I had begun to feel. After a long time of holding each other and talking trivia and exchanging bits of humorous sexual banter, I turned to her, brushed a few hairs from her eyes, and said, "Are you okay?"

"Uh-huh," she answered with a warm smile. "I feel really good right now, like I never want this to end, ever! In fact, I'm hoping it's only just begun."

It would be some years later before the Carpenters released their major hit, "We've Only Just Begun," but when I first heard it, that conversation came immediately to mind.

As it turned out, Barbara's hopes were realized, though not as she might have imagined.

Sunlight dappled the room with little sprites of sparkling effervescence, as I looked over Barbara's shoulder. "I hate to repeat myself," she whispered in my ear, "but I think I'm ready." And with that, she took my hand and placed it between her legs, where my fingers met with a warm gush of fluid so arousing I nearly came again without being touched. But before I let myself get carried away, I managed to work up enough nerve to ask something I'd been wanting to ask all afternoon. "Could I look at you?" I said in a voice I realized was almost inaudible.

"Okay," she whispered back, as if we were discussing some clandestine conspiracy. "But I thought you had been looking at me on and off for quite a while now."

Continuing the conspiratorial whisper, I replied, "I have, in a way, but I want to take a closer look at you now. Down there." And I nodded toward her legs. "Is that okay with you?"

She seemed a little perplexed, but soon I felt her smile against my cheek. "Oh," she said. "You mean you want to see what your about to get into?" Her laugh at the pun was tinged with nervousness, as if she had only then realized she was naked and that I wanted to examine her as she had me before. Fact was, my request had little to do with sexual desire. As with my first view of her pubic area, and the realization that it didn't at all resemble the other Barbara's, I was curious to see if the rest of her vagina was different, or if all vaginas were alike.

Feigning, I thought, a bit of false modesty, she brought her legs together and turned away from me. "I don't know," she said. "I'm a little embarrassed about that. I mean, what if you hate it? What if it's so gross you won't want to get near it?"

I grabbed her by the arm, and spun her back toward me. "You want the honest truth?" I asked. She nodded with a little smile. "Well then, here it is. I've only seen one up close in my life, and it was … I guess it wasn't exactly what I expected. In fact, it was kind of ugly, but that didn't stop me from wanting to get into it. So you have nothing to worry about on that score. Besides, that one had already been used—and apparently abused—and yours is new, so it has to be prettier. Not to mention the fact that everything about you is ten times prettier than that other Barbara's."

"Do you think so?" she asked, and she looked serious. "You've never said anything like that to me before, that you think I'm pretty and stuff. Are you only saying it now to get into my pants, which, you will observe, are over there on the chair?"

I was taken aback by this. Not by her humorous comment, but by the fact that she was right. I had never said things like that to her before. Here was the most beautiful, most wonderful human being I had ever met, and yet I hadn't told her. "I'm sorry," I said, and I meant it. "I guess I thought you would know how beautiful you are. Stupid! I'm stupid and inconsiderate and dumb and anything else you can think of."

She took hold of my ears and pulled my face to hers. We kissed, and when we parted, she said, "Right! So what are you going to do about it?"

It wasn't the time for me to try to make up for my lack of compliments in the past. Mainly because it would sound like a bunch of contrived crap. Instead, I said, "Give me a while, will you? The task is so immense I couldn't possibly do it justice on the spur of the moment. But I can say one thing."

When I hesitated, she said, "Yes?" with a glint of humor in her eyes.

"Sorry, I was trying to figure out the best way to say it, but I guess there's only one way." I took a deep breath, let it out, and said, "I love you Barbara, more than anything on the face of the earth, and I want you so bad it hurts."

That seemed to do the trick, for the moment at least. As she pulled me on top of her, she whispered in my ear, "I'm going to hold you to that, you know?" And she began to spread her legs under me.

The desire to enter her was so strong I thought at first I couldn't resist it, but I started remembering all the things we had talked about: the pain and her inability to be in control of the situation and the fear that created for her. And as she spread her legs farther apart, I hesitated. After a moment, I said, "I still want to see you. Before we go any farther, okay?"

She thought for a moment, then put her arm across her eyes so she couldn't see, and said, "It's okay, Tommy. Go ahead. You can look now."

I tried not to rush as I moved down and took hold of her legs above the ankles. She stiffened a bit, but then relaxed, as I began to push until her knees were bent. I spread her legs a little more, and looked down at what would forever remain in my memory as the most beautiful vagina I had ever seen. Below that lovely wisp of light brown hair was a glowing, pink, almost invisible aperture, like a tiny vertical pair of lips.

For a while all I could do was stare, and when I got up the nerve to touch it, I felt almost like I was defiling a price-less work of art. As I began to spread those tiny lips in order to see more, she drew in a quick breath, and I pulled back thinking she might not want me to continue. But just then I caught a glimpse of a small triangular protuberance above the opening. It suddenly dawned on me that I must be look-ing at something my father's medical book had described as the clitoral hood, and that under that hood would be the magical organ itself.

"Are you okay with this?" I asked before continuing. She moved her hand away from her eyes then, and nodded. Try-ing to be as gentle as possible, I ran my finger down through her pubic hair, and as I approached that little hood, she jerked her legs together, squeezing my hand. At first I thought she was trying to stop me, but then I realized this was not something she had done on purpose. And as her legs relaxed, I began to move my finger in circles around what I was sure now was her clitoris.

A subtle vibration rippled through her entire body, so I pressed a little harder and started sliding up and down against the growing stiffness of that tiny button. She re-sponded with slow, steady movements and little kitten-like moans, while her hips began to rise and fall as if we were already having intercourse.

"Oh Jesus," she whispered in a voice both guttural and sweet. "That feels soooo good. Please do it harder."

Her vagina was now coated with a glistening film of fluid, and I swept my finger down to moisten it so I would-n't chafe her delicate skin. By then her lower body was mov-ing in gentle circles, and she seemed to be holding back, as if in fear of giving in to her approaching climax. This hesi-tant yet steady motion went on for what seemed like forever, never intensifying, but never slowing down. Eventually, with my finger growing tired and my hunched-over body position becoming painful, I asked, "Do you think you can get over the top of the mountain this way?"

As if emerging from a dream, she lifted her head and we stared at each other through the V of her legs. "I don't know, Tommy," she said in a breathy whisper. "But I sure wouldn't mind if you kept doing it for all eternity."

"Well," I said, "I'd love to, but I'm afraid I've gotten myself into a bad position here, and my body is telling me I'd better move or else I'm going to end up with some pretty serious cramps."

She sat up abruptly and her eyes shone with alarm. "Oh, shit," she said, shocking me with her language. "I had no idea. I mean, you can stop anytime you need to. We can do something else, or we can take a break. Anything you want." And with that, she grabbed my hair and pulled until I fell forward onto her chest. She rubbed my back while I tried to imitate with my knee what I had been doing with my finger.

"That feels good, too," she whispered, and we stayed like that for a while, me massaging her with my knee and her rubbing between my shoulder blades with her hand. It was a few minutes before she asked, "Well, what did it look like?"

I rolled off and reclined next to her, my head on her shoulder and my lips once again nibbling at her neck. "It was beautiful," I said. "It's the most beautiful thing I've ever seen." Then came a spontaneous afterthought. "I wanted to kiss it," I said, immediately embarrassed by the admission.

21

ROSIE

I first experienced oral sex with Barbara as we explored and experimented and learned about each other's needs and desires on that incredible afternoon in 1960. From then on, it became a routine part of my lovemaking repertoire. As I came to understand how arousing it could be, I honed my skills over the years, next with Alicia and then, in more elaborate, some might say even disgusting, ways with Annie (Paula, with her conservative upbringing, would have none of it). But by far the most fantastic oral sex I have ever had is with Rosie, who, until our first sexual encounter in 1972 had never experienced it, and who was so shy she almost refused it. However, before we got around to that, there were several other obstacles we had to overcome, not the least of which was something that would prove to be a mini preview of our future together.

When we arrived at Rosie's duplex apartment, following our somewhat unsettled breakfast with her two sisters, I was prepared for almost anything, including a long, platonic conversation about her current boyfriend, if that was the way things were going to work out. What I wasn't quite prepared for, however, was the scene that greeted us when we first opened her front door.

As we stood on the tiny porch and Rosie fumbled in her purse for her key, I began to notice a foul odor wafting in the early morning air. I didn't give it much thought, however, assuming some dogs must have recently visited her yard. It turns out I was right about the dogs, wrong about the location.

Rosie finally retrieved her key and when she opened the door that foul odor took on a whole new dimension of strength. "Oh, shit," she said. A statement that was, unfortunately, accurate. She reached around the doorjamb and turned on the living-room light to reveal a scene of such filth and chaos I was stunned into silence.

The narrow living room was destroyed, with stuffing from pillows and furniture strewn about among torn strips of shit-laden newspaper. There was shit on the floor, on the walls, on the lamps and chairs, and two squealing puppies were romping and sliding through this mess, tossing everything around like kids abandoned at a daycare center. When the light came on and the puppies saw the open door, they made a beeline toward us. Fortunately, Rosie was able to slam the door before they reached it. We heard their bodies hit as we turned to look at each other, Rosie in tears and me with what must have been an expression of astonished disgust on my face.

It took me a while to recover from the initial shock and tend to Rosie, who by that time was weeping with her head against one of the porch pillars, while the sounds of romping and destruction resumed behind the closed door. Trying not to display the reluctance I felt, I put my arms around her, whispering the old standard, "It's going to be all right" over and over to try and calm her down.

As I mentioned before, this was one of those signs that should have signaled things to come, especially considering the events that followed. But at that moment I was so confused and worried about Rosie that speculating on the future was the farthest thing from my mind. As I held her and patted her back, whispering as many encouraging words as I could think of in her ear, she began to recover somewhat, then started trying to explain.

"They … they were on the porch when we got home from work, my roommate and I. That is, today, I mean." She said all this through jerky little sobs that made her words hard to understand, but I got the gist of the story. It seemed these two puppies, which were not small, but looked as if they might be Lab mixes about six months old, had been abandoned on their doorstep earlier in the afternoon. Rosie, being the kind of person who could never ignore any creature in need, had convinced her roommate they should let the dogs inside, feed and take care of them until they could find good homes for them. She would have suggested they keep the dogs, but their lease did not allow animals of any kind and, as it turns out, they were behind on the rent to boot and were trying to convince their landlord to grant them more time.

I had mixed emotions about all this at the time, but her concern for the dogs—which I would later realize extended to all living things—wormed its way into my psyche until it overcame my doubts and left me falling hopelessly in love. Before that slow process took hold, however, there was a lot of other—to be precise—shit to deal with.

My second revelation about Rosie came a few minutes later, when we finally managed to enter the apartment without letting the dogs out and, after a prolonged struggle, collared them and took them out back, where, though she hated having to do it, we locked them in the small utility shed at the rear of the lot. When we got back inside, exhausted from the effort and standing in the aftermath of a shit storm, she broke down again. "What am I going to do?" she sobbed. "How can I fix all this?" It wasn't long before I realized that Rosie, despite her kind and loving attitude, had no housekeeping skills whatsoever, and her dismay over the dog mess was only part of the evidence. There were stacks of dirty dishes in the sink, and sometime later, when I entered her small bathroom for the first time, I was greeted by a stained, filthy toilet and sink.

What made this scene even more disconcerting for me was the fact that I had been married for seven years to a girl whose mother made her paste wax the front steps, who had snow white carpet in her living room zigzagged with clear plastic runners intended to keep even the cleanest of shoes from defiling it. "The apple doesn't fall far from the tree," they used to say, and that certainly applied to Paula and her mother. Among our friends, Paula's penchant for cleanliness was legend. I used to joke that, at our house, you could light a cigarette, tap it into an ashtray, take another drag, and by the time you returned it, the ashtray would be magically emptied and wiped clean. A generalized exaggeration, to be sure, but it did happen once at a party we held, and that sealed the legend.

Needless to say, I was appalled by the filth in Rosie's apartment, and when I realized she had no idea whatsoever how to even begin to clean it up, I almost bolted for the door. What I did instead shocked me when I thought about it later, but I already had that thing nagging at the back of my mind that kept saying, "This is a wonderful person. Don't fuck this up like you did with Barbara." So I led Rosie to a small, unscathed patch of couch, sat her down, and began searching the apartment for cleaning supplies, a difficult task because she seemed not to know where they might be.

The whole process took over two hours. First I had to find the cleanser and bleach and a mop and some rags, but I soon managed to assemble all these things and began the arduous task of cleaning up what looked like the aftermath of a nuclear explosion at a sewage plant. Though cleaning was new to me, I realized I must have learned by watching Paula, who never allowed me to participate in the house cleaning because she didn't trust me to do it "right." Finally, with the house smelling like a Clorox factory, the dishes clean and stacked on the drain board, and only a few fading stains remaining on a lamp or pillow, I plopped down next to Rosie, who had sat in stunned silence during my labors.

"There," I said, slapping my hands together. "All fixed." She seemed unable to speak at that moment. She kept sweeping her gaze across the now-clean room, then back to me, then back to the room.

Finally, she returned from her reverie and said, "That was amazing! I think I'm in love." And she was. For that matter, so was I, though it took a few weeks for that fact to dawn on us.

Exhausted, I sat on the couch next to Rosie and leaned back, feeling a little proud and cocky that I had been able to handle what at first looked like a hopeless situation. I also began to realize that, if we got together, if I won this tiny vision of beauty and kindness who, in many ways reminded me of Barbara, there was going to have to be a role reversal of sorts. That is, I would most likely have to be chief cook and bottle washer, the opposite of my previous role as lazy husband and beneficiary of all the free cleaning and cooking services I had enjoyed for seven years without much thought.

Over the next few weeks I pondered the commitment I would have to make, which became clearer the more time we spent together. My first assumption: that Rosie simply did not possess Paula's domestic skills, proved to be true. And I—of necessity and not because I was ever asked— became a surrogate maid for Rosie and her roommate, Pauline, who was equally inept at anything that might have required paying attention during high-school home economics classes.

As disturbing as this prospect was, I eventually began to accept my new role. And, as our relationship matured through long, honest discussions and ever surprising revelations about Rosie's kindness and caring, I also decided never to resent that role. What I learned about her heart during that time would have been far and away enough to convince me I should hang in there, but it was the second half of her one-two love punch—the sex—that closed the deal.

Do you have anything to drink?" I asked, as Rosie sat next to me marveling at the transformation I had made in her living room

"Oh, sure," she said, obviously feeling she had been a bad hostess. "There's some Cokes in the fridge and I think there might be some orange juice. Let me get something for you." She started to rise, but I pulled her back down to the couch. "I don't drink soft drinks," I declared. "And I wouldn't want the orange juice unless you had some vodka to take the edge off."

By that time, the booze from the club and the exertion of cleaning had combined to give me a pretty good waking hangover, and what I needed was a little "hair of the dog," as Annie would have put it. Of course, under the circumstances, that particularly descriptive phrase would not have come to mind. "Wait here," I said, laying a hand on her arm to reassure her she needn't do anything, while I rose and headed for the door.

"You're not leaving are you?" she asked in a panicked voice. "I mean, I sure wouldn't blame you if you did. It's just that I feel so bad about all this I couldn't live with myself if you disappeared on me before we at least had the chance to talk."

I paused at the door and looked back at her. "I don't think I could leave you right now even if I wanted to," I said. "But I've got half a quart of CC in the car and I could use a drink right now, so I'm going to go get it, if that's okay."

She seemed flummoxed by this, but then gathered herself and said, "Oh, sure. I didn't know. I mean, it's fine with me. I'll get you a glass and some ice." With that she stood and walked to the kitchen alcove. I watched her for a moment as she held an aluminum tray under running water, then continued on my journey to the car and the booze and, I hoped, to some small measure of relief from the pounding in my head.

I returned with the bottle a few minutes later, and to my great surprise, Rosie took on what seemed like a domestic duty; that is to make my drink and serve me. I would later come to realize that, in spite of her ineptitude at general housekeeping, she would always insist on acting as my personal server in situations involving food or beverages.

After a couple of drinks and a few minutes of relaxation on the couch, I was feeling better, so I turned to her and said, "Okay, what's the deal with your boyfriend? You said there was one little problem. Would you like to talk about it?"

"I guess so," she said. "I mean, if you don't mind. I know you must be exhausted and I have no right to ask you for any more favors, but—"

"Hey, don't sweat it, okay. I'm fine, and after all, isn't that what we we're supposed to be doing, discussing your love life?"

"Yeah. Sure. But, I don't know. After all this crap, I thought you might not want to anymore."

"He's married, isn't he?" I said, hoping I'd guessed correctly. She looked at me with shock, then lowered her head in embarrassment. "Look," I continued, "that was a guess, but even if I'm right, there's no need for you to be ashamed or anything. Hell, I'm married myself, though I am getting divorced. What I'm trying to say is, I don't make moral judgments about people I like, and I like you a lot. If you've found somebody you love, and if that somebody happens to be married, I have no problem whatsoever with that."

She thought for a while, then said, "That's what he keeps telling me, too. Thât he's going to get a divorce and then we can be together. He never came out and said we'd get married or anything, but I thought that's what he meant."

I chuckled a little, then asked, "How long has this guy been telling you that?"

She seemed reluctant to answer, but finally she said, "For about a year."

Without thinking, I said, "Jesus, Rosie, do you hear yourself? Do you really think after a year of his claiming he's going to get a divorce and not doing it he actually means it?"

"Well, I don't know," she answered. "He's always telling me how she doesn't understand him and how it's not working out between them, and how much he loves me and all. I mean, why would somebody make all that stuff up?"

I hadn't given much thought to her age before, but her naiveté was so obvious in that statement I had to stop myself from laughing out loud. Here was someone so innocent and trusting she didn't even recognize the standard crap married guys feed to their extra-marital lovers. In many ways Rosie was still a child, trying her best to find the right guy. She believed the bullshit because she couldn't imagine anyone would lie. It was pathetic in a way, but it also it spoke of innocence and trust so sincere I felt the need to protect her from this creep.

"Listen," I said. "I know you like this guy, and that he's a good dancer and probably good in bed and all, but have you ever really talked to him? I don't mean when you're setting up a meeting, or when you're working out dance moves or he's telling you he can't make it on a particular night. What I mean is, do you *know* him? His heart, his life, his flaws, his ambitions?" She started to answer, but I held up a finger to stop her. "Wait, let me try to phrase that better."

I thought for a moment, then said, "After a year of intimate relations with a guy, there are some things you should know or at least understand about him. For example: What are his life ambitions? Why did he decide to become an air traffic controller? Why did he marry his wife? What are his views on religion and politics? Does he think of sex as primarily a recreational activity, or as a union of souls that binds two people together? And, speaking of sex, does he jump on and jump off, or does he make sure you're satisfied and stay with you even after he's gotten his kicks?"

I could see from her expression she had never thought of these things, and when her eyes started to glisten with moisture, I began to regret my pointed questions. I held out my hand then, not in a way that demanded she take it, but with what I hoped was an apologetic offering of commiseration. She considered the gesture for a moment, then slid her fingers in between mine, clasping until our hands locked in a closed embrace.

"I know you're going think I'm stupid," she said. "But I want to be honest with you, so please try to understand, Okay?" I nodded and squeezed her fingers. "The thing is that stuff never comes up. Most of our conversations are about how and where we're going to meet or, when I get sad, how he's going to leave his wife for me. Now that I think about it, I don't know much about him." She looked down at our hands, then shook her head and continued. "And you're right about the sex. He's always in a hurry, and he never seems to care about my needs. He's only the second guy I've ever been with like that. The first was a kid at school, and neither of us knew what we were doing. I really didn't know there was supposed to be something more to it." She turned to look at me with a sad little frown.

I stared into those little-girl eyes, filled with expectation, almost pleading, and I suddenly began to feel like that older brother I had intended to impersonate. I took her other hand and we sat there for a moment, like a mother and daughter about to have a heart-to-heart talk. It took me a while to think things through, and when I began to speak I surprised even myself.

"First," I said, "I don't think you're stupid. There's a difference, you know, between being stupid and lacking experience. We all learn from our life experiences, and when we're first confronted with something, we often have to go through it and then look back on it to understand what it was all about. Unless we have a parent or friend, maybe a brother or sister, who's been through the same thing or learned about it in some other way and can share their experiences."

"Uh-huh," she said, her eyes brightening a little in expectation.

"So," I continued, "how about I try to be that person for you? At least tonight?" I looked around then at the soft glow of sunlight beginning to seep through the curtains, and added, "Or maybe I should say, 'today.'"

"Okay," she said. "I mean, yes, please. If you don't mind."

"I don't mind, Rosie. I wouldn't offer if I did. Okay, first lesson: I want you to think about something. How long have we known each other?"

She looked confused, but then answered, "Well, I've known you, or at least I've seen you with the band, ever since you guys started playing at the club. But, I guess if you mean personally, it would only be about two weeks now."

"Right," I said. "Now does that tell you something? Think about it for a minute."

Her eyebrows lowered in concentration, then she shook her head from side to side. "Not really," she said.

"See now, that's one of the things you to have to learn. Look, I don't want you to take this the wrong way, but you shouldn't even be accepting my offer of advice or help."

"No?" she asked. "Why not?"

"Because you don't know me well enough to trust me. All you really know about me is that I'm cute and have a nice singing voice, and that's certainly not enough to make me a safe bet. What if this is all bullshit? What if all I want is to get you into bed? Did you consider that possibility?"

She thought for a minute, then said, "Yeah, maybe at first, but you seemed so honest and nice I stopped thinking that after a while. Besides," she added before I could respond, "I guess I wouldn't have minded. Much, anyway."

This was getting complicated. My thoughts and intentions spun around in my mind and I finally had to ask myself what I was doing. There was no question I wanted to have sex with her; to deny that would be lying to myself. Still, there was this thing, this affection that kept dueling with my libido. "Listen," I said, finally, "I have to be honest about this or it won't mean a thing. My first intention *was* to sweet talk you and get you to trust me so I could get into your pants."

She seemed a little shocked, but then she smiled. "Really?" she said. "That's interesting." Then, after another few seconds, her eyes narrowed. "Are you saying that's what Dave's been doing? Sweet talking me for the sex?"

"Right," I said. "That bit about his wife not understanding him and things not working out between them? That's one of the oldest lines in the book, and I guarantee you it's bullshit. And then there's the old 'I'm going to get a divorce' bit, the promise that someday soon he'll be free and you won't have to sneak around. It's crap, Rosie, believe me. It's never going to happen."

"Yeah," she said. "I was kinda getting that idea. But I guess I wanted to hang onto the possibility as long as I could." Then her eyes narrowed. "So what about you? You said the same thing a few minutes ago, that you were getting a divorce. Was that part of your plan, too?"

"Now you're getting it," I said with a smile. "That's the kind of healthy cynicism you need to learn if you're going to make it through life without being conned."

"Okay, I understand, but you didn't answer my question."

"You're learning, kid, and I'm proud of you."

"Thank you very much. I'm glad you're proud of me, but you still didn't answer my question. And don't call me 'kid!'" she said..

"Sorry," I said. "I'll try to remember. But I guess you got me on the divorce thing." I saw a hint of sadness creep into her eyes. I waited for her to say something, but she remained silent. "Tell you what," I said, "you sit here for a minute, and let me get something from the car, okay?"

"Okay," she said. I squeezed her hands and let them drop, then stood and headed for the door. I returned a few minutes later with an envelope, which I tossed into her lap.

"There, open that up," I said.

"What is it?" she asked.

"Open it," I answered.

She shrugged and drew out a thick sheaf of papers. She studied them for a while, then looked up at me in surprise. "It's your divorce papers," she said with amazement. "You *are* getting a divorce!"

"It's not final yet, but yes, I'm getting a divorce."

I don't know if I'd say that little drama was the *coup de grace* for Rosie, because I hate to think of it that way. Fact is, it was a totally unplanned bit of serendipity. I happened to have pulled the preliminary papers from my mailbox the day before, and had accidentally left them in the car after scanning them at the Post Office. When she challenged my claim about the divorce, I remembered they were still there, so I purposely injected some dramatics into the conversation. Unintentional as it may have been, I'm pretty sure that clinched the deal for us, and before long we were making out, as if neither of us had had sex in months. Which, in my case, was true.

The almost instantaneous switch from conversation to passionate lovemaking seemed to indicate that our desire for each other had been building up for a while, as we abandoned all pretense of simple friendship and fell into a frenzy of kissing and fondling that left us gasping and panting like animals in heat. When we finally managed to slow down a little, I realized how uncomfortable things had become. The couch had many broken springs that gouged us with every move, and I didn't want the experience to end up being remembered only because of its oddity and weird positioning, like so many adolescent fumblings in my past had been. So, when it seemed clear that intercourse was inevitable, I whispered, "We need to move."

"I don't know if I can," she whispered in response. She seemed to be unsure what I meant, so I decided to take command of the situation. As gently as possible, I withdrew from her embrace and lifted her into my arms.

"Which one is your bedroom?" I asked. She looked into my eyes with the tiniest bit of fear, then glanced at one of the bedroom doors. I carried her across the living room and kicked open the door, then gently lowered her feet to the floor.

By then it was light outside, and that fact served to introduce me to another of Rosie's endearing traits: her incredible modesty. Our band had several sets of different colored matching outfits that served as comfortable, attractive uniforms. When I started to remove the top of mine, Rosie looked around the room nervously. "Wait," she said almost pleading. "Wait a minute, okay?" I had already laid my top on the dresser and was about to pull down the elastic-waisted bottoms, but when she said, "Wait," I stopped and watched as she went to the lone window and pulled down the blinds. When they wouldn't go all the way down to the sill, she grabbed a blanket and rolled it up to fill the gap. Next, she pushed and adjusted the blinds to block as much light as possible, then walked over to close the door. When she was through, the room was dark, and it had begun to dawn on me that she was shy about removing her clothes in front of me. And, even though it was now about as dark as late twilight, she climbed under the covers without even removing her blouse.

I began to wonder if there might be something wrong with her; some scar or blemish she didn't want me to see, but I would later come to understand this was just Rosie. In fact, during our entire marriage, I only saw her naked maybe five or six times when the lights were on, and those were brief glimpses as she emerged from a shower without realizing I was in the bedroom, or when I accidentally interrupted her while she was dressing. I also realized, when she averted her eyes as I stepped out of my clothes, that her shyness wasn't only about my seeing her.

I climbed under the covers with her, but before I touched her I wanted to make sure she was okay. "Is this all right?" I said in a near whisper. "I mean, I thought with all that went on out there in the living room—"

"Yes," she interrupted. "Please don't think I'm silly or anything. I want to make love with you. I do. But I've never been comfortable taking off my clothes in front of anyone, even girlfriends or my mom or my sisters. Is that okay?"

"It's fine," I said. "I sure don't want to embarrass you or anything. This is fine, really." With that she reached over and laid her arm across my chest and we kissed. What happened then was in complete contrast to her initial shyness, with one exception: when I started to work my way down towards her legs with my kisses. Until then her responses to my touch and mouth were unbelievably sensuous. In fact, I soon learned Rosie was an orgasmic wonder who could have a climax at almost any time. She even came sometimes when all I did was massage her breasts. Plus, she was what we used to call a screamer, and her vocalizations, though not loud but more like subdued exclamations and sensuous moans, coincided precisely with her excitement level, which made it easy for me to anticipate her every orgasm. Needless to say, this was a tremendous ego boost for me, and it was all I could do sometimes not to come myself without even entering her.

Another thing that enhanced our sexual unions, as if there needed to be anything more, was the fact that we fit together as if we'd been cast in some kind of male-female mold. Our bodies seemed to be perfectly formed for one another. She was the tiniest bit smaller than I in the genital department, which meant I could always fill her completely, and our embraces created an almost artistic joining of two torsos.

It was Sunday, the band's day off, and her roommate had stayed over at a boyfriend's house for the rest of the weekend, so we had all day for sex. And we dedicated ourselves to it as if it was the last time either of us would ever get laid. Time and time again we fell exhausted beside each other on the bed and agreed we'd better stop before we ended up hurting ourselves. And time after time we decided to keep going. There was no elaborate positioning or unique methodology, as with Annie. Our nearly perfect orgasmic explosions were repeated over and over without any overt effort toward variety or experimentation. There was variety, all right, but it occurred naturally and was never purposeful. The only stumbling block came when I tried to approach her orally.

It was around two in the afternoon when I first made the attempt. As I kissed and suckled her breasts, reveling in her almost frenetic sensual responses, I eventually began to move downwards, kissing her stomach and then her navel, but when I started to move farther, she reached out and grabbed hold of my hair to stop me. Surprised, I looked up to see what the problem was, and she stared down at me with such fear that I pulled myself back up to her chest.

"What's wrong?" I asked, stroking her face with my fingers. She turned her head away from me then, in embarrassment it seemed, and it finally dawned on me: she had not done this before. And like many young girls who had never experienced oral sex, she probably saw it as taboo or gross or forbidden. As it turned out, however, it wasn't only those trepidations that caused her reluctance, but her innate sense of fairness.

"You've never done this before, have you?" I asked, trying not to sound condescending. She shook her head, still not looking at me. "Does it scare you for some reason?" This time she did a tiny shrug of her shoulders, but she didn't speak. "Can you tell me why?" I asked, as I rolled off to lie beside her. She tried to bury her face in the pillows, but I scrunched a hand, palm up, under her chin and lifted her head to look into her eyes. Unfortunately, they were closed. "Rosie?" I said softly, "Do you think you could look at me? I won't bite, I promise." That elicited a little smile and after a moment she opened her eyes.

"Look, honey," I said, "I'm not going to do anything you don't want me to. I mean, you don't have to worry about my pressuring you to do anything. Do you think we could talk about it? Maybe you could tell me what scares you so I can understand." We stayed there like that, looking at each other, then finally she pulled me close and snuggled against my neck.

"I don't know," she said in my ear. "You're right. I've never done it. And it seems gross or unnatural to me. But that's not the only reason."

I waited, but when she seemed unable to go on, I said, "Please, honey, tell me. What's the other reason?"

She sniffled a little and hugged me tighter, then said, "It's … it's because I don't think I could do my part. I mean, do it to you, you know? And that wouldn't be fair."

"Is that what's worrying you?" I said. Then, not waiting for an answer, I went on. "Listen, when it comes to making love, there's no such thing as fair. Nothing says you have to do anything because I do. We make the rules, and only if we both agree. We should never, make demands on each other. When we make love, it should be because we want to, and whatever form it takes should be okay with both of us. Understand?"

"I guess I do. But—"

"There's no buts about it, Rosie. That's the way things have to be. We're going to be honest with each other and I'm never going to do anything to make you ashamed or embarrassed, okay?"

"Uh-huh," she said, nodding vigorously against my neck.

"Okay, now, do you mind if I tell you some things? Some things about what I was trying to do?"

"No, I guess not."

And then I was stuck. I had managed to work my way around to a conversation about oral sex, but I had no idea what to say. It was like the time I wanted to explain to Barbara what an orgasm felt like, only to realize there was no way to adequately describe the sensation. How could I know how cunnilingus felt to a woman? Finally, without yet knowing exactly how to proceed, I decided to dive in.

"This is going to be hard for me, honey, and it might be a little embarrassing for you, but what we say or do will always stay between you and me, okay?" Again, she nodded, a little less vigorously this time, but still a nod. "Okay, let's see. Well, you know we use our tongues when we kiss, and you like that, don't you?"

"Uh-huh," she answered.

"And when we do that we do something you probably would have thought of as gross a few years ago. I mean, what if somebody came up to you when you were, say, ten years old, and asked if they could spit in your mouth. What would you have said?"

"Forget ten years old," she said with revulsion. "I wouldn't go for that today."

"But, think about it, when we kiss, we do almost the same thing. I mean, we exchange saliva, don't we?"

"I guess so."

"Well, saliva is a bodily fluid, and you don't mind me tasting that, do you?

"I never thought about it like that, but, no, I guess there's nothing wrong with it. But that other … bodily fluid is, well, different, if you know what I mean."

"Sure, I know what you mean, and I understand that you might think its nasty or something because of where it comes from. But it really isn't. And, if you're worried about me tasting it, you shouldn't be, because I've tasted it many times, and it's perfectly okay with me."

"You have?"

"Yes. Not only is it okay, I like it. The taste doesn't bother me at all, but the main reason I enjoy it is because it's so pleasurable for my partner. I'm telling you, oral sex can be one of the most wonderful things a woman can experience. Really. I'm not kidding."

She was silent for a while, and I could sense the conflict in her mind and her embarrassment. Finally, she said,

"Maybe. If you're sure it's okay, and if I don't have to ... you know. I guess we could try it if you want to."

I pulled away from her then, and held her by the arms. "You're sure now?" I said, looking into her eyes. "Because I don't want to do anything unless you agree."

She studied my face for a moment, then asked, "Is it okay if I don't want to watch or have you see me while it's happening?"

"Honey, you can do anything that makes you more comfortable."

And so, with Rosie's head buried under three pillows and her body shaking with fear, I introduced her to the wonderful world of oral sex. And if I thought she was an orgasmic wonder before, well, I guess you could say that this time she went off to another planet or dimension or something. And she didn't come back until I was too exhausted to continue. During subsequent performances over the years (of which there were thousands) her craving for my tongue grew stronger until she lost her inhibitions to the utter delirium and orgasmic volcano of cunnilingus. She was so enamored of the act and so appreciative of my efforts, she eventually almost begged me to let her "do her part," as she had first put it. And the oral facet of our sex lives became one of the most enjoyable for us both.

Regardless of the rumors about the sexual prowess of KISS bassist, Gene Simmons and his supposedly long tongue, I learned early on that deep vaginal penetration with the tongue is not the most stimulating thing for a woman. Oh, I guess if you had an eight or ten-incher, and could learn to use it in such a way that it not only penetrated but stimulated other areas at the same time, that might be a major turn on for some women. However, 99% percent of us have average sized tongues (around four inches or so) and what with the restrictions of position and other factors, vaginal penetration is limited to about three inches at best. I eventually realized that when, where and how you use your tongue is critical. For that I can thank Barbara and her candid instructions on that day back in 1960.

With Rosie, however, knowing how, when and where was never a problem. As in all things sexual, her reaction to my tongue was immediate and clear as a bell, which meant that, without words or even gestures, she could guide me in the exact direction she wanted to go, and when she got to her destination, at least orally, she could remain on that peak of pleasure for so long it was I who often had to stop in order to avoid neck cramps or other potential injury. She would sometimes get so lost in her pleasure she would fall into a prolonged moan that worried me because it almost seemed to border on insanity. She was, of course, at least a little embarrassed afterward that she had let herself do that in my presence. Not that she could have done it alone. One thing Rosie never learned was masturbation of any kind

I tried several times to teach her with gentle instructions and a helping hand, so to speak, but she never liked it and always begged me to take over. "You do it, please, Tom," she would say as she withdrew her hand. I could never understand why anyone would be reluctant to sexually stimulate themselves; after all, who knows better what feels good than the person it's being done to? I finally chalked it up to Rosie's ever-present shyness and let it go. After all, she had me, any time she wanted, and even in our later years, the intensity, frequency and duration of our encounters would probably have set a Guinness World Record, if such a thing existed.

22

BARBARA   1960

Given the time, the year, the era, my admission of wanting to kiss a vagina was gross. The idea was simply beyond the pale. No one I knew had ever done such a thing, or at least, no one had ever talked about it. Vaginas were, to my knowledge, rather stinky things that caused one's fingers to smell badly after an evening of heavy petting. Like dead fish, we used to say over beer and laughter while discussing our sexual conquests, minor as they may have been. But something changed for me that day, something that altered forever my opinion of touching a vagina with my lips. And, if I have to say so myself, that change provided considerable pleasure for several ladies, both young and old, as the years played out.

I gazed at Barbara's lovely vagina, wondering how something so unattractive to me during my first encounter with Barbara Wilson could suddenly manifest itself as a thing of ultimate beauty. I was struck by an almost irresistible urge to lean down and not only kiss it, but suckle and lick and make love to it with my mouth. It occurred to me at the time that such an activity would probably be pleasurable for a woman: a soft, non-abrasive massaging with a moist, resilient and sensuous organ like a tongue. Of course, I wasn't stupid enough to do it right then, but I had already blurted it out, and there wasn't much I could do to change that.

After a brief, shocked silence, Barbara seemed to be considering what I had said. And with a little smile and that adorable tilt of her head, she said, "So, why didn't you? Kiss it, I mean?"

"Uh, I don't know. I guess I thought it might gross you out or something."

She hesitated for a moment, then said, "How about you? Wouldn't it gross *you* out? I mean you're the one who'd be tasting all that stuff, not me." Then she did something that shocked the hell out of me. I had rolled off to lie beside her and had reached between her legs to resume the vaginal massage, when she suddenly grabbed my arm and pulled it away. Afraid she might be mad or something, I raised up on one elbow to look at her, but she paid no attention to me at all. What she did was take my hand, turn it a little from side to side to examine it, then with a flourish, she stuck two of my fingers into her mouth. Her face took on a contemplative look, and when she removed my fingers, she turned to me and smiled.

"Well," she said with a quirky grin, "it isn't the best thing I've ever tasted, but it wasn't all that bad either. A little salty, but other than that, pretty tasteless. Maybe you should try it sometime." I started to stammer and shrink with embarrassment, but she continued. "I'm pretty clean, you know, down there I mean. I use a dou ... that is I clean myself inside fairly often. Besides, we were swimming for a long time this morning, and with the chlorine and all. Well, you know."

I finally got past the stammering, though I was sure my face had turned beet red, "Are you asking me to ...?"

"I'm not asking anything," she said. "I'm telling you some things you probably want to know anyway. Besides, it was you who said you wanted to kiss it. I don't think the thought would ever have entered my mind unless you had said that."

I lay back on the bed next to her and stared at the ceiling, and she turned to snuggle against my neck. "I think your face is bleeding," she whispered.

"Where?" I asked, reaching up to run a hand over my nose and cheeks.

"All over," she said with a chuckle.

"Well," I said, "I guess I am kind of embarrassed by all this, you know?"

"You're embarrassed!" she said, lifting her head to look at me. "What about me? How do you think I felt? That was one of the weirdest things I've ever heard, at least at first. But then when I got to thinking about it ... well, it's a normal bodily fluid, isn't it? And we exchange bodily fluids all the time when we kiss, don't we?"

"Yeah," I said. "I guess." And then something dawned on me. As if to counter her argument, I looked her in the eyes and said, "You know, I've got some bodily fluid myself. Lots of it. You know that because you cleaned it up for me."

That seemed to stop her in her tracks. She flopped down next to me, shrugged, crossed her arms over her chest and said, "*Touché.*"

We were quiet for a while, then she said with a dreamy lilt in her voice, "I wonder if people actually do that kind of stuff when they have sex. I'll bet they do, but they don't talk about it." She hesitated a moment, then continued. "Now that I think about it, the kids at school were talking about some sex report by a doctor named Kingsly or Kinsley or something like that. Anyway, according to the rumor, this doctor—" she emphasized the word 'doctor' "—concluded that whatever people decide to do when they're having sex is okay, as long as it doesn't cause injury and both partners agree to it."

"Okay," I said. "So what're you trying to say?"

"Well, I was thinking, maybe if people can get past the gross part, using your mouth isn't as weird as it might seem at first. I mean we do a lot of kissing using our tongues and all, and that would've seemed gross a few years ago." Her dreamy state seemed to dissipate as she added, "You think I'm weird, don't you? You think I'm a slut or something because of what I did."

"Stop it!" I said. "I told you before, I could never think that way about you. I think you're, well, curious, that's all. Besides, like you said, it was me who first brought all this up by saying I wanted to kiss you down there."

"Yup, that was you all right. But forget that for now. My curiosity is satisfied, though yours probably isn't. However, if your curiosity ever gets the better of you, I won't stand in your way. By the way, don't we have a little goal we have to reach? And again, at the risk of repeating myself, Tommy, I think I'm ready."

My curiosity, or maybe I should say *our* curiosity, would eventually get the better of us that day. Whatever it was, we both learned a lot about things we would probably never even have thought of had it not been for the incredible set of circumstance that led to our having several hours alone in my brother's room. Not only were we granted a generous allotment of time, we received an extra bonus when Mom called about 4:30 that afternoon. The phone startled us out of what we were doing at the time, but after we recovered and I ran out in the hall to answer, the result was fine.

It seemed Mom had spoken to Thelma and was calling to fill me in on the condition of her son Gerald. He was okay, she said. In a good bit of pain, but okay. She asked how we were doing and offered the obligatory cautions, ending with, "I'm going to have to trust you kids for a little bit longer than I expected." It seems they were having some problems with the new computers at her work, and she had to stay until they got the payroll taken care of. In those days, computer problems were legion, what with the unreliability of early mainframes and the difficulty of training operators in the nuances of the primitive and complex software they had to use. In fact, "Blame it on the computer" had become a catch phrase for the few businesses that had made the jump to the new technology.

Since Barbara was scheduled to join us for dinner that night, Mom felt bad about not being home to cook, but she said there were lots of leftovers and some TV dinners in the big freezer if we got hungry before she could make it back, which she estimated would be around seven or so. Of course, we were thrilled at the news and couldn't have cared less about food at the time. For some odd reason I never quite figured out, the fact that we were going to be alone for such a prolonged period didn't seem to worry Mom too much. I guess it might have been because she liked Barbara and that Barbara was a "church girl," so she must have thought that made everything a lot safer when it came to the possibility of illicit sexual activity. What Mom and lots of other parents got all wrong was thinking that, because kids went to church and professed their faith in Jesus, their hormones were magically suppressed. In fact, some of the most promiscuous girls I ever knew were girls I'd met at church. And oddly, one of the least promiscuous, in her early teen years at least, was not a church-person at all, at least not until I started inviting her to accompany me to church on Sunday mornings.

23

THE FUNERAL

Seeing Alicia, especially in a religious setting at Barbara's funeral, brought on a rush of memories. Back in our teen years, almost everyone attended church, except our Jewish friends who attended synagogue. Alicia, however, was the odd one. Her parents weren't religious, and she didn't have to go to church on Sunday mornings.

Because my father had been a minister before becoming a doctor, we attended church, religiously I guess you'd say. Mom and Dad were devout Bible-based Christians, and we kids were required, under threat of force, to accompany them to church every Sunday. Only if we were deathly ill (something my father could easily determine) were we allowed to skip church.

Alicia and I often talked about religion in those days, and eventually she started coming to church with me. I think this was because she was lonely on Sunday mornings with no other kids to play with. Her dad was not happy about it, but her mother said she should at least be exposed to some form of religion and then be allowed to make up her own mind. I was a Christian back then, a Bible reader and regular contributor to Bible study discussions during Sunday school. But that was before I began to question things.

My doubts were predicated on the fact that I had a good pair of ears and used to mingle with the adults before and after church, listening to their conversations. I was surprised to find that these conversations were not about God or Jesus or religion; they were mostly about business or gossip, and many comments weren't at all what I considered Christ-like.

At the time, I had the silly idea that church was a place to go and practice one's religion, not a club where people went to make business deals or engage in critical, sometimes cruel, gossip. I was also of the opinion that in order to be a true Christian, one had to try one's best to emulate Jesus. The Jesus I knew would never use the House of God to promote business or talk about others behind their backs. After all, hadn't we learned in the Gospel of John that Jesus nearly went berserk when he found the Synagogue filled with moneychangers? And didn't Jesus tell us we should love our neighbors as we do ourselves?

Alicia, who was always somewhat ambiguous about the whole religion thing, would listen to my growing concerns about the sincerity of church attendees and agree. "That's what my dad always says," she told me more than once. "He says religion is one of the most destructive things that ever happened to mankind, and that religious fanatics are going to be the downfall of the human race some day."

I came to some of the same conclusions when Barbara disappeared and my parents divorced a few months later. I stopped going to church and more or less became a non-believer. I had spent hours kneeling beside my bed begging God to bring Barbara back to me, then later, to keep my parents together. But, as with Barbara's fervent pleadings to erase her pregnancy, God didn't seem to be listening.

My transformation, which devastated my mother (a "real" Christian), was enhanced by my later association with Annie, a confirmed and angry atheist, whose logical and pointed arguments were hard to refute. Later in life, I would do a little bit of a turn around and become a Unitarian Universalist, which allowed me to join a spiritual community while still developing my own belief system.

Once inside, away from the graves and out of the rain, we all gathered in the church basement, where coffee and snacks were served while we waited out the storm. I eventually left the minister to mingle and attend to his duties of comforting the bereaved, and it wasn't long before I located George and Alicia in the crowd. I ran up to hug my first girlfriend, trying in vain to hold back tears.

"Hey," said George after the hug had gone on for a while. "You had your turn a long time ago, so leggo my wife." He said this with guarded humor, so I held Alicia out at arm's length and said through my waning sobs, "Thanks so much for coming. You can't imagine what this means to me."

She looked deep into my eyes, as if she were trying to absorb some of my grief. "That's what friends are for, Tommy," she said. "I would no more have missed this than I would *your* funeral."

We found a table and settled in with cups of coffee, while the crowd noise faded around us. We were silent for a while, then George piped up. "I guess you feel about as awkward as we do, huh?" he asked. "I mean, you probably don't know many of these people either."

"No. Well, I know her dad and I know Charles." I glanced around to see if I could catch sight of Charles, but I couldn't find him. Then, turning back, I said, "But the most important thing is that I knew Barbara."

"Where's Rosie?" Alicia asked, and that question brought the lump back to my throat.

"You know Rosie," I said once I felt I could talk without breaking down. "If I'd asked her to come, she would have, but she knew this was going to be personal and emotional for me. Though she didn't say so, I know she stayed home so I wouldn't feel inhibited about what I was going to say here."

"She's a love," George said, and Alicia nodded in agreement.

"I don't think I could have quite handled that if it were George," she said. "But, then again, my goodness quotient can't hold a candle to Rosie's."

The conversation drifted into trivia for a while, and then Alicia asked, "Where're you at religiously nowadays, Tom? Still a UU, or did you give up on that, too?"

"Oh, I'm still a UU all right, though I don't attend a church. I'm a member of what they call The Church of the Larger Fellowship. It's a bunch of us UUs around the world who, for one reason or another, can't or don't want to belong to a brick-and-mortar church."

"That's weird," said Alicia.

"Yeah," I admitted. "We're mostly an online community of folks with the same values and views about free religious inquiry. And it allows me to remain a part of the UU movement, which I still think is the best thing going when it comes to organized religion. How about you?"

"Oh, you know me. Never had much use for religion of any kind. Was Barbara religious?" she asked.

"When she was young," I answered. "But things changed some for her later in life. Still, she was religious. She and I were pretty close, you know, at least way back when, and we often talked about our doubts and questions and all."

I had never told anyone about what happened between Barbara and me back in the early sixties, and I never mentioned to a soul the pregnancy or my illegitimate son—except to Rosie. When I did tell Rosie, she went on a quest to find him. She eventually got up the nerve to contact Barbara, and the two of them became friends. But even working together on the project they were never able to come up with anything more than isolated and tantalizing clues. Until, that is, the day they located our son, dead, in a military graveyard.

It wasn't long before the rain began to slacken, and the minister started herding the crowd back to the memorial garden, where a team of volunteers worked to dry off the white wooden folding chairs. As we made our way toward the doors, I caught sight of Charles and signaled for him to come over. George and Alicia knew Charles casually, and we all shook hands.

"How've you been, Charles?" I asked as we walked back out into the humid air.

"Oh, you know," he answered, and then he turned his head away and his shoulders started to shake. I put a hand on George's back and gave him a little shove, indicating that I needed a minute alone with Charles.

Charles and I moved to an alcove away from the shuffling crowd under a huge stained-glass window, and I waited until he had recovered somewhat. Finally, he said,

"You know, Tom, I did everything I could to take care of her, to protect her and make sure she had what she needed."

"I know that Charles," I answered. "And I'm sure everyone appreciates what you did."

"It was the alcohol, Tom," he continued in a shaky voice. "I couldn't get loose of it. And I started getting, well, kind of violent, I guess you could say. I mean, I never hit her or anything, you've got to believe me, but I think she started to get scared that I might someday, and eventually things fell apart."

I laid a hand on his shoulder. He looked at me then, through his tears, and said, "If only we'd had kids. At least then I might have a piece of her now to hang onto."

My thoughts flashed back to that day in 1975 when Rosie had said something about there being a little piece of me out there somewhere, and I began to think how frustrating the search for my son had been over the years.

"I know what you mean, brother," I said. "I know exactly what you mean."

24
BARBARA   1968

I sat in stunned silence while Barbara's words hung in the
air as if spoken by God. *David Lee Tate*, I thought. *My son,
David Lee Tate*. Thunder cracked and I looked up at the little
white chandelier as it shook above us in the darkened living
room. When things began to come back into focus, I turned
to Barbara. "Where the hell is Mexico Beach?" I asked.

"It's a little town up in the Panhandle, on the coast not
too far from Panama City."

"How long were you there?

"About seven months, until the baby was born." She di-
verted her eyes and her shoulders began to shake. "I never
got to see him, Tommy," she said in a quavering voice.
"They said it would be best if I didn't. After I was out of the
hospital, they shipped me back home with a cock-and-bull
story about how I had rheumatic fever and had been at

some convalescent center. They didn't even let me go back to school, telling people I wasn't strong enough yet. I had tutors and ended up graduating about a year later than I should have, but I missed out on all the stuff my friends got to do, like prom and all. Mostly, though, I missed seeing you, something my dad absolutely forbade me to do."

"Yeah, I'll bet," I grumbled. "What happened after high school?"

"Dad introduced me to Rob at church and we started seeing each other. From then on it seemed like a whirlwind thing, with both our parents convinced we would get married. Rob was nice and all, and handsome, and we got along well, but I never really loved him, at least not like I did you." She smiled at me and continued. "He joined the Marines shortly after the wedding, so we never got much of a chance to get comfortable living together. He was gone for basic training, and when he got back they shipped him off to Vietnam. He came home after his first tour, and we tried to have kids." She reached into her purse, drew out a photo wallet and handed it to me.

I flipped it open to see several photos of her and Rob, him in his uniform and her pregnant. On the next few pages there was a baby, then a little girl, the spitting image of Barbara. A few more photos followed, showing the girl at various stages."

"We call her BB. She was so tiny when she was born, and she used to roll up like a little ball when she slept, so Rob started calling her BB and it stuck. Her real name's Barbara. She's four now, a great kid, lots of spunk and energy and smart as a whip. She's at her grandma's today."

"Damn," I said. "Damn, damn, damn!" All I could think of was that this beautiful little girl could've been ours; that by now we would have two kids, a boy and a girl, and would be looking ahead to the "happily ever after" I had dreamed about ever since that day in 1960. Barbara seemed to sense what I was feeling, and she let me go on caressing those photos and moaning quietly.

Eventually, I remembered what I wanted to ask, and I handed the photo wallet back to her. "Did you ever find out anything about David?"

Tears filled her eyes as she answered. "They said I shouldn't. That it would be best for him if he never knew." She sniffled a little, then continued. "I wanted to, Tommy. I really wanted to. But I guess I finally decided they were right, so I let it drop." Before I could respond, she added, "In case you're wondering, the Tates were nice people. They took good care of me and they weren't judgmental at all. One thing that helped make me feel a little bit better was knowing that he, that David, would have a good home."

Oddly, at that moment, I started thinking about God; about how our prayers had been ignored and how cruel it was that all this had been allowed to happen. I wanted to say something, probably blasphemous, but she spoke up first.

"What about you?" she asked, "How has your life been?"

"I thought you had your 'sources,'" I said with a sly grin.

"I do, and I've kept pretty good tabs on you, but that doesn't mean I know what's been going on in your mind, in your heart. Are you happy? Do you have regrets?"

"Regrets!" I said, raising my voice without meaning to. "Hell, Barb, I regret practically my whole life, mainly because it hasn't been with you. Paula and I got married because she was pregnant, and it's been a struggle to say the least. Besides her running around, which you apparently know about, she's cold and conservative, and we don't have much in common except the kids. The kids are neat, though.

Bright and athletic and good looking. I'd show you some pictures but I don't carry any with me."

"That's okay, I know what they look like."

"Yeah, I guess you do. Tell me, who are these mysterious sources you claim to have?"

She thought for a while, then said, "Maybe I shouldn't tell. I mean, I don't want you to get mad at h—at whoever they are."

"Oh, I'll get mad all right, especially if it's someone I know well. But I'll tell you this, I *will* find out, even if I have to go to every one of my friends and harass them until somebody tells me."

"Okay, okay," she said. "Please don't do that. But if you think for a minute, you should be able to figure it out."

I thought about it, and then it dawned on me. In fact, it had been right there in front of my eyes for years and I'd never suspected a thing

"It's George!" I said with finality. "That sonofabitch!" George was the only person I had ever confided in about my search for Barbara. He had gone to Dixie Hollins, Barbara's high school, and he knew her casually way back when. "That, that—"

"Oh, Tommy," she interrupted. "Please don't blame George. I swore him to secrecy. I made him promise on his mother's life that he wouldn't tell. He told me how hard you had tried to find me and how upset you were, and I knew that with my dad monitoring my every move it would only cause problems for both of us if we got together during those first few years. George wanted to tell you, but I convinced him it was best not to."

I sat there shaking my head, but then she took one of my hands and squeezed it. "It was only recently that I started to feel different and realized you had a right to know what had happened. It was the hardest thing I ever had to do, leave you hanging like that, but I did think I was doing the right thing at the time." We looked at each other, me no doubt with anger still showing on my face, she with sorrow and regret radiating from hers. And, of course, I melted again. In a way, I could understand why she'd felt she didn't have much choice under the circumstances. And I was happy to learn that at least she'd been keeping an eye on me.

"So," I said, "when did all this detective work start? I mean how did you guys get together? You weren't in high school anymore, so how did you two hook up?"

"It was at one of your performances, shortly after Rob and I met. Remember that folk festival they used to have out in Seminole by that little lake?"

"Sure," I said. "We played there every year until they stopped having it."

"Well, I don't remember the exact year, but Rob is a big folk music fan and we were there on a date. It was a Saturday, I think, and the crowd was pretty big by the time we got there, so we couldn't get too close to the stage. I heard you announcing a song over the microphone, and I knew it was you, even though your voice had changed a lot since I'd last heard it."

"Yeah," I mused. "The boy soprano hits puberty and everything goes to hell. You remember how crackly my voice was when we first met, back when you were dating Brad? That's why I used to talk so softly all the time. It was either that or I'd be skipping from one octave to another with no control. When I finally came out of it, I was a tenor, to be kind, and I ended up nearly a baritone."

"I know," she said. "I've heard you sing several times, and you have a beautiful voice, Tommy. You do."

"How? What?" I stammered, but she ignored me.

"Anyway, when I recognized your voice, I got nervous, afraid you might see me or something. But when I urged

Rob to go, he said he wasn't about to waste the money we'd spent for admission. We listened to you and George for a while, and Rob was impressed. He wanted to get closer to the stage, but I talked him out of it. After you'd finished, I watched you guys pack up your guitars and was relieved to see you leave the stage at the back and head across the street to a house over there."

"That was the Holloway's house. They were the ones who used to put on the festival, and the musicians always gathered there afterwards for a barbecue and jam session."

"Anyway," she continued, "George apparently wasn't joining you, because he jumped off the front of the stage and started making his way through the crowd in a direct line towards us. Then I had an idea."

"An idea, huh?" I said. "Looks like it worked out better than that other idea you had way back when."

She looked perplexed for a moment, then she released my hand and punched me on the shoulder. "That's not very nice," she said in mock anger. "Besides, if I recall correctly, you thought it was a great idea at the time."

I nursed my aching arm while we both laughed at the memory. "Okay," I said finally. "So what was your big idea?"

"Well, I wanted to know how you were and what you were up to and all. So I told Rob I needed to find a bathroom and asked him if he would get us some Cokes. I went one way and he went another, and as soon as he was far enough away, I headed toward George. When I got to him I blurted out that I needed find out some things about you. I begged him not to tell you, at least until he and I had talked, and he finally agreed. But he did say that I'd better have a good story, or he was going to tell you he saw me."

"Good ol' George," I said. "At least he started out on the right track. Then what happened?"

"He gave me his phone number and I called him the next day. We met that same day, and after I hammered him repeatedly about not telling you, I made him fill me in on as many details of your life as he could remember. He agreed to talk to me from time to time after that, so I started calling him every few months or so, and that's how I kept up."

"So, what about last Saturday at the beach? Was that planned, too?"

"No, that was really strange. I had already decided I wanted to see you. In fact, it was George who kept insisting I wasn't being fair and that I owed it to you to meet face-to-face and explain things. I was actually trying to figure the best way to go about it, when he saw June and me at the beach and you almost tripped over us a few minutes later."

"Serendipity," I said, skepticism dripping from my voice. "Funny how those things seem to happen."

"Come on, Tommy, you know I would never lie to you," she said, again smacking me in the arm. "I mean, I may have avoided contact, but I have never deliberately lied to you."

And she hadn't. In fact, there was not a single time I could remember when she hadn't been totally honest with me. It was a pact between us that I never violated either. And it was the realization that she, too, had never forgotten it and was simply incapable of lying to me that led me to believe her when she said she had no idea how to find our son.

Barbara and I stayed in touch regularly after that. I would have pushed her to resume our intimate relationship, but I knew it would only cause her anxiety and sorrow. So, even though I was perfectly prepared to end my marriage and reunite with her, I held my ground, continued the charade of "happily married man," and suffered in silence.

25

BARBARA 1972

Tommy?" said the voice on the phone. It was Barbara, and it was clear she was distress. "Tommy, are you there?"

"I'm here," I said in a near whisper, thinking Paula might be within earshot. Then I remembered she had gone for her evening run and I raised my voice. "I'm here, Barb. What's wrong?"

I heard her gasping and trying to get some words out, then finally she said, "He's dead, Tommy. Rob's dead." I could feel her grief radiate through the phone like the heat from a blowtorch. "Oh, God, honey," I said. "How? When?"

I knew Rob had been reassigned to Vietnam. He was an officer by then, having been recommended for OCS after his first tour and graduating with honors. "They came to my door," she said. "They said he was killed on patrol in the

Mekong Delta. They said he died with honor and all that crap. Assholes!"

I was relieved to hear anger in her voice, which meant she at least had that to hang onto for the moment. "What can I do? Do you want me to come over?"

"No. Hell, I don't know what I want. I'm freaked right now, you know, and I needed to talk to someone. Is this all right, I mean you won't get in trouble or anything because I called, will you?"

I thought then about my initial hesitation, the fact that I had lowered my voice so Paula wouldn't hear, and that made me angry. "Hey," I said. "I don't give a good flying fuck. If Paula was here and she said one goddamned word, I'd tell her to stick her head up her tight little ass."

"Oh, Tommy, you shouldn't say things like that," she said, her voice straining against the tears. And before I could answer, she lost the battle and her voice shook with waves of pent up emotion.

"Listen," I said, raising my voice to be heard over her crying. "Where's BB. Is she with you right now?"

"No," she managed to squeak between sobs, "She's spending the weekend with Mom and Dad."

"Okay then, I'm coming over. It should take me about ten minutes. I'll honk twice when I get to your driveway. You hang in there, you hear? I'm on my way."

Normally a ten-minute drive, it took me only about six before I turned into Barbara's driveway. I started to honk the horn, but then I saw her on the porch swing, rocking back and forth in the dim light, oblivious to her surroundings. My heart was about to explode with emotion, but I realized what she needed me to be at that moment was strong and supportive, not some blubbering imbecile, so I resolved not to fall apart as I ran up the front steps and knelt to take her hands in mine. I waited without speaking, and finally, almost with surprise, she looked at me.

"Thanks, Tommy. Thanks for coming," she said in an eerily calm voice. We stared at each other for a while, then her eyes began to wander. "I don't know what I'm going to do. I mean, what about BB? What is she going to do without a dad? She loves him so much. I don't know how I'm going to tell her. And what am *I* going to do? I don't know if I can make it on my own." Then the emotion took over and she began to cry. Not the wracking sobs I might have expected, but quiet little gasps she seemed to be trying to hold back.

"It's going to be okay," I said, realizing her grief, though part of it was over Rob's death, was mostly from a fear of the unknown—fear for her daughter; fear of being alone. "I won't let it be any other way. I won't, Barbara, you can take that to the bank!"

That moment was one of the most conflicted I have ever experienced. Here I was, trying to comfort the woman I loved more than any other on the face of the earth, while thoughts of the opportunity to press my case pushed at my mind like pounding surf against a crumbling seawall. *Don't even think about it,* one half of my mind kept saying, while the other half desperately wanted to take advantage of the situation. In the end, the nobler half won out.

Over the next few days, working behind the scenes, I arranged with my friend Billy Anderson to have his father keep tabs on the body as it was shipped back to the states. And I personally spoke to the minister at Barbara's church about arrangements for the funeral. Rob's parents had died in a car accident about six months earlier, leaving only debts. Then there was a bunch of bureaucratic horseshit from the military, which wanted to dictate where and how he would be buried, but Barbara rejected all that. And, because of the military red tape, there was almost no money available up front.

By that time, I had given up worrying about Barbara's asshole father and what he thought of me, and when he tried in his inimitable way to intervene, I told him to fuck off; that this was something I was better equipped to handle now. He grumbled a bit, and threatened to tell Barbara what I had said, but I could see he didn't want to take time out of his own affairs to act like a real father for a change. Eventually he faded into the background.

Barbara was adamant about not wanting a military funeral. Nor did she want Rob buried at Arlington. She wanted him buried nearby so she and BB could visit the grave and keep his memory alive in their minds. She had come to despise the Vietnam War, as had most of us at the time, and she didn't even want Rob to be buried in his uniform.

I worked on Billy's father, who had always liked me, and got him to give Barbara a substantial break on the casket and funeral (which meant his obscene profits might have to fall to merely disgusting). He even managed to pull in a favor and find a burial plot in a nearby cemetery for about half what it might've cost. In the end, after a long legal battle, Rob's military benefits covered most of the expenses, and what wasn't covered I decided that Barbara didn't need to know about. So I signed a personal note with old man Anderson for the rest of it.

Through that time, I never once allowed my desire for Barbara to show. She was so riddled with grief and concern and fear I knew it would be wrong to complicate things. There was also BB to think about. She and I had never met, and bringing a strange man into her life at that moment would have been the worst thing Barbara could do. I knew this and so did Barbara, which is why I tried to stay out of sight, making arrangements while remaining in the shadows.

After it was over, and Rob had been laid to rest in civilian dignity, I waited awhile, then tentatively broached the subject of getting back together. But I was still married and Barbara could not bring herself to even consider the idea of being a home wrecker, as she put it. I tried again to convince her my marriage was destined to end soon. I even offered to file for divorce, but she would have none of that.

"Tommy," she said one night some weeks after the funeral, as we sat on the same porch swing where I had found her the day she called with the news. "You know I love you, and you know I want to be with you more than anything in the world, but it's too goddamned complicated. I mean, you're married and BB's still grieving and right now I've got to figure out how to survive. Please, honey, please don't push me."

Unfortunately, her fears of being alone and of BB growing up without a father, led her into a whirlwind affair with an old family friend from church. Charles, I would later learn, was BB's Sunday school teacher, and when the opportunity presented itself, he swept in with the promise of financial support and stability. They were married less than six months later.

I would remember that night a few years later, as I listened to John Denver's new album, "Farewell Andromeda," and first heard the song, "I'd Rather be a Cowboy." There was a line in the song that tore at my heartstrings like fiery claws. The song itself didn't remind me of Barbara at all, since it

was about some country guy whose girl had left him for the
Big City, but that one line said it all when I thought back on
the weeks following the death of Barbara's first husband.

"I love her, yes I love her," John Denver sang, "just
enough to let her go."

26

BB   1982

Hey, kiddo," I said as I strolled up to the cement bench where BB sat in the bright sunshine outside the Eckerd College Library. She had called me earlier and asked me to meet her, that there was something she wanted to talk about.

A few years after Barbara and Charles divorced, she decided it was finally okay to bring me into her daughter's life. BB was eight at the time, and growing into a lovely, vibrant kid, with an enormous intellect and her mother's innate capacity for empathy. Brown haired and freckled, she had a smile that could light up Yankee Stadium at midnight. That, plus her outgoing personality would, I thought, have the guys falling at her feet before long. My speculation proved to be correct, however BB didn't seem to have much time for boys. She had never been able to put her dad's death behind her and her hatred for war and all things military led her into political activism as an avocation. That fury occupied most of her time outside of school and kept dating to a minimum.

"Hi, Uncle Tommy. Thanks for coming." She shuffled some books and papers together and stood to give me a hug. "How much time have you got?" she said as she released me and picked up her pile of school materials.

"Got all day, if you need it," I said. "What's up?"

At the time, I was working as a free-lance graphic artist and my hours were my own to manage as I pleased. After sensing in her voice that something important was going on in her life, I set aside the afternoon and told Rosie I might not be home for dinner.

"Good," BB said. "Can we go somewhere private and talk?"

"Sure, honey, anything you want. Where should we go?"

"Well, I'm finished with classes for the day, so why don't we head over toward my house and maybe take a walk down at The Bay?"

Barbara and Charles had bought a home in the old northeast section of St. Pete, a few blocks from the house I grew up in. When they divorced, Charles had insisted she remain there and, as was the case with Barbara and me, The Bay had become one of BB's favorite haunts.

I arrived at The Bay a few minutes later, with BB right behind. We left our cars at the curb and held hands as we walked across the wide expanse of grass to the waterfront. It was a beautiful autumn day, with a slight breeze to enhance the perfect 75-degree temperature.

"You sounded upset on the phone," I said as we approached the seawall and sat looking out over the rippling water. "Is everything okay?" She didn't answer right away, and my feeling that this might be something serious grew.

"Yeah, I guess," she said, finally. "I was talking to Mom about some things last night, and she said I might want to speak to you. I've been thinking about a lot of stuff lately, mostly religious stuff, and Mom seemed to think you might be able to help me make some decisions."

"Whooee," I said. "I wonder what made her think that. I mean your mom has always been better at that kind of thing than I am. Hell, I don't even go to church anymore and I'm probably as confused about religion as anybody could be."

"Yeah, Mom told me you weren't the most religious guy in the world. Actually, neither is she, or at least that's the way it seems to me. Even though we still belong to church and attend services and all, it seems more because of the community and our friends than for religious reasons." She looked down at her knees and shook her head. "I don't know, Uncle Tommy. I'm going through some stuff right now, and I need someone to talk to besides Mom. Don't get me wrong, we have a great relationship and all, and I try to be as honest with her as I can, but there are some things that are difficult to bring up. You know what I mean?"

"Sure, honey," I said. "I wasn't trying to get out of talking with you when I said that. I don't know if I'm qualified to be a religious advisor, but hell, I'll give it my best shot."

"Do you believe in God?" she asked abruptly, catching me off guard.

"Hey, why don't you start out with a tough one?" I said with a sigh.

She chuckled a little, then said, "Well, I could maybe start off with the old chicken-and-egg bit, but you know yourself it would all still come around to that one basic question. So, do you or don't you?"

"Okay, let me think a minute." Over the years I had pondered this simple question, and I still wasn't absolutely sure. Having grown up in a devout religious family, I found it hard to let loose of the spiritual feelings I remembered having as a kid. But so many of the so-called facts never seemed to add up. I saw myself as a logical thinker, and the answers to my questions about God and all the other trappings of religion never seemed to have adequate, logical foundations. Barbara and I had discussed these questions from time to time, too, but we were always left with no real conclusions. "Did you ask your mom that question?" I said, stalling for time.

"Yep," she answered flipping her hair back and looking up at the fluffy white clouds. "She said she didn't know, and that she didn't want to get into it."

"Right," I said. "So she put it off on me, huh?"

"That's about the size of it," she answered.

"Well," I started, stretching the word out. "If you're asking if I believe there's some all-seeing, all-knowing, all-powerful 'force' in the universe that oversees and controls things, I'd have to say I don't. But I can't know the unknowable, so my view might be about the same as your mom's."

"Great! Then I guess you're going to give me the same dodge she did."

"Now, wait a sec. I wasn't finished." I thought for a minute, then gathered my gumption and continued. "Look, if there is such a thing, which there might be, why don't we call it 'love,' and leave it at that? It's so much simpler than trying to believe in something like a wise old white-bearded man sitting on a throne somewhere in the sky directing things." She didn't respond so I added, "For some folks, that's the only way they can get a grasp on the idea, and if that imagery works best for them, it's fine with me. We're all still talking about the same thing, aren't we? How we define it for ourselves is really of no consequence. I will say, however, that if this force exists and is intelligent, then he/she/it has a warped sense of humor at times, and a sadistic streak as well." That elicited a smile and I began to think I might be on a roll.

"Okay. I get it," she said. "But I guess what I really want to know is, does this force or whatever, if it exists, does it have rules, like the Ten Commandments or something? I mean, do you think in order for us to be in harmony with this larger-than-life entity, we have to do certain things and not do certain others? Do we have to *be* a certain way, and if so, whose word to we take when it comes to figuring out what that way is? Do we take the word of Jesus, or Buddha, or Confucius, or any of the other seers and prophets and philosophers? Is there some source of absolute truth that can tell us how we should act and live?"

So much for the roll. "Boy," I said, "you've got me there. A lot of these so-called rules you're looking for are repeated in the teachings of those folks you mentioned. Things like 'Do unto others as you would have them do unto you,' or 'love thy neighbor as thyself,' they show up in one form or another in most religious traditions and philosophies down through the ages. Unfortunately, though, there isn't one single set of rules that I know of, even though all the different sects will tell you theirs is the only true way."

"Yeah," she said. "That's the problem, at least for me. I've read a ton of stuff lately on religious history, not only from official church sources, but also from those of secular historians and archaeologists and anthropologists and the like. Problem is, they disagree about the fundamental 'truths' of the universe about as much as religions do."

I knew BB was looking for an answer to a specific question, searching for an ultimate authority to help her make some important life decision, though I couldn't imagine what that might be. What could be so monumentally important to her that she would agonize over it like this? Finally, I decided to ask.

"Is there something specific, some question in particular you're looking for an answer to?"

She looked at me with reluctance and embarrassment radiating from her eyes. "So," she said, avoiding my question, "as far as you can say, there is no ultimate authority on how we should live our lives."

"No," I said. "I think life's too complicated for one authoritative cut-and-dried set of answers for everything. I think we have to figure things out for ourselves. I'm not saying we shouldn't read and listen to historical philosophers and seers and theologians. Most of them had good ideas, but they couldn't know us or our time or the pressures and complex decisions we have to make in today's world. About all we can do is take what we think are the most important of all their ideas and apply them to our lives as best we can." I considered what I had said, which had come out before I could think about it, then went on.

"I tend to look more toward the Eastern and Native American philosophies nowadays, but that's just me. I can't see things through your eyes or your mom's or anybody's for that matter, so I have no idea how the world looks to you or others. I do believe most thinking people—that is those who don't blindly hang onto some religious dogma, but who think for themselves—I believe most of those free thinkers understand right and wrong and try to live their lives accordingly. Of course, there are people who think they know what's right, but because of some mental impairment or greed or downright stupidity, they don't manage to conduct their lives as they should. But if my observations over the years have been correct, those folks are few and far between. Most of us get it about right when we decide for ourselves how to live."

"Really?" she said, brightening up a bit. "You mean those of us who are smart enough to study and think about things, that we can decide on our own what's right and wrong?"

"That's exactly what I mean." I reached over and took one of her hands. "And I know you're one of those people, BB. I know it for sure."

"Thanks for the compliment," she said, squeezing my hand. "But what if a person can't decide? What if, even with all the study and inquiry, a person still can't figure out if a thing is right or wrong?"

This was getting tougher by the minute. I'd never doubted my ability to discern right from wrong, though I knew I had made bad choices. Finally I figured out a way to answer. "You know we all make mistakes, don't you? That we're all human, and humans aren't perfect, right?" She nodded. "Well, that's one of the ways we learn about right and wrong. Isn't it?"

"Yeah. I guess," she said.

"Okay, so look at it this way: if all we ever did was wait until we were absolutely sure any decision we had to make was correct, most of us would never be able to make a decision at all, and the world would grind to a halt, don't you think?"

After a while, she seemed to get it. "You mean we have to go on and do what we think is right at any given time, and be who we want to be, even though we might be wrong?"

"Yep. And if you think about it, you'll realize that you— that we—do that all the time and we're destined to make some mistakes. The trick is to be honest with ourselves and others and when we realize we've made a mistake, we try to correct it, or at least try to do better the next time. Even your mom, as wonderful a person as she is, she'll tell you herself she's made her share of mistakes. What makes her such a great person is not that she's perfect, it's that when she makes mistakes she always figures out what she's done and then tries her best to fix it. It's one of the most important ways we learn and grow, you know, by making mistakes."

She shifted uncomfortably against the hard concrete sea-wall, then stretched her legs out straight and brushed her jeans with her hands. "Yeah," she said after a few moments. "I guess I know. But what if …?" She stopped then, as if she was about to say something she didn't want to.

"Come on, Kiddo, spit it out. You know me and you know I love you. Whatever it is, you can tell me, and you can be sure I won't ever tell a soul."

She stared out at the water and a tear began to drip from her eye. Then she turned to me and reached out to put her arms around my neck and draw me close. "Oh, Uncle Tommy, I don't know how to say this."

"Well," I said, "About the only way I know to say anything is to come right out and say it."

I felt her nod against my shoulder, then she whispered, "I think I'm gay, Uncle Tommy. In fact, I'm pretty sure."

Talk about your atomic detonations. They didn't hold a candle to what was happening in my mind at that moment. I was shocked to say the least, but I knew I had to hide it. I took a deep breath, hugged her hard, then sighed. "Boy," I said in her ear, "you really know how to stop a conversation on a dime." She continued to sniffle against my neck, so I stared to rock her and rub her back. "Listen." I said after a while. "If that's the way you feel, there's nothing you did or thought or didn't do to make you that way. Believe it, BB. I know what I'm talking about. Being gay is not a choice or a mistake or anything like that. It's the way things are."

I had known gay people all my life, mostly from the music world. In fact, one of my best friends when I was growing up was gay, though I never knew it until he committed suicide in 1975 and left a note explaining. I also knew gays and lesbians were outcasts in society, their lives made a living hell by bigots with their righteous ignorance and stupidity. That's what worried me most about BB. Not the fact that she was gay, but knowing how hard her life could be.

"I love you, honey," I finally said. "And you know your mom does, too." She snuggled even closer as if trying to hide from the world in the crook of my neck. "Now, listen to me, will you? I want you to know I'm willing to run some interference for you here. I mean, you're probably mostly worried about telling your mom and what she's going to think, right?"

"Uh-huh," she managed to blubber.

"Well, I can help you with that. I mean, if you want me to."

Finally, she seemed to calm down a little and drew back to look at me. "I don't know," she said, turning her head to stare out over the water. "I don't know what I want right now." I touched her hair and she turned back to face me.

"You do know you're going to have to tell her, though, right?" She nodded. "And you know the longer you wait, the harder it's going to be?" I let that sink in for a moment. "So, don't you think it's best if we get it over with? And I do mean 'we,' kiddo. I'm willing to help. We can tell her together or I can break the news first, which would at least give her the chance to absorb it without doing or saying something she might later regret." When she didn't respond, I continued.

"Look, your mom is going to be shocked, there's no way to get around it. She'll be sad and confused and worried at first, but not for the reasons you might think. After she gets past the initial bombshell, her concern will be for your happiness, your safety, and that's the *only* thing she'll be worried about!"

"I guess so," she said after thinking about what I'd said. "And I sure would like to skip the bombshell part." A tiny smile began to tug at the corner of her mouth. "Do you think it will be all right? Do you think she'll be mad at me because I wasn't the first to tell her?"

"She might be a little angry at first, but I know your mom, and I know for a fact she'll get over it. Honesty is the important thing, honey, and you *are* going to be honest with her. But I don't see anything wrong with us trying to break the news as easy as we can."

"And and you're okay with telling her? I mean that's not going to be so easy either, is it?"

That was an understatement if there ever was one, but I knew this was something I had to do, for both of them, and I had already resigned myself to it. "It won't be easy, but, well, there are some things about your mother and me that you don't know."

I didn't realize it at the time, but my off-the-cuff statement about what BB didn't know might not have been the best thing to say. However, it did make her stop thinking about her problem. She almost immediately seemed to forget what we had been talking about, and her eyes narrowed. "Really?" she said. "And what might those things be?"

Caught! Here I was talking about honesty and trying to reassure BB that the best course is always to lay out the truth as soon as possible; and here she was, challenging me to be honest with her. Until then, all she knew was that Barbara and I were old friends. We had never given her any reason to believe our relationship was anything more than platonic. After all, we had both been married to other people, and I still was. In fact, she and Rosie had become good friends. But BB had me, and I didn't see any way out of the situation other than to lie through my teeth, and I could no more do that to her than I could to her mother. So, employing as many qualifiers as I could without making the story less than believable, I explained about Barbara and me. No graphic details, of course, and I didn't mention our out-of-wedlock child, but she got the gist of things. When I finished, she looked perplexed.

"But why? Uncle Tommy. If you loved each other so much, why didn't you get married?" She considered her own question, then added, "You know, I've always dreamed about you being my dad, but you were married and Mom, well, she seemed to be through with men, at least in the sense of wanting to have a permanent relationship with one. And now you tell me you guys have been in love with each other for years? God, how bad is that?"

"Yeah, right," I said. "Pretty bad, huh?" I went on to explain how circumstances never allowed us to get together and how our love for each other had evolved into a strong friendship.

"Still," she said as we approached our cars, "it must've been tough on you, on you *and* Mom, I guess."

"You have no idea, kiddo," I said, opening the door for her. "You have no idea!"

27

BARBARA

1960

It's funny how, considering my incredible horniness, I felt reluctant to take things to their conclusion at that moment right after I had admitted I wanted to kiss Barbara's vagina. Fact is, I wanted more than anything to go ahead, to get past the initial trauma of intercourse as quickly as possible. But I was scared. We had, I thought, resolved all the major issues about pain and control, and I felt sure she wanted it as bad as I did. But even though I had actually had intercourse before, it began to feel like the first time for me, too. And in many ways, it was.

I had never been in this situation with someone I cared about the way I cared about Barbara, and the emotion was getting to me. I had no idea what to do to make the experience good for both of us, and I guess what frightened me most was the anticipation of setting off into the unknown.

Whatever it was, I couldn't seem to forge ahead with abandon, as my hormones urged me to do.

Barbara seemed to sense this, because she raised up on an elbow and looked at me, "It's okay, Tommy. You don't have to be worried. We'll get through this one way or another, and in the end it'll be wonderful. Right?"

I nodded, but I made no move to start. I was trying to think of something more to say, some way to delay things a little longer, but it I knew Barbara had made up her mind. She leaned over to kiss me, and it was deep and powerful and as sensual as any kiss I have ever experienced. At the same time, she turned her body toward mine and wrapped her legs around me like a viper enclosing its prey. Then, with a subtle movement, she managed to turn onto her back and draw me on top of her, spreading her legs and tugging at me so I had no choice but to move up into a position that suggested immediate entry.

As she continued to pull me upward, I finally gave in and started to push, but that didn't seem to be working. I couldn't gain enough traction on the bedspread, which slid backward under my knees and kept me moving in place. (Years later I would remember this frustrating moment when I first saw Michael Jackson doing the "Moon Dance" on TV). It was that old flat missionary position, which we would later figure out wasn't all that conducive to a proper and adequate first sexual coupling. I realized Barbara had only some vague descriptions and a bit of street talk to go on, and I didn't have much more.

Intercourse with the first Barbara had always been in that straight missionary position, with no attempt to do anything else that might make the experience more comfortable or easier. Fact was, easier was not even a consideration back then, because entering her, even in the conventional position we always used, was never a problem. Had I given it serious thought, I would've been able to come up with some way to penetrate deeper and in a more satisfying way, but back then all I cared about was getting to my climax, and she didn't seem to mind. I later came to believe her lack of caring was due to her rape and a subsequent inability to understand how much pleasure a woman could derive from sexual intercourse.

So, there I was, wriggling against the shifting bedspread and failing to achieve any degree of penetration. In fact, I wasn't even sure I had aimed correctly. Without being able to see anything, it was like groping in the dark for a moving target neither of us could seem to home in on. Finally, she whispered in my ear, "This isn't working, Tommy."

I gave up then and relaxed, falling on her with all my weight. She exhaled sharply, and when I realized what I'd done, I pushed up with my arms to relieve the pressure. "Sorry," I said. "I didn't mean to—" She stopped me with a smile.

"There has to be a better way," she said, again with that practical tone creeping into her voice. "Let's think about it for a minute, okay?"

"Okay," I said. "But I want you to know I'm sorry. This is the only way I know how, and it always worked before."

"Well," she said, "before, you were with someone who had a huge, you know. And, at least the way you described things, you were pretty small at the time, which probably made things a lot easier."

I nodded, not wanting to revisit my inadequacies of the past, but not able to disagree either. With the frustration of the moment, I had begun to shrink again, so I asked her if it would be okay for me to get off for a minute while we talked.

"Of course, silly," she said. "What do you think, I'm going to hold you hostage until you succeed in defiling me?" She said this with wry humor, and to make sure I didn't take it the wrong way, added, "Don't worry, I'll still love you in the morning."

"Damn it!" I said without thinking, and slapped the bed with my hand.

"Hey!" she said. "We're not finished here, and you haven't done anything wrong, so get over it!" After a moment, she continued. "Look, we've got what—" she looked over at the clock "—two, maybe three hours left? Unless you're tired of all this and you want to go for another swim or something."

"Tired! I'm definitely not tired. Hell, I'm so horny I can't stand it. And I sure as hell would have done anything I could think of to make it work that time. But I can't think so well while we're, you know, doing that stuff. Oh, crap. I don't even know how to say it right."

"Don't worry, I know exactly what you mean, and I'm sorry for trying to be so practical. I hate myself sometimes for that, but I can't seem to help it."

Fact was, that was one of the things I had begun to love about her, and it's something I had only seen in her that day. Learning about each other, about how we handled things and reacted to things and dealt with them was one of the coolest parts of our relationship. And, although I didn't know it at the time, it was something that would stick with me over the years: a type of frank honesty I came to understand as the essence of real intimacy, and about the only glue that could hold a relationship together for any length of time.

28
ROSIE   1972

Jesus," Rosie said between waning gasps. "That was in-credible!" I had just finished introducing her to the wonderful world of cunnilingus and had collapsed on the bed next to her with my arm draped like a dead snake across her chest. I could feel her body shudder in little waves that slowly receded until finally she was still.

As we had several times before that Sunday, we both dozed off for a few minutes, and when I woke up she was staring at my face in the near dark of her bedroom. She leaned over to kiss me on the forehead and when she pulled away I could sense a subtle sadness in her body language. "What's wrong, honey?" I asked. She shook her head, unable it seemed, to speak. "Come on, now," I said reaching out to touch her cheek, but she pulled away..

"What does all this mean, Tom?" she asked "Is it just going to be the most fantastic day I've ever known, or is there maybe something else going on?"

I pondered her question for a minute and when I didn't answer right away I could feel a tenseness growing between us for the first time. Even though we had known each other only a short while, and this was the first time we'd been intimate, I had already almost decided it was not going to be a brief encounter, or even an extended affair. Still, I had just come off a failed seven-year marriage and was reluctant to jump into anything new.

"Listen," I said as sincerely as I could manage. "I'm a little brain-fucked right now, and I don't know exactly what to say. But if you're asking if this is going to be a one night stand, then my answer would have to be that I sure as hell hope not."

"Really?" she said. "You mean that?"

"I do. I wouldn't say it if I didn't. But there are some things I'm worried about right now. Like dealing with another long-term relationship so soon after I screwed one up as badly as I did my first marriage."

"Did you?" she asked. "I mean do you think it was you who screwed things up?"

Her question started my memory working overtime in search of a truthful answer. My first inclination was to blame Paula for everything, what with her infidelities and all, but if I was honest with myself, I knew I shared in the blame. In many ways it had been nobody's fault, unless I counted that one time when we had unprotected sex, which led to her pregnancy and our semi-shotgun wedding. The fact was, we were kids having kids, and neither of us was mature enough to handle a commitment like that. I was still an irresponsible beer-drinking hell raiser, and that didn't change much after the wedding. Had it not been for Paula's common sense and domestic skills, and her willingness to take over the management of our home and finances, we wouldn't have lasted a year.

I thought back over all the times I took off with the guys and left her alone to handle things, and how she never complained. And I began to realize for the first time that a lot of her infidelity had been my fault. Had our roles been reversed, I, myself, might have strayed out of loneliness. Then there was our naiveté when it came to what a successful marriage requires: the commitment, the sacrifices, the compromises, the acceptance of each other's personal habits. We were living in a dream world made up of sex and the idealistic assumption that once we were married we would live happily ever after without much effort.

As these thoughts ran through my mind, I found myself resolving to do everything I could to make sure nothing like that ever happened again, especially to this lovely creature who lay next to me waiting for an answer.

"I guess, if I'm going to be totally honest with you, I would have to say yes, I did more than my share to screw things up. And the possibility of that happening again scares the hell out of me."

"Oh," she said. "I see. I mean I understand." Her voice radiated resignation, as if I had told her she couldn't have something she wanted. Then, she brightened a little. "But, Tom, didn't you lecture me earlier about how we learn about life through experience, by going through stuff and then looking back?"

"Yes, but—"

"Well, you went through your marriage and you made some mistakes, so why can't you figure out what those mistakes were and try not to make them again? I mean you have experience to teach you, which is a lot more than I have, and surely you're smart enough to change if you think you need to."

I agreed, of course, and a plan began to form in my mind that would eventually become the foundation of our successful partnership. "You know what," I said. "I think you hit the nail on the head. I'm not sure if I understand everything that went wrong, or even if understanding would guarantee those things don't happen again, but I can sure as hell give it a try."

"Do you mean?" She hesitated for a second. "Are you talking about us, or were you talking in general about the future, your future?"

And right then, at that instant, I made up my mind. I reached out to caress her hair, and this time she didn't turn away. "I don't want to make any assumptions here because you haven't said anything about how you feel, but I *was* talking about us. I'd like to be with you, Rosie, and I don't mean only for sex or for a few months. If that's okay with you."

She surprised me by not responding, and I fiddled with her hair until I began to think she didn't want to answer. After a while, she said, "You know, that's what I thought I wanted a few minutes ago, but I'm pretty scared myself right now. I don't have any experience to go on like you do, so I would be starting out from scratch, and I don't know if I can live up to your expectations over the long haul. Do you understand what I'm trying to say?"

Her trepidation was certainly warranted, but for me, it spoke of only one thing: honesty, a frank openness that kindled memories of Barbara and caused a chill to run up my spine. I was momentarily at a loss for words, but I finally got my brain to start communicating with my mouth again. "I have only one expectation, Rosie, and that is honesty. I think that's the key. All the life lessons and experience, though they may help, could probably be thrown out the window if we promise we'll always be completely honest with each other. Do you think you could make that kind of promise and stick to it?"

"Do you?" she asked. "If you think about it, you've already admitted you tried to deceive me at first, which wasn't honest."

"No, it wasn't, but that was before I started feeling the way I do about you now. And when I began to understand how important your friendship was to me, I came clean, didn't I? In the end, I *was* honest with you. And from now on I make you this solemn promise: I will do everything in my power never to lie to you again. How about you?"

She looked down, then reached up to take my hand from her hair and hold it in both of hers. "I'll try, Tom," she said. "I promise, I'll try my best."

"Okay, then, that's settled." I pulled on her hands a little to urge her toward me and we kissed. Then she laid her head on my shoulder and whispered, "Can we start right now, being totally honest with each other I mean?"

"Absolutely," I said.

"Okay, then. I know you must be exhausted and all, but I'd really like it if you did that again?"

Rosie was right about my being exhausted, but I wasn't about to refuse her, so I once again worked my way down between her legs and for the next ten minutes or so, reveled in her extraordinary responses to my tongue. This time I ended by lifting her legs in the air and entering her hard with the deepest penetration possible. And, even though I had thought there was no way she could ever exceed the intensity of her last orgasm, this time she somehow seemed to find an even higher level.

After we recovered, we began what would be a weeks-long process of telling each other everything we could think of about ourselves. It was during that time that she made one of her most difficult admissions, telling me she had once had an illegal abortion. She was devastated by the experience, and when she told me, she cried for a long time, saying she knew I was going to hate her for it. Of course, I wasn't a bit shocked, something she seemed to find disconcerting.

Over those weeks we not only told each other about our pasts, I asked her to please tell me if there was anything about me she disliked or that turned her off. She thought for a minute, then shyly said she didn't like the fact that I bit my fingernails. So, after some 20 years of biting them down to the quick, I quit on a dime and never resumed the habit for the rest of my life. It was that sacrifice on my part that provided me with the final bit of evidence I needed to assure myself what I felt for her was real. As for me, when she asked the same question, I thought and thought, but I couldn't come up with one thing I would change about her. Oh, the thing about housecleaning came fleetingly to mind, but after I gave it some consideration, I decided that would be far too much to ask. Besides, by then I had settled in to my new role, and had even started watching some of those cooking shows on TV to acquire a few skills in that department. Rosie, it turns out, couldn't boil an egg without it ending in disaster.

All in all, things worked out well for Rosie and me. For the first few years, when my kids were still young and used to spend summers with us, we had what we came to refer to as the "annual argument." This always seemed to be maliciously planned and executed by the kids, who were jealous of my attention to Rosie at first. But as they grew older and came to know her better, even that faded away and, other than an occasional mild disagreement, we almost never argued.

There was only one thing that worried me about coming clean with Rosie, and that was when I told her about Barbara. In keeping with our promise to each other, I didn't hold back, and I admitted I would probably always reserve a small room in my heart for my first true love.

"But you can have all the rest," I told her, and she said she could handle that. In fact, her only concern seemed to be for me and the sadness she saw in my eyes every time the subject came up. Eventually, she and Barbara became friends, and I often felt a little paranoid thinking they might be trading stories about my sexual expertise or lack thereof. In fact, it was Rosie I first told about BB's admission that she was a lesbian, and she insisted on being there when I broke the news to Barbara.

About a week after I had talked with BB at The Bay, we finally told Barbara. In the meantime, I had insisted on meeting BB's companion. She turned out to be one of BB's classmates who reminded me a little of Sally Field: thin and petite and about as shy as Rosie, at least at first. Later I would come to realize her initial shyness was mainly due to having to come out of the closet, and that she really was a pretty outgoing person, one of the first of what would later be referred to as "rabid feminists."

Rosie and I invited Barbara over for dinner and, after we'd eaten and were sitting around drinking coffee, I tried to break the news to her as gently as I could. Her reaction was about what I'd expected: shock at first, then tears, and finally resignation. And, as I had predicted, from there on out her only concern was for BB's welfare and the problems her sexual orientation might cause her.

"Is she with someone now?" Barbara asked after Rosie had gotten her calmed down and made her take a Valium.

"She is," I answered. "And you're going to like her. Her name is Terri, and she's a real no-bullshit kind of person. She and BB are talking about joining the Peace Corps together."

That last little revelation was probably not the most diplomatic thing I could have said, because it only added to Barbara's worries. But it was the truth and, as always, I had never been able to be less than truthful with Barbara. The thought of them being shipped off to some primitive and impoverished country scared her, but I told her BB had inherited her empathy for others and wanted to do something that would make a difference. After a while, she seemed to take some pride in the fact that her daughter was willing to make such a sacrifice, and before long she resolved to call BB right then and start the process of assuring her she wasn't angry or anything. BB, I knew, was waiting for a call from me, so I told Barbara that would be a great idea.

"I love you, honey," were the first words Barbara spoke on the phone and, even though I could only hear half of the conversation, it was clear there was a lot of crying on both ends at first. Eventually they got past the tears and by the time she hung up, she had spoken to Terri and they had planned to meet the next day.

Even with all the pressures of that time, Terri and BB stayed together, and after their first Peace-Corps tour, they joined up with NOW and went on to become high-profile activists in the Feminist Movement and with several other organizations. They later settled in the DC area, from where they would often travel around the world in various efforts to combat poverty or genocide or whatever else they felt needed their attention or assistance.

We tried to send them a telegram when Barbara died, but they were somewhere in Darfur and couldn't be reached in time. Two days before the funeral, I got a call from BB. It was a crackly connection and I had a hard time making out what she said, but the essence was they were devastated and wanted to come home, but the situation was too dire for them to leave. Before we hung up, the line cleared a little and the last thing she said before we were cut off was she didn't want Barbara's ashes buried. "I should be back in a couple of months or so, Uncle Tommy," she said as her voice began to fade again. "You hang on to her for me, okay? When I get home we can talk about what to do." Then the line went dead.

29

THE FUNERAL

When I finally got Charles calmed down, and everyone was seated again, I resumed my position at the podium. I looked out over the small crowd as they squirmed and settled, and wondered where I was going to start. I remembered I had been interrupted in the middle of a soliloquy on Christianity and Barbara's adherence to its principals, but when I thought back, I realized I had gotten preachy and I didn't want to go in that direction. After all, this was about Barbara, not religion.

"Well," I began, in an attempt to break the ice after the delay, "it appears God is about as sad as we are on this occasion, since He seems to have shed a few tears of His own over Barbara's passing." A few smiles in the crowd told me this had gone over okay, so I dove back in.

"I did a little research on eulogies before I decided what to say here, and I discovered the general rule is never to say anything bad about the deceased. In fact, as we all know, eulogies are usually long lists of at least slightly exaggerated compliments. So my first inclination was to do something different, to break the mold, so to speak.

"I thought and thought, trying to come up with something uncomplimentary to say about Barbara, and in the end, I couldn't think of a thing. Still, in case she might be listening, this particular eulogy is going to be different. It's going to contain the plain, unvarnished truth. Even though it may sound exaggerated, I can assure you it's not.

"Truth was always incredibly important to Barbara. Honesty was so much a part of her character, it was like some kind of soul tattoo that could not be erased, even though the pressures of modern life tried at times to laser it off.

"Barbara's character was an enigma. She was simple in her ways and mannerisms, yet complex in her thinking. She had an enormous capacity for love, and almost none for hatred. Her tolerance for the foibles of humanity seemed boundless, however, that tolerance was often strained to the breaking point by things like greed, violence, political dishonesty, and other injurious aspects of human nature. She could talk religion with the best, yet, in her later years, she swore off religious debate for fear her words might do harm to the joy a person derived from their spiritual beliefs.

"When I say character, I mean that set of traits that make up the essence of a person's being. Most of us value the same things in people: honesty, integrity, responsibility, authenticity, moral courage. Barbara had them all. Throw in a good helping of love, humor, generosity and selflessness and you get only a glimpse of her."

I stared out at the space above the heads, some of which were now nodding in approval of my words. Encouraged, I took a deep breath, and continued.

"We all have our ideas about truth. The 'little white lie' or the bending of truth to spare someone grief or heartache—these are generally considered okay under the proper circumstances. The problem for most of us is that we stretch those concepts to include lies that can be harmful, sometimes maliciously, sometimes inadvertently. And Barbara was not immune to these human shortcomings. The difference in her case, as I alluded to earlier, wasn't that she didn't make those mistakes from time to time, but that she always seemed to look back and discover them, then do her best to fix whatever damage might have resulted.

"In addition to this uncanny ability and willingness to judge her own actions in retrospect, there are many transgressions we all indulge in—or at least I have—that she would never allow herself. For example, how many of us parents have asked a child to answer the phone and tell someone we weren't home? How many have told a 14-year-old to say they're twelve in order to get a cheaper price at the movies?" I looked around to see several heads nod or lower in acknowledgement.

"Well, Barbara would never do such things. Not because she was particularly pious, but because she knew those actions would speak far louder than the words she might use to justify them. She realized her daughter would learn from her actions that she was a dishonest person, not always to be trusted, and that lying was acceptable.

"I'm not going stand here and recite a list of all the good things Barbara did in her life, even though such a list would certainly be impressive. Most of her kind acts went unnoticed. When something needed doing, she didn't wait around for a committee to appoint someone or for others to step up, she went ahead and did it, never for the recognition she might receive, but because it was the right thing to do. You see, Barbara wasn't interested in feeling good about herself or in garnering the admiration of others, she was only interested in *being* a good person. And she was. In fact, with her only possible equal being my mother, she was quite simply the finest person I ever knew.

"I think that statement about says it all, so I'm going to get off my soapbox now. But before I do, I want to read you something that sums up what Barbara was all about. This is paraphrased and, unfortunately, I cannot credit the author, since the original version came from one those e-mail pass-alongs with no attribution. But I'm sure whoever wrote it knew someone like Barbara."

I pulled from my pocket the slip of paper I had been carrying, tried to clear the huge lump in my throat, and read:

The Best Person I Ever Knew
She taught us all by example to:
Live as Christ lived
Love without question or favor
Give without expectation of reward
See and nurture the potential in everyone
Accept defeat without seeking revenge
Suffer without complaint or rancor

She will always be with us
She's the whisper of the leaves as we walk down the street
She's the smell of bleach in our freshly laundered socks
She's the cool hand on our brow when we're not well.
She lives inside our laughter and she's crystallized in every teardrop.
She's the place we came from and the map we follow with every step we take.

She was my first love and my first heartbreak, and nothing on earth can separate us.

Not time, not space

Not even death.

30
BARBARA   1960

I lay beside Barbara in the aftermath of our second failed attempt to consummate our relationship, and tried to figure out what we were doing wrong. It was obvious that the position, with me between her outstretched legs trying to scrunch up on the shifting bedspread, was not going to work. An idea had begun to dawn on me and I was about to say something when the phone rang and scared both of us out of our wits. Instantly, we were on our feet running to retrieve our clothes, when Barbara stopped.

"Hey," she said. "It's only the phone. There's nobody here. Nobody can see us. Forget the clothes and answer the phone before whoever it is thinks something weird might be going on."

"Right!" I said, and quickly opened the door. I went to the phone stand in the hall and lifted the receiver. "Hello?" I said, trying to keep the nervousness out of my voice. It turned out that it was my mother, and we not only had nothing to worry about, but we had something to celebrate, since she was calling to tell us she was going to be later. When I hung up, I spun around and ran smack into Barbara, who had followed me out and was standing right behind me. I caught her before she fell, and then, with a movie-star flourish, I put one arm around her back, swung her legs up into the other, and carried her to the bed.

"Gee," she said as I brushed a stray hair from her face, "that was like being carried over the threshold on our honeymoon." I looked down at her, lying naked on the bed, and felt a rush of emotion so strong it nearly buckled my knees. After hopping up beside her, I explained that Mom had called to tell us Gerald was going to be all right, then gleefully told her we now had extended time.

"And," I said in conclusion, "I have an idea."

"Well," she said, "I hope it's better than the one I had."

"I'll let you be the judge of that," I said, and proceeded to explain what I had in mind.

I had been thinking about this earlier, when I had examined her. That position, I reasoned, with her knees bent nearly double and her legs apart and almost vertical, might be ideal for us to try, at least until we got past what was turning out to be the pretty awkward first entry. I explained the idea to her and, though she seemed a little nervous about it, she agreed we should try it. Of course, being another somewhat mechanical procedure, coupled with her growing nervousness, by the time I had repeated the earlier exercise of pushing her legs up and apart, she was dry as a bone. I hadn't given this any thought prior to beginning, but when I looked at her closed eyes and the anticipatory grimace on her face, I worried we were going to run into the same problem we'd had the bathroom.

"Uh, Barb?" I said. "I think we've got a little problem here."

Without opening her eyes, she said in a tone of mild exasperation, "Yes? And what might that be?"

"I think we're running into the same problem we had in the bathroom."

She slowly opened her eyes and lifted her head to look at me between her legs. "Bodily fluids again, right?" she said as a smile began to crack the corners of her mouth. I nodded. "Okay," she said. "Why don't you lend me some of yours?"

At first I didn't understand what she was getting at, but then it dawned on me and I began looking back and forth from her face to her vagina in what must have appeared to be a nod of agreement. When she saw this, she closed her eyes and laid her head back in anticipation.

Feeling trapped now, but still curious, I made up my mind and lowered my head between her legs. At first, with reluctance tugging at my psyche, I kissed her on the insides of her legs, moving closer and closer with each kiss. Before I made it all the way, her body had begun to move in a circular motion and then forward as if urging me toward the goal. When I finally got there and gently kissed her she let out a soft high-pitched moan. Finally, I entered her with my tongue and began trying to push it as far inside as I could. She responded, though only a little, and when I tried to emulate intercourse by moving in and out, she reached down and placed her hands on either side of my head. When she started to pull upward, I thought she might be angry and wanted me to stop, but I soon realized she was trying to tell me something.

As she continued to pull, I soon found my tongue resting above the opening. She made adjusting moves of my head, then started lifting it and pushing it back down in a slow, rhythmic motion. "Like that, Tommy," she whispered, and before long I got the idea and started moving my tongue slowly up and down against her clitoris. "Yes," she said a little louder. "Like that." After I had gone on for a while she again whispered, "Now, harder." I increased the pressure and she started to moan, her body straining against my mouth, rising and falling in rhythm with my movements.

By that time I was so excited I was about to explode and my own movements against the bed were bringing me closer and closer to an orgasm, but her responses were so sensual and encouraging I didn't want to break it off in order to enter her. Soon she began to moan louder and make other little sounds, punctuated by an occasional whispered "Yes" and "Ooohh" that grew higher and higher pitched as our movements increased in speed. Finally, she started to let out little quiet shrieks and, even though I didn't want to, I came against the bedspread. As I gradually began to slow down, she caressed my hair and her panting became shallower. When I finally stopped moving, I said, "I'm sorry, Barb, really I am."

She didn't seem to hear me at first, but when she began to emerge from her delirium, she asked in a half whisper, "What do you mean?"

"Well," said, "I sort of finished before we could—"

"Tommy?" she interrupted. "I had one. I had an orgasm, and it was the most wonderful thing I've ever felt."

I lifted my head up to find her staring down at me. "You did?" I said. "Are you sure?"

"Oh, I'm sure all right. I'm absolutely sure. So there's nothing in the world for you to be sorry about." Then she added with a smile, "Except maybe the bedspread."

We would go on to many more experiments that afternoon, almost forgetting about actual intercourse. With a little encouragement and assistance from me, she learned how to masturbate, and as I kissed and made love to her lips and neck, she managed to have another orgasm. And then, because I hadn't had one with her, she seemed to come to a decision.

She began touching me and pulling the skin of my penis up and down as she had done earlier, then she whispered in my ear, "It's my turn, now," and started kissing me on the chest. I wasn't quite sure what she meant, but as she moved lower and lower I soon got the idea, and when I felt her take me into her mouth, I nearly jumped out of my skin. She pulled back then and looked at me. "Are you all right? With this, I mean?" she said in a concerned voice. I tried to speak but my own voice deserted me, so I nodded my head.

"Okay, then," she said before starting again, "But I want you to help me. I don't know exactly what to do, and I don't want to do anything wrong. Promise?" Again, I nodded.

That, of course, was my first experience with fellatio, and it was weird at the beginning. She seemed to know instinctively what to do, but before long there was a problem. I reached down to touch her head and she stopped to look at me. "What is it?" she asked with concern, almost panic, in her voice. I tried to answer, but ended up giving her a sheepish smile and shrugging my shoulders. She seemed to sense my embarrassment and reluctance, so she moved back up until she was snuggling against my neck. She rubbed my chest and whispered, "That wasn't very good, was it?" Again, the sheepish smile, which I figured she could probably feel against her hair. When I didn't speak, she said in a more normal voice, "Tommy, I don't have a clue what to do to make it better, but I want to, I really do. Or I want to quit if it's not going to be good for you. And you promised to help me, didn't you?"

Finally I managed to stutter an answer. "I don't want you to be worried or anything," I said. "And I definitely don't want you to quit. But, well, it's your teeth."

"Oh my God," she said. "I'm sorry. Gosh, Tommy, I never even thought about that. Did it hurt bad? Oh, shit, oh shit." And she buried her face in my shoulder so hard I thought she might suffocate.

"No, no, Barb. It didn't hurt that bad, but I thought if I didn't tell you we might get, you know, carried away, and I might end up with abrasions or something."

"I'm so, sooo sorry," she said. Then she seemed to make up her mind about something. "Look," she said, raising up on an elbow, "I can't see you too well when I'm down there, you know? So how about this?" She laid a hand across my legs, and started to tug until she had swung them over the side of the bed. She took my hands and pulled me into a sitting position, then knelt on the floor between my knees and looked up at me. By then I had lost my erection, but that didn't seem to bother her. She smiled sweetly and explained.

"This way, can see your reactions and you can help me even without speaking if you don't want to. I mean, you can let me know what hurts or feels good, and I can change things to make it better. At least I hope I can."

I didn't answer. I was so shocked and turned on by her offer, all I could do was stare.

"Is this okay?" she said as she started to kiss me up and down. I nodded, and when she took me in her mouth again I let out an involuntary sigh of pleasure. This time she was careful, and I couldn't feel her teeth at all. She started bobbing her head, smoothly taking in more of me, withdrawing until I was nearly out and then moving back down. As she did this, she lifted one of her legs and placed it on the outside of one of mine, drawing it in until I felt the top of my foot come to rest against the moistness between her legs. As she started to move back and forth in rhythm with her head movements, I reached out and grabbed her by the hair, urging her to take me deeper and deeper into her mouth. It didn't occur to me at the time that I might be choking her, and she didn't resist, so I kept this up until she was accepting almost my entire length. By then, she had reached under and was massaging my testicles as well, which made the overall sensation so intense, I came with a shriek.

When my contractions started, she pulled back a little, still keeping me about halfway in her mouth. By that time I was shrinking and I began to realize it must be pretty gross for her, but when I tried to pull her head away, she resisted, and she even started squeezing a little with each fading contraction, as if attempting to empty me completely. At the same time her sliding movements on my foot became more and more intense, until her body began to shake and jerk with seemed like another orgasm.

We stayed like that for a few moments, our bodies shuddering in the aftermath, then she released me and looked up. Her mouth was closed, and I assumed she would want to get up and go to the bathroom to spit out my semen, but she made no move to do so, and eventually she smiled and spoke.

"Was that all right?" she asked.

I gathered my shattered wits and shuddered. "God, Barbara, it was incredible! Did you, uh, I thought you might have—"

"I did, Tommy. Again! It wasn't exactly like the last time, but it was really nice. I could sense your excitement growing and that made me feel, well, sexy I guess you could say, so that's why I did what I did. I know it probably seemed strange to you, but I needed something myself, and that was the only way I could figure to do it. Do you think I'm weird?"

I pulled her into my arms and we fell back on the bed, with her head resting on my chest. "I don't think you're weird at all, honey, and I'm happy you managed to find a way to enjoy it." And then I remembered something. "What was it you said about that doctor's report earlier? Something like whatever people want do when they're having sex is okay, as long as it doesn't cause injury and both partners agree to it?"

"Uh-huh."

"Well, you wanted to do that and I agreed, or at least I didn't stop you. You don't think it could cause you any injury, do you?" I asked.

She thought about it, then said, "No. If we're careful, I think it's okay."

As the day wore on, we would try many other things that would have seemed odd to us earlier. Including her straddling my knee and moving back and forth, my brushing her breasts with my erection, and the old 69 position for oral sex, which, as famous as it was, didn't work out so well for us. The reversed position made it difficult for me to use my tongue in ways that would most satisfy her, and because she was not very stimulated, I didn't enjoy it much either.

It was about 4:00 when she realized we hadn't gone all the way yet, at least in the traditional sense. What with all the other things we were doing, and the fact that we had both managed to have orgasms, it seemed to have receded into the back of our minds. We were lying beside each other, snuggling and making up fantasies about our future lives together, when she once again broached the subject.

"I hate to keep saying this," she whispered, but I didn't let her finish.

"I know. I know. You think you're ready, right?" We laughed and hugged, and it wasn't long before things started to get passionate. Not sexually at first, but kissing and caressing and snuggling until I finally reached down between her legs and both of us seemed to sense this was going to be it.

Though I would later experience several new and higher levels of erotic, nearly insane excitement with Rosie, that coupling and the few that followed remained in my memory as the most satisfying and loving moments of my life. Little did we know they would soon lead to heartbreak, frustration and the disappearance of our only child.

Honey?" Rosie said over the phone. "I think I might have found something."

"Where are you and what are you talking about? I said, irritated. "You were supposed to be home over an hour ago."

"I'm at the college. I've been using their computers to do some research after class."

I had recently convinced Rosie she needed to learn how to use a computer, but rather than let me teach her, she had chosen to take an adult-ed course at the local community college. Though Rosie and I almost never argued, the one time we had started fighting like cats and dogs was when I decided to teach her how to drive. Until that time in 1992, Rosie had never had a driver's license, and the idea that I should be her driving instructor turned out to be a pretty bad one. She was understandably nervous and it took her a long time to catch on to the nuances of handling a stick shift. And, as it turns out, I was less than patient with her. After that, whenever she wanted to learn something new, she sought outside help.

"Right," I said, still peeved that she hadn't called earlier to let me know she was going to be late. "So, what is this great discovery?"

"Well, you know they have some incredible research tools here, and I've been fishing around with the help of a librarian, tying to find some trace of David. I found a bunch of Tates in several university student and faculty data bases, but never anyone that looked right. Until today, that is."

After I'd told her I had a son out there somewhere, Rosie had embarked on a crusade to find him. And when I later introduced her to Barbara, the two of them would often run down leads together, always hitting dead ends. Then the subject would lie dormant for a while, until something sparked their interest again, and off they'd go on another wild goose chase. I'd gotten used to this, and the phrase "I think I found something" had become like the boy who cried wolf. Still, I wanted more than anything to find my son, so I always went along with whatever new leads they came up with.

"So, what did you find?"

"Well, I know it's another long shot, but you mentioned something about Fitchburg, Massachusetts, and that's only about 50 or 60 miles from Boston, right?"

"I guess so, but Rosie—"

"Wait. Listen. There's a professor at Boston University listed as D. L. Tate and he's 41, which means he was probably born in 1961."

"That's interesting, honey. But the problem is you forgot what I said about Fitchburg."

"Oh. What was that again, exactly?

"Fitchburg was where the absentee owners of the house were supposed to live. The Jenkins, not the Tates. The Tates rented a house from them in Mexico Beach, remember?"

"Yeah," she said, sounding dejected. "I remember now." Then she brightened, "But what if they were good friends or something? What if when they tore down the house, the Jenkins found them a place up there near them?"

I knew better than to throw cold water on her efforts, but this was a stretch. "I don't know, honey, that sounds a little far fetched to me. Besides, I was never even able to locate the Jenkins in Fitchburg, so who knows where they really were?"

"I guess," she said. "But I'm going to call Barbara anyway."

I hated for her to get Barbara's hopes up again, but I resigned myself to the inevitable, swallowed my skepticism and said, "Okay. Just make sure this time she knows it's a long shot and try not to get her too excited, okay?"

Later that week, Barbara came over for dinner, and all she and Rosie could talk about was this new lead on finding David. I had to admit that D. L. Tate was pretty close, though I still didn't think there was much hope because the logistics were so far out. The fact was they had traced down several David Lee Tates in the past, none of whom had turned out to be the right one. Still, when they decided to call Boston University, I didn't put up a fight. They agreed it was too late to call that night, but the next day they started on their new quest.

Unfortunately, this particular D. L. Tate turned out to be Daniel Lewis Tate, and he had been born and raised in Boston.

The three of us met again a few weeks later at our favorite Cuban restaurant, and Barbara and I had a long conversation about our previous efforts to find our son, trying to think of new scenarios that might make a little sense. Finally, I brought up something I'd been thinking about for a long time. I hadn't wanted to suggest it, but we had tried for so many years to find David without success that I decided to mention my idea.

"I don't want you to get mad at me," I began, as we sat at the table in Pepin's eating salad and drinking sangria while our paella was cooked from scratch. "But have you ever considered the possibility your folks and the Tates pulled off a hoax?" Barbara looked at me and her eyes narrowed. "Now, wait, hear me out before you go off," I said. "All I mean is that maybe they wanted to make sure you would never find him. You told me yourself that back in those days it was an accepted fact that birth mothers should never know their adopted kids. And even though yours was not a legal adoption, they might have thought it would be best if they followed the thinking of the day."

"My mother would never have done that, Tommy. She and I always told each other the truth. Always! I can't imagine her even considering such a thing."

I was stepping into sacred territory here, and I knew it. Her mom had been gone now for several years, and I was about to defile her memory. Still, I decided to press on. "Look, Barb, what you have to understand is, if my theory is correct, your mom was doing what she thought was best for both you and the baby. In her eyes she wasn't doing anything wrong. Besides, even though you two had a great relationship, you know what a powerful influence your father was on her back then. If it was his idea, which I bet it would've been, he probably put tremendous pressure on her to go along with it."

She considered that, then said, "You mean they could have conspired with the Tates to make me believe that was their name when it really wasn't?"

"That's exactly what I mean. Look how much it would explain. Think about it. Over the years the three of us have done a tremendous amount of research. We've looked at birth and death records, marriage and divorce records, legal and criminal records, deeds, school records, everything we could think of. And now Rosie has scanned the rosters and faculties of almost every college and university in the country. We've found a few candidates, but none of them panned out. How else can we explain why these people disappeared without leaving a single trace?"

I could tell she was reluctant to consider it, but I also knew I had her thinking. The waiter brought our dinner then, so we waited while he got everything organized on the table. When he left, Barbara said, "It still sounds pretty far fetched to me, but there's one way I can find out." We both looked at her in expectation. "I'll ask my dad." And with that she dug into her plate of food as if she'd been starving.

After a while, when we were finishing dinner, I decided I had to respond to her idea, so I wiped my mouth, dropped my napkin in the middle of my near-empty plate, and cleared my throat. "Look, Barb, I know you love your dad in spite of all the trouble he's caused, but you know as well as I do that even if my theory is correct he'll deny it. I mean, he's had, what, over 40 years to tell you if he were going to? Besides, Phillip is one of the most stubborn human beings ever to grace this earth, and once he makes up his mind about something, he never changes it."

"Mmmm," she murmured. "You're probably right, but there's one thing you haven't thought of. You know how he's always discouraged me when I tried to find David or the Tates, right? Why would he even worry about that if he knew Tate wasn't even his real name and the Tates didn't exist? Hell, he gets angry whenever I let it slip I'm on the hunt again, and that tells me your theory is probably wrong."

She had me there. Phillip was an asshole, but I didn't give him credit for being that clever. I looked at Rosie and she shrugged. "It makes sense, don't you think?" she said.

"Yeah, I guess so." I glanced back and forth at both of them, but by then they knew they had won. My theory simply didn't hold up in the face of Phillip's vehement admonitions not to look for one David Lee Tate.

We were silent while Barbara and Rosie finished their dinners and refused dessert from the elaborate cart the waiter brought by, which, at any other time would've had them salivating. When we got to the parking lot and finished with our goodbye hugs, Barbara turned back as she opened her car door. "Of course, you know I'm going to ask him anyway," she said.

We watched her drive away and after she was out of sight, Rosie turned to me and said, "I think you might have opened a can of worms, there."

A few days later, Barbara called Rosie to relate the news that she had asked her dad about the name-change hoax. He denied it, of course. Still, I wasn't quite ready to let go of my theory. If the Tate name had been a carefully planned deception, that would explain too many things. It wasn't long, however, before something happened that would blow a big hole in my theory.

David is dead, Tommy," Barbara said over the phone. "He died in the Gulf war. He was an officer, a decorated officer, as if that means anything, and he went MIA in 1990 outside of Kuwait. Six months later, the military identified his remains using DNA analysis. They said it was friendly fire."

I was shocked by her words, especially since she seemed so sure. "Wait a minute, now. Wait a minute," I said. I could tell she was on the verge of tears, so I softened my tone a little. "How to you know this? How can you be so sure?"

"Well, I can't be one hundred percent sure, but everything adds up. He was the right age and his hometown was given as Panama City, which is not far from Mexico Beach. His parents were both deceased, and he didn't use a middle name, only the initial "L." But his name was David L. Tate, and everything else fits, at least far better than anything we've found before.

Military records were one thing the three of us had overlooked, I guess because Barbara and I had projected our own attitudes toward the military onto our son. Of course, he had never had our influence as parents, so that didn't make any sense. I would later learn it was Rosie who came up with the idea to check military records, but she'd decided it would be best if Barbara broke the news to me.

"Is there anything else?" I asked.

She hesitated for a moment, then said, "Yes. I have a photo of him." *Oh, shit*, I thought. "It was taken when he was in officers' candidate school, at graduation." She was crying now, and I wanted to comfort her, but I also wanted to know more. I wanted to see that photo. I was choking up myself when Barbara said, "Can you come over?"

"Damn straight," I said. "I'll be there in 15 minutes."

The photo was one of those graduating class things, and all the heads were small; too small, I thought, to make out much of anything. Looking at that picture with Barbara was like looking at a newborn baby while the family cooed and said how much it looked like Mom or Dad, which was basically horseshit as far as I was concerned. To me, all newborns looked alike: wrinkled, bald for the most part, and not resembling anyone I could ever think of. This, however, was not a baby, but a handsome young man in the prime of his life, who would shortly go off to some Godforsaken desert country and die so a few oil barons could reap even more obscene profits.

Barbara pointed out several identifying features, at least they were to her. His nose, she said, looked a lot like mine, though I couldn't see it in the tiny face that stared out at me from the group picture. He also had brown hair, like both of us, but it was his eyes, she said, that convinced her. Not so much the color or shape, but something only a mother would detect. She kept looking back and forth between my face and the photo, and finally she said, "I'm sure, Tommy. I'm really sure."

As it turned out, though, Barbara and Rosie might not have been quite as sure as they'd led me to believe, a fact that came to light a few days later while Rosie was packing us up for the trip to Arlington. She seemed to be thinking out loud when she said, "You know, I don't think Barbara is completely convinced about this."

"What do you mean?" I asked.

"I don't know exactly, but I get the feeling she's worried about you. She knows how hard it's been for you with all the false hopes and dead ends over the years, and I think she might want to put an end to it—to spare you anymore heartache, you know?"

I thought about that for a moment, but I had gone over and over the facts myself, and I was convinced we were right this time. Besides, I didn't think Barbara would have said those things if she hadn't seen something that made her sure. "I don't think so," I said, as I helped close the overstuffed suitcase. "She seemed confident to me, especially about the photo."

"Yeah, I guess you're right. Still, as much as I'd like for you to be sure, something keeps niggling in the back of my mind. Maybe it's that I don't want to give up. I've probably become so enamored with the process of playing detective that seeing things resolved this way would be a little anticlimactic."

And so, we finally laid our son to rest, at least in my mind. At the cemetery, after a prolonged search, we found the nondescript white headstone that marked David's grave. The inscription was simple.

"David Lee Tate," it said. "He served his country with honor and bravery, and he made the world safer for us all."

I wasn't sure about that last part, but I was so caught up in the moment I managed not to make any sarcastic remarks. Barbara and Rosie exchanged furtive glances and when Barbara looked at me we embraced. Rosie eventually joined us, and after many tears and lots of silence, we trudged back toward the car.

"You know," Barbara said as we headed out of the immense cemetery toward the beltway, "sometimes I can't handle this country. Sometimes I want to renounce my citizenship and get the hell out." Neither Rosie nor I chose to comment, but it was clear we felt the same way.

The rest of the trip was strange, with no one speaking or asking for music. We hit I-75 and before long reached Dumfries, where we had reserved two rooms at a chain motel. We ate bland food in the motel restaurant, again without speaking much, except to order and make a few comments on the plastic atmosphere and less than appetizing cuisine. Back at our rooms, we all hugged and went inside. And after the doors were closed, Rosie provided me with one of those classic moments that once again convinced me I had made the right snap decision on that fateful day after the shit storm in her apartment.

"Tom," she said, as she started to get undressed for bed, "I think you should be with Barbara tonight." I turned to look at her in the waning twilight atmosphere of the room, and my heart nearly burst with love and the residual emotion of the day.

"Oh, honey," I said, trying my best to hold back the tears. "She'll be okay. She will. She may be devastated right now. Hell, so am I. But she's strong. She'll make it through this." Of course, I knew she wasn't suggesting I make love to Barbara or anything, though when I think back on that moment, I'm not absolutely sure she would've minded if I had. She listened to my shaky response with quiet resolve, then she walked over to me, gave me a long hug, and held me out at arms length.

"Don't worry about me," she said. "I'll be fine. But I don't think Barbara will be. Not tonight, and definitely not alone." Then she turned me around, led me to the door, opened it and gave me a little shove on the back.

I still marvel at the unbelievable gesture Rosie made that evening. Talk about selflessness; talk about sacrifice. These were the same qualities that made me fall in love with Barbara. To be lucky enough to find those qualities in two women; well, that was too much to ask of God or whomever. But I didn't ask. I never begged for a new relationship that would be as satisfying as mine with Barbara. Rosie and I found each other; that's all there was to it. Fate? Maybe.

Despite the fact that it was almost a knee-jerk reaction on my part; despite the fact that it seemed like one of those Vegas quickie deals that tend to end the next day; despite all that, it worked. And as I felt Rosie's hand push me toward someone she should have been jealous of, someone who should have been her ultimate rival, I fell even more deeply in love with my wife.

When I knocked on Barbara's door, there was no answer, so I stood there like a simpleton until the quiet around me gave way to the vague sound of the shower coming from inside. I pushed tentatively on the door, and when it gave a little I realized it was ajar. I entered the room and, speaking loud enough to be heard over the running water, said, "Hey, don't come out naked. I'll try not to look, but I can't make any guarantees." When she peeked out of the bathroom, I covered my eyes in an exaggerated move that elicited a chuckle. A few minutes later, she emerged in a cloud of steam, her hair wrapped in a white motel towel and her body wrapped in another.

We looked at each other for a long time without speaking before she broke the silence. "What are you doing in my room?" she said, affecting a bit of humorous shock. "Has your wife thrown you out or something?"

"Actually," I said, "you pretty much hit the nail on the head there."

"Uh, Tommy, I need to put something on here. Could you?"

"Oh, sure." I looked around the room and realized about the only place I could go would be the still steamy bathroom. "How about if I turn around?" I said, and spun on my heel to face the front windows.

"Do you think I can trust you?" she asked in an almost provocative voice.

"Well," I answered, "I'm not sure. But what the hell, Barb, it isn't anything I haven't seen before."

"Right," she answered. "Okay then, I guess you can turn back around."

I was a little shocked at that, but when I finally worked up the nerve to turn around, I realized she had used the time while we were talking to slip into a floor-length white cotton nightgown with little flowers all over it. Though she and I had struck a note of humor, as we stood there looking at each other, her smile faded and I saw her shoulders begin to shake. I took the few steps necessary to close the gap between us, and wrapped her in my arms as she began to sob. Before long her grief mingled with mine, and I found myself crying as well. After a few minutes the tears began to subside, and she held me at arms length.

"What's going on, Tommy?" she asked, as she leaned over and pulled some tissues from the box on the dresser. She handed me one and wiped her nose with the other.

"Rosie thought you might need some emotional support tonight," I said as I dabbed at my eyes. "Actually, I think she knew I would, too."

"Jesus!" she said. "How did you ever find such an incredible woman?" I took her by the arm and led her to the bed, where we sat side-by-side holding hands.

I thought about it then, the opportunity, the wonderful bit of serendipity that had led us to that moment, but I knew in my heart I couldn't take advantage of it. We slept together that night, for the first time in our lives, but there was nothing sexual about it. For the next hour or so, we lay side-by-side and talked about old times, about opportunities missed, about what our lives might have been like were it not for the circumstances that had kept us apart. We also talked about that day in 1960, and we laughed at our fumbling adolescent attempts to achieve that first penetration. And then, in the most chaste way possible, we drifted off to sleep in each other's arms.

32
BARBARA   1960

Barbara was ready. Really ready. In fact, she'd been ready for most of the afternoon. We had tried at least three times to end her virginity, and we'd learned a lot along the way about each other's bodies and needs and desires. If any two people were ready for the real thing, we were.

We'd not only learned how to satisfy each other in many ways, we found out that some things don't work, like unromantic settings that omitted foreplay.

So there we were, side-by-side, reclining on my brother's big double bed, determined to get on with it. We started making out, not sexually at first, but in a way that conveyed our growing love for each other. It wasn't long, however, before we were almost desperately making love. I began to massage her, and she responded by touching me with gentle squeezes and soft encircling caresses.

At first, I only stroked her with my open hand, waiting for her to relax and let her natural lubrication begin. When it did, I started to move one finger up and down until her hips began to rise and fall in response. I had thought earlier it might be a good idea to try and stretch her a little in order to better prepare her what was to come, so I decided to use my thumb. I felt that by doing so, I could not only stretch her with the greater thickness of my thumb, but could also keep stimulating contact above. Slowly, I began to insert it, going deeper with each thrust and pulling up to apply steady, moving pressure. .

Her breathing became heavier as I continued, and when I made the deepest penetration I could, pushing my hand in almost up to the wrist and lifting, she let out a tiny shriek. "It hurts, Tommy," she said with the hint of a quaver in her voice.

"I know it does, honey," I whispered, "but I'm trying to make it as easy as possible. Do you want me to stop?" Again I made a deep thrust and she breathed in hard between clenched teeth.

"No," she answered. "No. I want you to do what you think is best."

After a few more thrusts, I thought she was as ready as she would ever be, so I moved on top. "Can you lift your legs for me?" I asked. She slowly began to pull up her legs and I moved in toward her. Looking down at myself, I realized that in my excitement I had grown huge, and I knew this was going to be pretty painful for her. So, in order to give her some small sense of control, I took her hand and placed it between my legs. "I want you to help, now, honey. I want you to put it in."

"Okay," she said. She was clearly scared, but she took hold of me and helped guide me until the tip had begun to spread her outer lips. She let her hand fall away then, and when I looked at her face, the fear radiating from her closed eyes and resigned lips made me stop. But I knew this was it and there was no going back now.

"Are you ready?" I asked. She nodded, and I saw the muscles in her neck tighten in anticipation. When I began to push and felt the vice-like clamp of that beautiful, unspoiled opening surround me, the thought of how much this was going to hurt her was almost too much to bear. But before I could pull back, she reached out to grasp my arms, urging me not to withdraw.

Her grip became stronger with every millimeter I moved forward, and when I realized my gentle pushing was not going to be enough to get past the narrow entrance, I said, "Okay, now honey, hold on tight" She nodded and squeezed my arms, while I made one quick, shallow thrust, enough to pop past that tender barrier. She screamed then. Not a loud or blood-curdling scream, but one that caught in her throat and quickly devolved into a series of short pants.

"It ... really ... hurts ... now," she said between labored gasps.

"I know, honey," I said, reaching up to stroke her hair. "But this is the part we have to get past, remember? I'm pretty sure it's going to get better if we don't give up now." As I said this, I continued to push deeper and, even with the pain, I could tell her body was beginning to respond. I was about half way in, when I asked, "Is it getting any better?"

Her head had started to jerk back and forth, as if she were trying to shake off the pain, but when I asked this, she steadied herself and began to nod. "It still hurts, Tommy. A lot," she said in a strained whisper. "But I don't want you to stop now. This is going to sound funny, but it kind of hurts and feels good all at the same time."

"Do you want more of me inside you?" I stopped to listen to her answer before continuing.

"Yes," she said with determination.

"Okay," I said. "Hang on now." And with that, I thrust deeper, then deeper yet. She started to cry, little kitten-like sobs that pulled at my heart, but at the same time, I could feel her hips rise up to meet me. Finally, I said, "Do you want it all?" And when she nodded I let my full weight go and buried myself as deep as I could. This time her scream was for real, and without pulling back, I reached up to touch her lips with a finger. She opened her mouth and took my finger in, biting down so that my pain mingled with hers. I was happy to feel the pain, because it allowed me to experience at least a portion of her own, and, with its growing intensity, made me aware of each minute increase in her discomfort.

As I increased the pressure against her without pulling back or thrusting, her hips began to move in rhythmic circular motion, and I felt the warmth of her fluids as they flowed around me. Soon, her exclamations began to fade into delirium, and she released her grip on my finger.

"Is that okay?" I asked, brushing her closed eyes with my damped finger, then moving down to touch the tears that now covered her cheeks. When she answered, it was with a breathy sigh.

"Yes," she said. "It's … better now." Encouraged by this, I started to pull back in order to begin moving in and out, but she squeezed my arms in protest. "Don't, Tommy. Please don't take it out right now."

"I'm not, honey," I assured her. "But it's time for us to start, okay?"

Until then, I had been concentrating so hard on doing everything right, I hadn't paid much attention to my own arousal. But now my emotions, coupled with the physical sensations, were beginning to build toward what I knew would be a point of no return. I didn't want to finish before her, so I did everything I could to hold on until I felt her body responding. And once I was sure she could handle it, I increased the speed and depth of each thrust. Soon she was gasping loudly, and when I felt my orgasm coming on, I whispered, "It's time now. Do you think you can …?"

"Oh, yes," she said, in a voice so desperate, so full of yearning and passion that I pushed even harder, until I felt myself pressing against the very limits of her depth. When she jerked and began to writhe in pain, I tried to withdraw and give her a chance to recover a bit, but before I could move, she lifted her legs and wrapped them around my back, pulling me even further into her.

"Please," she screamed, as our bodies came together again and again with nothing between them to stop my ever -deepening penetrations. "Now! Please!"

I was frantic with the need to finish, but even in that state of impending orgasm, I found that I wanted something more; something outside the realm of animal desire; something that would seal this moment forever in our collective memories. So, without slowing or pulling away, I managed to lean over far enough to touch her lips with mine. Her head was jerking from side to side, her hair slapping against my face like a whip, but when she realized what I was trying to do, her movements gradually slowed until she was smiling up at me with a look of such intimate affection it brought tears to my eyes. Our lips met in a kiss filled with so much love and compassion it would forever remain etched in my memory as the single most incredible moment of my life.

Our orgasm was not abrupt, as mine had always been before. Instead it seemed to begin like the distant mournful song of a whale, increasing in volume until it drowned out all sense of reality and melded our souls in a torrent of emotion and love that made me feel I was approaching insanity. Our contractions joined in harmony as we finally reached the pinnacle of endurance and came together in a prolonged eruption of relief and satisfaction.

The laws of the universe, of time and space, seemed to be suspended, as we remained in that incredibly intense netherworld for what seemed like hours. And during those moments of slowly receding sensation, we whispered to each other. I would never be able to recall the words, but they would always remain in my memory as powerful expressions of love and amazement, of satisfaction so complete I would have willingly died right then without the slightest regret. For I knew that nothing in my future could ever equal what we'd experienced; that if I lived for a hundred more years, I would never experience anything that could approach the purity and perfection of our first union.

Unfortunately, regret would come later, without warning or preamble. Devastating regret that would haunt me for the rest of my life. Still, I was often comforted in times of great sadness simply by recalling those few mystical dream-like moments, as our bodies blended, not only physically, but spiritually, and it seemed we became one single entity with no dividing line. To this day, even having experienced Annie's unique sexual creativity and Rosie's unbelievable orgasmic capacity, I have never been able to come close to the overall feeling of completeness Barbara and I experienced on that incredible afternoon.

When we came to our senses, which seemed to take forever, I looked over at the clock to find we still had at least two hours left. And when I finally rolled off, we both noticed the blood. Without speaking, we wriggled off the bed, avoiding the large damp spot, and stood facing each other. Then, with that heart-wrenching tilt of her head, Barbara once again took command, grabbing my hand and pulling me toward the shower.

Neal's shower had one of those flexible spray nozzles you could remove from its clip and use like a hand-held wand, and Barbara used it to clean the blood from my body. Then she handed it to me with a smile, and the pulsating magic in that wand turned out to be extremely pleasurable for her. In fact, probably the most pleasure she got from our little shower adventure was when she placed it between her legs and turned around to let me enter her from behind.

After we dried off, we returned to the bed and surveyed the large spot of blood. Barbara sighed and shook her head. Then, without asking for my help, she stripped the bedspread and linens and took them to the laundry room, where she washed and dried them, while we jumped back on the bare mattress and, like the kids we really were, used the time waiting for the laundry to play and laugh and tickle and experiment. We tried a couple of new positions, once with her on top and the other time lying side-by-side. They were interesting, she would say, but nothing like the first time. Later, with the bed freshly made and the clock showing we had only half an hour or so, we commiserated with each other over the fact that we didn't have enough time to continue without worrying about being caught.

As the clock ticked down, we hugged and snuggled and professed our eternal love for each other. Finally, with full hearts, exhausted bodies and promises of things to come, we reluctantly headed back down the long, dark stairway.

As we sat on the patio in our bathing suits and waited for Mom to get home, we held hands and talked about the ten kids we were going to have and how much fun it was going to be growing old together. When we heard Mom's car pull up, we had one last kiss, a long deep emotional one that put the perfect cap on the day.

That was our last romantic kiss.

33

THE FUNERAL

With the exception of a few sniffles, the crowd was silent after I finished my little speech and read the paraphrased poem. But before I left the podium, there was one last matter that needed to be dealt with. A matter I knew was going to anger Phillip and probably make the rest of the day miserable for me. Still, I wasn't about to ignore BB's wishes, so I steadied myself and cleared my throat to let everyone know I hadn't quite finished.

"There's one final thing I need to say," I began. When I had their attention again, I continued. "Day before yesterday, I got a phone call from Barbara's daughter BB. For those of you who don't know, BB and her companion are right now somewhere in Darfur, doing whatever they can to help stop the genocide. BB asked me to tell you she does not want her mother's ashes to be buried until she can get back and decide what should be done with them."

I looked over at Phillip and saw the blood rise in his face. The original plan, or at least his plan, had been to have Barbara's ashes buried that day in the church's memorial garden where the ceremony was taking place. But that plan was now being preempted by his granddaughter, with whom he had what might kindly be called a strained relationship. In fact, BB hated his guts, mainly because of the way he had treated her mother over the years. This hatred was amplified by the fact that he had virtually cut BB out of his life when he first learned she was gay, and from then on it was all she could do to hold her tongue in order to spare Barbara the heartache of knowing the two of them would never be close. Despite that, and the fact that I knew Phillip would do everything in his power to see to it BB didn't have the last word on the disposition of her mother's ashes, this was something I was prepared to fight for. BB had faxed me a witnessed note stating her wishes, and if it became necessary, I was ready to produce it.

"BB asked me to hold on to Barbara's ashes until she returns in about two months," I said, as I reached down to lift the small white urn from its perch on a little wooden stand. "And that's exactly what I intend to do." This last, I knew, had come out a bit angrier than I intended, but when I said it I was staring into Phillips eyes, and I wanted to get the point across as strongly as possible.

As I relinquished the podium to the minister and walked down the small strip of grass between the two sections of folding chairs, Phillip turned in his chair and reached out to grab me, but I drilled him with a look of such intense resolve, he withdrew. I'm not sure if it was that look, or that he simply didn't have any energy left, but he never approached me again that day.

The minister said a few words and ended with a prayer, after which he directed the crowd to the basement for the reception. On the way in, I grabbed Charles and George and Alicia, and we found a small table where we could sit together. I had no desire for refreshments, so I sat and stared at Barbara's urn while the rest of them fixed their plates. After they returned and took their seats, Alicia was first to speak.

"You know, Tom," she said with a forkful of potato salad halfway to her mouth, "that was about the best eulogy I think I've ever heard." George and Charles, both with their mouths full, nodded in agreement. After Charles had swallowed he reached out to touch the urn.

"What do you think BB will want to do with them?" he asked. "I mean, I wonder why she didn't want her to be buried."

"You know, Charles," I said, "I really have no idea. Maybe it was to make sure Numbnuts over there—" I jerked my head in the general direction of Phillip "—didn't get to have his way. She wasn't specific on the phone. The connection was bad, and I think we got cut off before she could finish. But she did make it clear that we should at least wait until she got back before we decided on anything. In fact, she later faxed me a statement to that effect, in case I ran into any problems."

There were head nods all around, and right in the middle of Alicia's, she stopped and stared over my shoulder. I turned to see Rosie at the door, nervously peering in as if to make sure it was okay to enter. I jumped up and ran to her, and when she saw me she seemed to relax. I kissed her and, still seeming reluctant to come inside, she asked, "Is it over? I didn't want to get here until you were, well, through, you know?"

"It's over, honey. This is the part where everybody feeds their faces on free food and talks a lot of bullshit about how well they knew her and how much they're going to miss her."

"Cynic!" she snapped. "Don't say things like that! How do you know what these people feel? Just because you knew her so well and cared about her so much, that doesn't mean others didn't. Besides, you need to watch your language, because there's someone I want you to meet." She moved aside and I saw she had been hanging on to the hand of a young boy, a slightly Asian looking kid maybe eight years old or so. By that time, George and Alicia had joined us, and I turned to look for Charles, but he was nowhere to be seen. "Why don't we all step outside for a minute," Rosie said, as she turned and started to walk away, trailing the boy's hand behind her.

I looked at George and Alicia, but they seemed as baffled as I was, so we all followed Rosie out the door. We walked over to the alcove under the stained-glass window where Charles and I had had our little talk, and stood in a loose circle. "What's this all—"

"I told you, there's someone I want you to meet," Rosie interrupted. "Timmy, this is my husband, Tom. Tom, this is Timmy. He just flew in from overseas."

The little boy held out his hand and I reached to shake it. "Hi," he said. "It's nice to meet you."

Puzzled, I stared at him for a moment, then realizing I was being rude, I managed to say, "Well, Timmy, It's nice to meet you, too." Rosie smiled then, and her smile seemed to be contagious, because as I looked around, it had migrated to the faces of George and Alicia. I was about to ask what was going on, when Rosie piped up.

"Tell Mr. Tom here what your last name is, Timmy," she said. And when I looked down at him, Timmy seemed to have caught the smile bug as well, though his was somewhat shy and reserved.

"Tate, sir," Timmy said. "My name is Timothy Lee Tate." Before that had a chance to sink in, Charles appeared from around the corner, accompanied by a tall gentleman dressed in a dark suit and carrying a briefcase. They joined our circle and the man set the briefcase on the ground, then held out his hand. After a momentary hesitation, I took it and felt the strong confident grip of someone who might have been a weight lifter at one time in his life.

"Hi," he said, in a voice that seemed familiar. "I'm David. David Lee Tate."

I held that hand for the longest time, while I tried to absorb what was happening. And then I slowly started to pull my son toward me. He stepped forward and we awkwardly embraced. Then Timmy came up and grabbed one of my hands. I looked down into his bright curious face and he smiled.

"Dad says you're my grandpa," he said. "Is that true?" I looked around at Rosie, who nodded.

"Yes," I said, ignoring the tears that streamed down my face. "I'm your grandpa."

The seven of us decided to meet back at our house. When we arrived, Rosie called out for Pizza. Though David wanted to hear all about Barbara, I insisted he fill us in on his life first. His dad, he said, had been transferred to Japan with the electronics firm he worked for shortly after David was born, and that's where he had grown up. When they thought he was old enough to understand, his parents told him he was adopted, however, they withheld any details in order to protect Barbara. He had met and married a Japanese girl while in college, and Timmy was their only child. Sadly, his wife died in the hospital after Timmy was born, of complications from a staph infection.

As I listened to David's story, it was all I could do to keep my composure. I kept thinking Barbara wasn't really gone; that her spirit was right there in my living room. As Barbara had said about the tiny photo of the other David Lee Tate, their eyes made it impossible to deny who they were. David's were so much like Barbara's I couldn't stop staring at them. And when Timmy jumped up on his lap, I studied his as well. Though slightly almond shaped, there was no doubt in my mind I saw Barbara in them. Not only that, but he had a sprinkling of freckles, a feature I didn't think was typical of most Orientals. I reached out to him then, and he climbed off his dad's lap and walked over to me. "Do you mind if I give you a hug?" I asked. He glanced at his dad for reassurance, and when David nodded, he approached me and let me take him in my arms.

With his head on my shoulder, Timmy asked, "Why did you go away, Grandpa? Where have you been?" I did my best to keep my composure, but I wasn't successful. When Rosie saw what was happening, she came over and put her hands on my shoulders to try and calm the shaking.

"Timmy," she said, "your grandpa didn't go away. He would never have left you. It's complicated to explain, but I promise we'll tell you everything soon. Right now, however, Grandpa is so happy to see you that he's having a hard time finding the right words."

"That's right, son," David said. "Why don't we have some pizza now and talk about this later? After all, we've got lots of time."

The pizza idea seemed to do the trick, and Timmy jumped down, stopping for a moment to look at me before bounding off toward the dining-room table, where three large deep-dish pizzas sat waiting. We all gathered around the table, while George and Alicia dished out slices onto paper plates. Through all this, Charles never said a word, but I could tell by the broad smile that seemed to have parked itself permanently on his face he was enjoying the same ephemeral sensation I was—the feeling that Barbara was present.

After we finished with the pizza, Timmy helped George clean the table and take the plates and boxes and dirty napkins to the garbage. I heard them singing in the kitchen as they washed glasses and silverware, and was amazed to realize Timmy had a beautiful soprano voice. While I began to fill David in on the events surrounding his birth, George and Timmy emerged from the kitchen and went into our master bedroom. Before long, I heard George playing his guitar and the two of them singing.

I told David all about his mother and what a wonderful person she had been. And I nearly went into a tirade about her father, but Rosie stopped me. "You have to understand, David," she said. "Tom has been terribly frustrated about all this, and he sometimes lets his anger get the upper hand. The most important thing now is that you've found each other. All the rest is in the past and should be forgiven and forgotten. There is one little detail, however, that Tom has failed to mention. Tom?"

I had been so absorbed in my story that at first I didn't know what she was getting at. But when she mouthed "Bee Bee" at me, I realized what she meant. Nervously, I turned to David. "I know you probably don't need any more shocks right now, but I think you might like to know that ... well, you have a sister."

That caught him off guard, but he quickly recovered and started asking all kinds of questions. I explained that BB was the product of Barbara's first marriage, and that her father had been killed in Vietnam. Then I told him how BB had dedicated her life to political and social activism, and that she was presently in Darfur. I also said if he wanted to get a good idea of what his mother had been like, meeting BB would provide that. He pumped me for as many details of her life as I could think of, and when he asked if she was married or had any kids, I found myself facing a dilemma.

We had not yet had time to discuss politics or social leanings, so I had no idea where he stood on gay rights, but I didn't see any way to skirt the subject. When I told him, he didn't seem shocked at all, though he did remain silent for a while before answering. Finally, he looked at me and smiled. "Mom's sister is gay, Pop—is it okay if I call you 'Pop?'"

"Sure," I said. "I'd like that. Where is your aunt, anyway?"

"She's in LA right now. She's an opera singer. A damn good one, too. I think that might be where Timmy gets his singing talent." I glanced at Rosie and she smiled. Just then, George and Timmy emerged from the bedroom and George announced they were going to perform for us.

We settled in the living room, while George and Timmy pulled up chairs and sat before us. It was one of the most heart-rending musical experiences I had ever known. They apparently found a song they both knew, and during the hour or so George and I were talking, they had put together a version so polished it was astonishing. The song was *The Flower That Shattered the Stone*, which had originally been performed as a duet by John Denver and the Japanese singing star, Kosetsu Minami. Their voices blended perfectly, and when they went into harmony, it was as if they had been singing together for years. George sang in English, then Timmy followed in Japanese, and they ended the song by harmonizing in English:

> *In the hearts of the children a pure love still grows*
> *Like a bright star in heaven that lights our way home*
> *Like the flower that shattered the stone*

When they finished, we all glanced around at each other in silent awe, our faces wet with tears. As Rosie and I hugged and sniffled, I realized the serendipitous significance of the song: the bright star that had lit David and Timmy's way home, was Rosie.

I caught sight of BB and Terri as they exited the monorail arriving from Concourse 3 at Tampa International Airport. When they saw me, they broke into a run, and we had a three-way hug, followed by lots of tears and anguished, stuttered words. After a while, Rosie walked up and put her arms around us. "I hate to break this up," she said, "but we need to get down to baggage claim before they think you've abandoned your luggage." Reluctantly, we separated, and followed my wonderfully practical wife toward the escalators.

I knew BB and Terri had to be exhausted after nearly 36 hours of plane hopping and delays on their way back from Darfur, but I had plans for them. And when I suggested we get something to eat, they enthusiastically agreed.

"I'm as hungry as a male lion without a female provider," BB said. "Can we go somewhere that serves anything that doesn't resemble airline crap?"

As we drove across the Howard Frankland Bridge, on our way to St. Pete, I suggested Pepin's would be the best place, since BB and Terri both ate little meat and Pepin's served several of their favorite seafood and vegan dishes. Before we arrived, I confessed I had an ulterior motive.

"We're meeting some people," I said as we exited the interstate and turned onto 4th street. "I know you guys are tired and probably don't need any more excitement right now, but this is something I didn't think you would want to wait on."

"Yeah?" said BB. "What's the big mystery?"

"Well," I answered, "how would you feel if I told you you had a brother?"

There were a few moments of open-mouthed shock, while BB and Terri exchanged curious glances. Finally, BB said, "This is a joke, right? Mom never had any other kids. I know that for a fact. What's going on here?"

I started to explain, but I was nervous, worried BB would be angry because Barbara and I hadn't told her before. When Rosie squeezed my hand, that gave me a measure of confidence, so, as gently as possible, I began to relate the story of how Barbara had become pregnant and how her father kept us apart. I didn't go into a lot of detail about our early relationship, except to say—with great trepidation that Rosie would be hurt—that we had fallen in love in our teen years, and that the baby was a result of that love, not some mindless adolescent sex for sex's sake. I also filled her in on the years of frustrating search and failure the three of us had gone through. I ended with the story about our mistaken assumption concerning the other David Lee Tate and our trip to Arlington, then turned to Rosie. "You need to take it from here," I said. And when she saw I was having a hard time continuing, she nodded. By then, however, we were pulling into the parking lot at Pepin's, so Rosie said we should go in and get settled first.

We piled out of the car, and when we approached the door, David and Timmy were outside waiting. I almost stopped in my tracks, but Rosie dragged me along, and when we made it to the entranceway, thankfully, she took over.

"BB, this is your brother, David," she said with obvious joy. "And this handsome fellow is your nephew, Timmy." They all stared at each other for a moment, but soon their inhibitions disappeared. As we entered the loud atmosphere of the restaurant, the conversation became jumbled, with everyone trying to talk at once and Timmy tugging on BB's arm in an effort to get her to lean over so he could hear what she was saying.

Over bowls of salad and plates of paella, we talked about the horrible situation in Darfur and the girls' futile efforts to affect some political resolution involving the UN and several other international agencies. We all seemed to be avoiding the subject of Barbara, which was fine with me. I knew there would be time for BB and me to grieve together. There was, however, something everyone seemed curious about, so before we finished, I asked Rosie to explain how she'd finally managed to locate David and Timmy.

"Well," she said, "you know I was never quite satisfied with the military angle. It was probably my prejudice, but I could see something in Barbara's eyes early on that told me she wasn't convinced either, so I never gave up the search. I was at the library, when one of the research librarians who'd taken an interest in what I was doing asked if I'd given any thought to the idea that the family might have left the country."

Rosie looked over at Timmy and BB, who were coloring a placemat together. After a moment, she continued. "Anyway, after Janice—that was her name—brought that up, we both dove into it with enthusiasm. Janice's brother works for the State Department, so she got him to search the passport records in Florida for 1961 and 1962. Sure enough, there was a family by the name of Tate, who'd left the country during that time with their newborn baby boy, and whose stateside address matched the one where Barbara lived in Mexico Beach. After a little more investigating, we learned the Tates had moved to Japan, and that's where David grew up.

"That was about three weeks before the funeral, and when I told David his mother had died, he insisted on flying over. I didn't tell Tom, although I had to bring George and Alicia in for moral support and logistical help. And then I ran into Charles, and I felt I had to tell him, too. It was tight, but we finally got the arrangements made and they flew in two days before the service."

David smiled at this, then cleared his throat. We all looked at him in anticipation. "I've got an announcement to make, if that's okay," he said. He fiddled with his fork a moment, then continued. "Timmy and I have made a little decision, haven't we, sport?" Timmy looked up from his coloring and nodded his head up and down. "Timmy's decided he likes it around here, so we think we might move back to the States."

I felt a lump rise in my throat and I reached out to grab his hand. Rosie took my other hand, and before long we were all holding hands around the table. "I'm asking Nissan for a transfer," David added. "But even if that doesn't work out, I think we're going to do it anyway."

Suddenly, everyone dropped hands and began to applaud, while Timmy and David sat there beaming. Finally, David signaled for quiet, and after everyone had settled down, he raised his wine glass. "To Rosie," he said. "Without whose perseverance, we wouldn't be here today."

EPILOGUE

Nine of us piled out of three cars and headed toward the glistening rain-speckled waters of Tampa Bay. It was a Wednesday, a day we all agreed would be best, since there would be fewer visitors to the park than on or near a weekend. A slight evening drizzle added to our privacy, though it couldn't deter us from what we had decided to do. George brought his guitar, and he and Timmy sang for Rosie and David and me all the way there.

The five of us took off, holding hands, across the long expanse of grass, and the others soon joined in. When we reached the seawall, we all jumped up to stand together, still hand-in-hand and staring out over the water. We probably looked silly to the few elderly residents and tourists who had braved the misty rain, but we couldn't have cared less.

After a few minutes, I hopped down onto the narrow sandy strip of beach that only showed itself nowadays at low tide, then I turned and reached up for Timmy and he jumped into my arms. David did the same for Rosie and soon we were all standing on the sand. I watched as BB and Timmy made their way into some ancient gnarled sea oats and emerged a few minutes later with a giant empty horseshoe crab shell. Timmy ran up to David to show him, then skipped back to BB so they could continue their explorations.

"Your mom loved this place," I said to David. "It was one of our favorite havens when we were kids. We used to come down here to get away from the parents, and we'd spend hours exploring like BB and Timmy are doing. I wish you could have known her, David. She was an incredible human being."

He didn't say anything for a while, but when everyone started climbing back up on the seawall, he turned to me. "I know her now," he said as he glanced up at BB and Timmy. Then he cupped his hands for my foot and boosted me up, like I used to do for Barbara.

It wasn't long before the rain stopped and the reflection of the sunset, that somehow always managed to circumvent the sky from the west and illuminate the eastern horizon, shown with a vague nebulous red glow across the water. One by one, we sat on the seawall and looked at that beautiful spectacle while George swung his guitar from his back and began to play.

BB and David rose then, both grasping the alabaster goblet. David removed the lid and released the urn into BB's hands. She hesitated for a moment, then said, "This is what Mom would have wanted," and swung it wide and hard toward the far coastline.

We watched Barbara's ashes drift and twinkle in the shimmering sunset, while the notes from George's guitar wafted out over the water and Timmy began to sing her favorite song. As the music echoed in the early evening air, I could feel her presence surround me like a ghostly ephemeral spirit.

"But I always thought I'd see you, just one more time again," Timmy sang. As his voice began to fade into the darkening silence, I felt a tiny sensation in the middle of my back; a touch, it seemed, but not substantial enough to be anything more than the wind ruffling my shirt.

I didn't turn, but as I glanced out over the still water, I realized the wind had disappeared.

·

ABOUT THE AUTHOR

R. LeBeaux is a pen name. The real person behind the pen is a semi-mature latent hippie, former rock musician, writer, editor, artist, music producer, publisher, and wood sculptor. His writing has been published in almost every nonfiction genre and he once served as editor/publisher of an international leisure sports magazine. He has authored nearly 2,000 articles that have appeared in over 30 national and international publications. His work has also been reprinted in hundreds of newspapers, on the Internet, and in educational materials for journalism and English classes.

In addition to his non-fiction work, he has published two novels (*Barbara* and *Cute*) and several short stories, written/directed numerous videos, TV programs and commercials, and produces music in his home studio. He currently serves as designer, co-editor and Webmaster for several Web sites, and as VP of Internet Services for Metro Direct Communications. At the time of this writing, he resides in West Central Florida with his anti-social parakeet, Bird. If you wish read about his novel, *Cute*, please visit: www.cutethenovel.com.

Printed in Great Britain
by Amazon.co.uk, Ltd.,
Marston Gate.